GOOD AMISH MEDICINE

AN AMISH ROMANCE NOVEL

RACHEL STOLTZFUS

GLOBAL GRAFX PRESS

CONTENTS

Apprentice Amish midwife, Kate Lapp is called to heal, but will God's path tear her from her community and love?

As an apprentice midwife, Kate Lapp assists her mamm in delivering the babies in their Amish community. But when a tragic complication forces Kate to face the limits of her knowledge, she does all in her power to learn about medicine. As she throws herself into her education, her obsession causes strife in her community and her relationship with her boyfriend, Mike.

Will Kate's growing desire to become a medical doctor force a rift between her and her community she cannot bridge? And when Mike deceives her, and a new English man captures her interest, will God's path prove something she never imagined?

Find out in Good Amish Medicine, an Amish coming of age novel of 74,000 words.

If you love Amish romance with strong women who are committed to healing their community, start reading Good Amish Medicine today!

"Kate! I need the blood pressure cuff and stethoscope now! Hurry!" Becky Lapp held one hand on their laboring patient's wrist, feeling the pounding beat of the blood through her body.

Kate grabbed the needed implements and shoved them toward her mamm. At the same time, she put a cool, wet cloth on the girl's head. "Mamm, she's so red."

"I know. I think she has preeclampsia." This last was whispered quietly.

Kate's blood seemed to coagulate in her veins. She had studied on this condition, so she knew how serious it could get.

"I'm going to separate her membranes and get

her labor moving faster. I wish we had some mag sulfate!"

"IV medication?" Kate's stunned voice reached a register higher than she'd spoken in many years.

"Ya! That helps to prevent seizures." Quickly, Becky got to work stimulating the membranes that would speed Mrs. Hoffman's labor along. Reaching high into her feminine area, she found the amniotic sac and, working quickly, she scrubbed her fingers between the sac and cervix. After finishing this process, she roused Mrs. Hoffman. "Anna? You need to get up and walk. We'll help you."

"I…can't. I'm too weak."

"Girl, we have to get your labor moving faster! This baby needs to be born now!" Becky was firm, which caught Anna's attention.

"I… okay." As quickly as she could, Anna stood at the side of her bed, teetering from side to side.

Kate and Becky stood on each side of their patient, taking much of her weight. They began walking her back and forth as fast as they could. After several minutes, Anna moaned and bent slightly. "Owwww, it hurts!" Her cries could barely be heard over the awful rumbling of the thunder outside the window.

"Breathe, Anna. Just like we taught you a few

weeks ago." Kate mimicked the breathing that would help Anna through her contractions.

Weakly, Anna followed along. For a few more hours, she did everything Becky and Kate told her to do. Still, her labor progressed too slowly. After trying everything, Becky sent Kate to the phone house to call for an ambulance.

"Mamm, the phone wouldn't work; I think the storm must have brought the lines down. Should we take her to the hospital?"

"This storm is too violent. I spoke with Mister Hoffman when I took my last break, and he tried to ready the buggy, but the horses are too panicked with the thunder and heavy, pelting rain. We'll have an accident. We have to progress here, as best we can."

Shortly after the discussion, Anna, who was back in bed on her left side, began having a seizure.

"Mamm!" Kate was scared.

"She's in full eclampsia." Becky's voice was sad. Anna still wasn't ready to deliver. All she and Kate could do was to try and keep her seizures from becoming too severe. If they had known Anna would develop preeclampsia, they could have given her one of several herbs to lower the risk of seizures. Soon, the seizures stopped, along with Anna's heartbeat.

Struggling against tears, Kate helped Becky to clean Anna up. She knew that soon the tiny life within their patient would die as well.

Kate took on the difficult task of telling Tom that his wife and baby had died. "Tom, I'm so sorry. That headache and the swelling she had were symptoms of preeclampsia. Unfortunately, we couldn't call an ambulance, or get her to the hospital because of the storm and lightning. We're sorry, Tom. She died just a while ago."

Tom rocked back, stunned by the news. "What…" He licked too-dry lips. "…about the boppli?"

"We were unable to remove him from the womb. She just wasn't ready to give birth, and she got so sick so fast." Becky stopped speaking before she broke down.

Kate was having a harder time of it. She was holding her breath and refusing to allow her eyes to blink. As a result, her entire face was strawberry-red by the time she and Becky left the house and got into the buggy. As soon as they were out of the Hoffman's yard, she let go, beginning to cry deep, shuddering sobs. By the time they got home, she was exhausted and weak from lack of sleep.

"Go to bed. Eat when you get up. But remember, we have another birth coming up next week." Becky's voice was firm, though still sad.

"Ya. I will." In her room, Kate struggled to keep from crying yet again. It was a little hard because of her tiredness. Finally, her eyes closed and stayed that way. Her shuddering breaths soon evened out and she was fast asleep. She slept for a gut four hours by the time she woke up. Still feeling tired, she knew she wouldn't be able to sleep anymore. Sitting up, she wondered about her effectiveness as a midwife. *What do we do when things go bad like last night? Just let them die? We can do some things to ease the process for the mothers, but because we aren't doctors, we don't have the knowledge or training to do other things. Like start IVs, which would have probably saved Missus Hoffman's life and her boppli. We do something that's so very gut, but if the mamm is sick… We don't have the training or experience. Maybe I should just become a doctor.* At this moment, Kate's struggle and dream were born.

Down in the kitchen, Kate stifled a huge yawn as she washed her hands. "What should I work on, Mamm?"

"If you're rested, cut the vegetables for the stew.

I'm making a chicken stew for supper, with zucchini and vegetables."

"Okay." She got to work, cutting the vegetables for the stew and for the zucchini dish. She knew exactly what Becky was making. To stay awake, she poured a large glass of iced tea and swallowed the contents in less than five minutes.

"Daughter, are you feeling better after last night? It does take some time, and this was your first bad birthing experience." Becky was concerned. She saw the circles etched under Kate's eyes and observed the still-slumped shoulders.

"I've been better. But I'll get past it. Somehow. Mamm? Why can't we insert IVs or epidurals?"

"You know why. Lack of education and training. That's why we have the hospital."

"But, when the weather is bad or the mother's health or labor gets bad so quickly, we don't have time to transport her. It takes a gut thirty minutes to get to the hospital by buggy. And to call an ambulance?"

"Ya. The ambulance would be an option if the phone lines are working."

"I know. I wish…" Kate's voice trailed off.

"What?"

"I…don't really know. All I know is that, if

Missus Hoffman had been in the hospital, she would be holding her baby right now. They'd both be alive."

"Or—maybe it was Gott's will."

"I know, but it still hurts. Bad."

Steve, Kate's daed, walked into the kitchen. Overhearing, he cleared his throat, a signal that Kate knew well.

"Yes, Daed?"

Daughter, you and your mamm did your best. Get over it, because before long, you'll have another delivery to assist." Leaving the room, his piece said, he went to wash his hands and change his shirt.

Kate continued to feel extremely confused for several days. She tried to take her father's advice, but she found it difficult to leave the events and memories behind. Even when she was on a date with Mike Newman, her boyfriend, she was unable to fully pull herself out of her sadness. The two were taking part in a rumspringa event, getting together with their friends to watch a movie that would ordinarily be disallowed.

Mike looked at her. "What's wrong?"

"Nothing. Just…stress from work."

"Is it Anna Hoffman, my cousin? I know she died in childbirth."

Kate sighed, her breath catching in her throat. "Ya. It is. She and her boppli died after she developed an illness that happens only in pregnancy. Mamm and I tried to save her. But nothing we tried helped; if only we'd had IVs and magnesium sulfate…"

"Mag… what?" Mike was totally ferhoodled.

"It's Epsom salts. Magnesium sulfate. It works to suppress the seizures that happen with preeclampsia and eclampsia."

"Well, why couldn't you give it to her? My cousin would still be living!"

"She didn't have an attending doctor from the hospital in Lancaster. Only through him or her could she have the solution prescribed to her."

"Sweetheart, you knew this when you first started apprenticing with your mother. Right?" Mike nuzzled Kate's neck, trying to distract her.

"Ya. Stop that! But we never— Mike, stop! We never anticipated that anything that bad would happen," she muttered, under her breath, "I should become a medical doctor; maybe then I could have done something useful."

Mike heard Kate's words, and he got angry with her. "Whoa! What do you mean? Are you serious?" Mike regarded Kate as one of the most beautiful girls in Lancaster, and he was still surprised she had agreed to date him. This made him a little insecure regarding his relationship with her.

Kate gasped and turned toward Mike. "Nee! I wasn't! I'm just frustrated, that's all." The evening went downhill from there. Mike became sullen and quiet. Kate, after trying to jolly Mike out of his mood, gave up. "Take me home. I'm tired."

Rather than putting an arm around Kate's shoulders, Mike kept both hands firmly on the reins. As he pulled up in front of the house, he set the brake so he could jump down and help Kate out.

Instead, she jumped down without any assistance. Without looking back at Mike, she ran to the house and went inside, securely locking the front door. After getting in bed, she began to think to herself. *Am I truly serious about what I told Mike? All I know is that I don't want to feel helpless when a mother is that sick again. Ever!* Even though she was in bed, and it was dark outside, Kate had a hard time drifting off to sleep. Giving up, she flopped onto her back, staring at the plain wood ceiling of her room. She thought about the realities of becoming a doctor. *It would mean leaving here and living among the Englisch. Getting my GED and going to college, then medical school. It would be years before I could start practicing as a doctor.* Slowly, she drifted off, beginning to enter disturbing dreams. She jolted awake when her mamm knocked on her bedroom door.

"Hurry! Missus Stoltzfus is in labor! I'll be downstairs." Becky hurried down, knowing Kate was already out of bed.

After dressing, Kate went downstairs. Nearly on autopilot, she poured two large Thermoses full of hot, steaming coffee, adding cream and sugar to both. Adding a container of chopped fruit to the lunch cooler, on top of the foods Becky had put in, she locked it shut.

After loading the buggy with everything, both women boarded and took off. "Okay, let's hurry up. We still need to get there."

On the drive, Kate was aware that she felt nauseated and that her heart was pounding hard. Her hands were clammy. "Mamm, I'm nervous. My heart's thumping. Is that nerves?"

Becky looked knowingly at Kate, smiling gently. "Of course, it is. We had a very rough time the other night. We both want this one to go well. You've observed Missus Stoltzfus' condition throughout her pregnancy. What do you think?" Becky had done this on purpose, wanting to distract

Kate from her fear and get her thinking professionally.

Kate was thrown off guard. Trying to think and coordinate her brain and mouth, she babbled uselessly for a few seconds. Finally, "Well, she hasn't had any signs of illness. So I guess—"

Becky interrupted. "You guess? Girl, don't tell me that delivery the other night has you hesitant! You know I'm giving my practice to you when I retire."

Normally, Kate would have been happy to hear those words. Tonight, she was chilled and not sure she wanted the practice after all. "Ya, Mamm, I know. I'm just nervous after what happened to Missus Hoffman."

Becky sighed. "Ya, I know. I'm sorry for snapping. Truth be told, I'm a little nervous myself. Let's just try to keep attentive to anything that might develop so we can act on it right away."

"Ya, and get her to the hospital, if need be."

"Exactly."

As Kate and her mamm gently assisted Mrs. Stoltzfus through her labor, it became clear that this delivery would run smoothly. After handing a healthy baby girl to her mother, Kate helped clean her up as Becky filled out the information on the birth certificate application. Loading their supplies in the buggy, they went home in a haze of exhaustion. Because it was so close to the time they would normally get up, they stayed up and made breakfast. After Steve left for the carpentry shop, Becky had Kate took a badly needed nap. "Three hours. No more. I'll get you up, and we'll get the cleaning done." Becky did a little of the cleaning, then, and when her need for sleep overtook her, she went upstairs as well.

OVER THE NEXT SEVERAL WEEKS, EVEN THOUGH the majority of their planned deliveries went smoothly, Kate still continued to think about leaving Lancaster and going to school. Her thoughts became more and more serious as she considered the processes she needed to go through. Her thinking evolved from misty imaginings about being in school and becoming a doctor. Now, she began to think, "How can we do gut if we don't have the knowledge or tools when something really bad happens to a mamm in labor? On this, at least, the Englisch have it right. Get educated. Go to college. Earn medical degrees so that, when a mother has problems, they can get our help and not die!" Often, Kate cried, grieving for the family, the mamm and the baby.

On the next Meeting Sunday, Kate went, but she dreaded seeing the Hoffman family. During the three-hour service, she realized it was difficult to look at the Hoffman kinder and their auntie, who was helping to take care of them.

After lunch, the woman's sister came up to Kate. "Kate? I was watching you during the service and you look so sad. Why? I was talking to my sister. She tells me that you and your mamm did everything you could think of to help our sister. Don't feel guilty!"

Even though the woman meant well, her words didn't help Kate very much. She still felt guilty. Her thoughts about leaving Lancaster to become a doctor became even more solid and persistent. That night, on the way home from the Sing, Mike tried to jolly Kate out of her mood.

Kate, feeling bad, shook her head and sighed. "Mike, I am so sorry. I spoke with Missus Hoffman's sister and she told me not to feel bad. But I can't help it! I just know there was more we could have done, if only we had had a medical doctor to sign off on the substance she needed."

Just as before, the two argued. Mike believed that women expecting babies don't need the services of Englisch doctors.

Kate got mad. "So, you're saying that, if our expectant mothers are having problems with their pregnancies, we should just let things go wrong?"

CHAPTER 2

"**N**ee! I'm saying that it's not Gott's will for us to rely on Western medicine. Our midwives are plenty." Mike was solid in this belief.

"'Gut enough.' Huh. Well, that tells me what you really think about my vocation. Thank you!" By now, the couple was in front of Kate's parents' front door. Kate jumped out of the buggy and hurried up the porch steps. She was so angry, she wouldn't allow Mike to say goodnight.

"Kate! I didn't mean it that way!" Mike's voice was high and frantic.

Kate whirled around. "Didn't you?" She shoved the door open and disappeared into the living room. She barely remembered not to slam the door.

Upstairs, she got ready for bed. Before blowing the lantern out, she pulled a medical text out from under her mattress. Her daed would have been angry if he knew she'd bought this book. Pulling just the sheet over her head, she stewed in her anger and began to read about pregnancy complications. It took a while, but soon, her eyes were too heavy to stay open. Sticking a folded sheet of paper in between the pages, she marked her place and, again, hid the book under her mattress. She dreamed.

"*Doctor Lapp, you're needed on Labor and Delivery. Doctor Lapp.*" *The PA system echoed as Kate, in scrubs and a white jacket, hurried to the L&D ward. Arriving at the patient's room, she entered, smiling gently.* "*Hello, Patricia. How are you?*"

"*It hurts!*" *The young mother squirmed in bed, trying to get away from the everlasting pain.*

"*Yes, I know. Let me check you.*" *Quickly, Kate ran her hands over Patricia's stomach and checked her dilation.* "*Well! Good! You're seven centimeters dilated. That's why it hurts. It looks like your epidural needs to be topped off.*" *Carefully, Kate changed the IV bag and added another injection of anesthetic to the IV port. Soon, Patricia relaxed and closed her eyes.*

"*Rest. The hard part is coming up.*"

Patricia slipped into a light doze that ended when she felt her abdomen tightening. As she felt the sensation, she smiled. "Doctor Lapp, this medication is so helpful. I can give birth without that horrible pain!"

"Ya…yes, as long as your labor progresses as it has for the past several hours, you'll stay on this. But—"

"Yes, I know. If things happen like they did with Selena, I need a C-section. But I really want to have her naturally."

"I know. Let's just see how this continues to go." Over the remaining four hours of Patricia's labor, Kate continued to monitor her carefully. She was painfully aware of what had happened to her first labor—Patricia's labor had seemed to stall, with her contractions coming one on top of another. When Patricia's old obstetrician had checked the baby's position, he had found the child's head had gotten stuck partway down the birth canal. Patricia was immediately taken into the OR for an emergency C-section. As a result, the baby had a permanent brain injury that led to some cognition problems. Today, as Patricia's doctor, Kate was determined that nothing would get in the way of a healthy birth and baby, even if it meant a second C-section for Patricia. "Let me check you again." Kate expertly checked the progress of Patricia's dilation. She also tried to determine where the baby was located. "Okay, everything is normal. Baby's head is well located and…" she looked at the fetal monitor. "Her heart rate is within normal range."

Thirty minutes later, Kate smiled at Patricia. "You're ready to push!"

Patricia gave Kate a look of apprehension. "I hope…"

"I know. I've been checking the progress of your daughter's head and she's where she's supposed to be. Now, when I tell you, I want you to begin pushing."

Forty-five minutes later, Kate, holding a healthy, newborn girl, grinned at Patricia. "See? You did it! Your daughter is healthy and appears to be completely normal."

Patricia, crying, extended her arms out toward the baby.

The next morning, Kate woke up. Remembering her dream, she was surprised to feel a sense of calm and even wellbeing. *Hmmm, maybe I'd better look at this a little more. I thought I'd feel upset or something.*

THE FOLLOWING WEEKEND, KATE AGREED TO GO out with Mike, even though the feelings between them were still tense and somewhat touchy. When she realized that Mike still refused to understand the situation she and her mamm faced with every delivery, she continued to withhold a part of herself from him emotionally. As Mike realized this was happening, he grew frustrated, only wanting their easy relationship to go on as it had before.

Every night, she would pull her textbook out from under her mattress, no matter how tired she felt. She studied a little more every evening, learning more and more about pregnancy and childbirth. Without reference texts or required prerequisite courses that medical students took, her progress was slowed, which led to her frequently feeling frustrated.

One night, she snapped the heavy text closed, and then winced at its sharp sound. Rolling onto her back after hiding the thick book under her covers, she closed her eyes and flung one arm over her face. She seemed to see difficult terms floating before her eyes. Even worse, chemical equations bedeviled her, their solutions remaining tantalizingly out of reach. Over the next few weeks, Kate's mood grew more and more quiet and somber.

Becky and Steve noticed Kate's change in mood. "Wife, what is going on with that girl? I had to call her name three times to finally get her attention."

"Please go easy on her, Steve. I think it's because she's so worried about our patients, after Anna Hoffman died several weeks ago."

"Well, if this is how she's going to get when a

pregnancy doesn't go as it should, maybe she should bake. Or quilt."

A look of horror crossed Becky's face. "Nee! Do you want other people to try to eat what she tries to bake? If she tries to sew, even on a machine, she's more likely to stab herself. It's better that she use her talent with me. And she is talented, just very young and impressionable."

Steve grumbled. "Well, her mood has affected everything here at home."

"Okay, then, I'll have a discussion with her." That opportunity came the next morning, as Becky and Kate were replenishing their midwife bags. Kate let out a huge yawn, and then looked at her mother with guilt.

"What's this all about? Don't you get enough sleep at night?"

Kate knew she needed to open up. Sighing, she spoke, "Ya, I do. I've been studying at night. I ordered a textbook a while back. Only now, I'm running into terms and chemistry stuff that I don't understand!"

"I see why you're doing it, and I think you have a gut idea. Why don't you think about going to the library and finding books that would help you figure this out?"

"Well, it's a gut idea. But what if someone goes into labor?"

"There is that, but if you go when we aren't supposed to have women going into labor, that might work better."

Kate just nodded. She knew it was a gut idea. But she was afraid. *What if I don't measure up to anyone else there studying the same stuff?* Kate's fear was well grounded. Because she had finished school right after the eighth grade, her schooling was nowhere near that of even a junior or senior in high school. She knew that, lacking a high school diploma, she didn't have as much education as Englisch students. This was a big reason she hadn't said anything to anyone about leaving the community to go to medical school.

For the next several days, Kate was mindful of her mood at home. It was only on drives to patient's homes when births were imminent, or at night when Kate was alone in her bedroom, that her mood became somber.

During one such labor, Kate was hyper alert to any problems that might potentially develop. She double-checked blood pressure readings and temperatures. When their patient was napping, Becky pulled Kate into the hallway for a quiet conversation. "Daughter, what is going on? You're taking blood pressures twice and re-reading temperatures. Are you losing your certainty about what you're seeing?"

"Nee. I just don't want to miss anything, no matter how small it is."

"Okay, but just don't do it so often that you slow things down. She's coming along well. Everything is normal."

Everything *was* normal until the mother's delivery stalled. Pacing back and forth with her, Kate spoke. "Mamm, I was reading in a journal that if a laboring mother's progress slows, have her bounce gently up and down on an exercise ball. We don't have one. So we should buy one before long. But there's another thing we can try before going to the hospital. Amy, lean forward on your bed. Gut. Now, start wiggling your hips from side to side. Like you used to do with Hula-Hoops when we were kinder, remember? Gut. Gut! Gently, now. We just want to loosen the baby's head so it moves farther down. I think it's already engaged in your birth canal." Tenderly, Kate talked Amy through the gentle exercise. "Keep doing it even when you have to push. You'll make faster progress. We're right here." Slowly, she kneeled and looked between

Amy's legs and nodded to Becky. "Okay, Amy, you're ready. I see the baby's head. On the count of three, I want you to push. We'll count up to ten. Take a break, and then when I tell you, push again. Okay?"

"Ya...I really do need to push!"

"One, two, three...now, PUSH! Gut, gut! Three, four, five, six, seven, eight, nine ten. Stop! Take deep, cleansing breaths and...one, two, three..." For the next hour, Kate and Becky worked with Amy. Finally, a small, wizened little boy was born. Laughing through their tears, Kate and Becky cleaned the little one and put him into his mother's arms.

Once mamm and baby were both cleaned and their vitals taken, Becky filled out the birth certificate and the two left. The sun was moving toward the western horizon, so they hurried home. While they were both very tired, they were also buoyed by the joy of a new baby for the King family. "This is their third. I wonder how many more they'll have?"

"I don't know, but that technique you had Amy try was wunderbaar! We didn't have to take her to the hospital for a C-section. I was really beginning to get worried."

That night, in her room, Kate still felt the

natural high she got after every baby's birth. Again, she replayed what her mamm had said to her. She hugged the feeling to herself, knowing she would have to recall it many times into the future. Sighing and feeling the onslaught of the day's efforts and tiredness, she slumped, ready to go to bed.

LATER THAT WEEK, THE RUMSPRINGA TEENS decided to go to town to listen to an alternative rock group that was playing at a local under-21 club. Even though she still felt anger toward Mike, she agreed to join him.

At the club, Kate sat in between Mike and Miriam. On Mike's other side was one of his best friends. Kate responded to some of Mike's observations, feeling nearly happy with him.

"How's it going? With the deliveries, I mean?" Miriam leaned close to her, talking so Kate could hear her.

"Better. But I'm still doing a lot of studying so I can get more confidence!"

Mike overheard. With a creased eyebrow, he questioned Kate. "I thought you were over all that by now."

"Nee. Mamm and I deal with lives all the time. If something goes wrong, we need to be able to get the mother to the hospital in time, if needed. And sometimes that does happen."

"But you're getting trained by your mother, right? And she's gut at what she does. Maybe you should—" Mike clamped his mouth shut, not wanting to say the words.

"Maybe I should…what, Mike?"

"Nothing. I just…I think I see where you're coming from now." Sliding out of the near-impossible situation his hasty mouth had almost dumped him in, Mike smiled at Kate, then turned quickly back to his friend.

Kate shook her head. She had heard his words. She'd also heard the doubt in his voice. She turned her back to him and continued talking with Miriam.

"Let's go to the girls' room. We can talk there." Miriam whispered near Kate's ear.

"Ya, let's go." Grabbing her small shoulder bag, Kate slid out of the booth with Miriam.

"What did he say?"

Kate was reluctant to say anything. "He said that he sees where I'm coming from with my confusion."

"But you don't believe him. Ya?"

"Nee. I don't."

Miriam shook her head, and sighed. "I never thought he was a gut boyfriend for you. He needs someone who is able to deal with things at their most basic. You think differently. So you need a different kind of boyfriend."

"Miriam! Are you saying I should break up with him?"

"If that leaves you free to meet someone who thinks more deeply, like you do, ya."

Kate sighed. "You know, I've thought about it a lot lately. He doesn't believe that I am able to be a gut midwife, which makes me doubt my career choice."

Miriam growled through clenched teeth. "You are a wunderbaar midwife!" Seeing two teen girls come in, she stopped speaking, just inhaling and exhaling so she'd calm down. After the two girls left, she continued. "And for Mike not to see that, means he is blind and mupsich!"

Kate giggled. She loved her friend so much. "I'm not breaking up with him quite yet. But it's getting to that point. Miriam, I need to tell you something." She told her friend about the break-through she and her mamm had had with their most recent delivery. "I want to go to the library to see if I can study up and learn what I don't already know. So I'm not as uncomfortable with emergency or unexpected situations."

"Ya, I think that's gut. Do your parents know about the book you bought awhile back?"

"Mamm does. I used a part of my earnings to order it, and it has helped. But there is much more information out there that I don't know. Like chemical equations—I've tried to figure them out, but without taking an advanced chemistry class…"

CHAPTER 3

Miriam's eyes widened. "You need chemistry?" Her voice soared to a high note on the last word.

"Um... Nee, not really. But I feel like, if I know the equation, then I can learn what a patient needs."

"Kate, that's what doctors do. Are you thinking of becoming a doctor?"

Kate immediately began to shake her head in denial. "Nee! Of course not! Because, I would have to leave here. And I don't want to leave my family or friends behind."

Miriam's gaze toward Kate was long and considering. She narrowed one eye, trying to figure out if Kate was telling the truth. Finally, she sighed.

"Okay. I believe you. Because, even though we haven't been baptized yet, you *know* what would happen."

"Ya, I do. I just don't want to lose anyone I love. At the same time..." Kate struggled with what to say next. "I.... I need..." She stopped. "I have to learn more about pregnancy and childbirth. So I can be more helpful when something goes wrong with a labor."

Miriam sighed. "Ya, your intentions are honorable and everything. But getting to where you want to be as a midwife will be right hard. Going to school? That won't be allowed. Because the elders may think you're placing yourself above everyone else."

Kate looked down. A tiny piece of the puzzle had just slipped into place. She swallowed hard, forcing the tears back. "I know. We'd better get back out there before the guys wonder where we are." Standing, she and Miriam washed their hands at the sink. Kate squeezed a small amount of the fragrant hand lotion in the bathroom and rubbed it over her hands. "Ohhh! So soft!"

Miriam followed suit. "Ya, but we'd better be careful about the smell." She quickly tucked her hands into the pockets of her apron, leading Kate to do the same.

"Where were you? You missed some of the best music!" Mike's forehead was slightly creased in frustration.

"We just went to the ladies' room is all. We're back." Kate gently bumped her shoulder against Mike's in a move she'd done many times before.

In response, he bumped back much harder, causing Kate to ricochet against the table, where her rib connected painfully with the edge. "Ow! Be careful!"

Mike swiveled silently to look at Kate, a significant look of anger in his eyes.

Kate, massaging her aching side, gasped. The look on Mike's face chilled her blood. At the end of the concert, she grabbed her handbag, looping the long strap diagonally over one shoulder and under her cape. "Miriam, do you and Jonah mind taking me home? Please?"

Miriam, about to ask why, saw the look of fear on Kate's pale face. "Ya, of course. Come." She wrapped one arm around Kate's shoulders and gestured silently to Jonah that they had to hurry. The trio rushed out of the club, leaving Mike behind.

"Hey, Kate! You're with me! Remember?"

Kate turned. "Nee, Mike. Not after you pushed me into the table. You know how I feel about violence." Her fear vanished as she reminded her boyfriend about her stance.

Jonah turned, standing right next to his cousin Kate. "Mike, stay back. We're leaving and you're not following. Kate made her intentions and wishes crystal clear." He wheeled back around and, arm around Kate's shoulders, he gripped her upper arm securely with his hand.

Miriam did the same. Putting slight pressure on Kate's upper back, she hurried her along, feeling strongly apprehensive. "Let's hurry." She and Jonah walked quickly, Kate sandwiched in between them. As they reached Jonah's buggy, they boarded quickly, just wanting to be on their way home.

"Kate, Miriam, I'm taking a different way home. I don't think Mike knows of this one, if you don't mind." He pulled a quick right, then another right, which hid them behind a thick stand of trees. To disguise their progress on the road, he weaved the team onto soft grass, deadening the sounds of the horse's hooves.

Miriam looked back frequently, praying Mike wouldn't catch up to them. Twenty minutes later, they pulled into Kate's yard. "You'd better get out fast, just in case Mike sees us."

Kate agreed. She jumped out and sent a hurried wave to her friend and cousin, then ran into the house, locking the door securely. Not feeling very secure, she ran into the kitchen and verified that door was locked.

"Kate! You're home early! What hap— why are you so pale?" Steve was immediately concerned. He had never warmed to Mike Newman, always sensing a need for control in the teen.

"Miriam and Jonah brought me home. Miriam and I went to the girls' room and Mike was unhappy that it took us so long. I nudged his shoulder, saying, 'hi.' He bumped back much harder. He pushed me into the table." Kate gave in to her fear, trembling and crying.

"Did he hurt you?" Steve put his hand under Kate's chin, making her look into his face.

"Nee... well, I bumped my ribs on the table edge, but that's it."

"Upstairs. Now. Becky! We need you!" Steve thundered up the stairs.

Becky came out of her room, blinking against the lantern Kate held. "What? Why, is Kate hurt?"

"She's home. She and Mike had a disagreement

this evening and she bumped her ribs into a table. Will you check her, please?"

Becky went silent. She hated any kind of violence—one of her close relatives had died at the hands of her husband. Quickly, she undid Kate's dress and spread the edges open. "Which side?"

Kate wordlessly indicated her left side. She was struggling not to cry again.

Becky reached for the lantern and brought it close. "Nee, I still can't see everything. Steve! Bring the flashlight, please!"

Hurrying with the flashlight, Steve clambered back up the staircase, not even out of breath. He handed the flashlight to Becky, waiting right outside Kate's bedroom.

Able to see much better, Becky gently prodded the discolored areas of Kate's ribcage. "Does that hurt? That? How about this?"

Becky nodded for each area. As Becky poked her bottommost rib, she winced and hissed in pain.

"I don't think it's broken. But I think we should go see the doctor or healer tomorrow morning. Maybe some poultices will ease the pain. But I want an X-ray, just to be sure. How did this happen?"

Gasping through her tears, Kate told her everything.

By the time Kate finished, Becky's mouth was tight. She shook her head.

Steve came in, hearing Kate's recitation of the evening and recent events. "I don't want you spending any more time with that boy. Under—" He stopped at a series of loud, insistent thumps against the front door. "Is that him?"

"Ya, it might be. Jonah got us home by hiding in between the tree lines. That's how mad Mike was."

"You two stay up here." He closed the bedroom door, leaving it cracked a few inches. Opening the door downstairs, he wiped all expression from his face. Seeing Mike glowering on the other side, his own glower returned. "What do you want?"

Mike was stunned. He'd never gotten this kind of reception here in the past. Then his anger returned. "Where is she? Kate?"

"Upstairs with her mamm, checking the ribs *you* bruised tonight."

"Hey, she pushed against me first!"

"Ya, so she said. But did she do so as hard as you did? Do you have bruised, even broken, ribs right now?"

Mike's mouth opened, and then popped shut. He felt shamed, as Steve had intended. "Uh."

"Nee. Go home right now, before I lose all my

self-control." Steve stood, blocking the front door with his bulk.

Mike, about to try and push his way in, quailed at the look on Steve's face. Nodding, he left. On his way home, he muttered to himself, knowing he was a coward.

Back upstairs, Steve told Becky and Kate what had happened. "He was mad. It was all over his face. I told him to leave before I lost all my self-control. Daughter, I think you should think very carefully about whether it's a gut idea to keep seeing him."

Kate nodded as Becky left for her first-aid kit. "Ya. I'll do so."

Returning, Becky shooed Steve from Kate's room. "I need to have her disrobe so I can rub liniment on her ribs and wrap them. This will have to do until tomorrow morning."

"I'll think about breaking up with Mike."

"Nee, girl! You'll do more than just think about it. I don't know why he's like that. Is that the first time?"

"Ya. He's never done this before. Oh, we've had disagreements. But this is the first time he's ever gotten remotely physical." She sighed. "I really like his mamm. She's so strong and so gentle. I can't imagine him ever hitting her."

"So, you want to see if he backs off on this." Becky's voice was flat.

"Ya—no. I don't know yet."

Becky sighed at her headstrong daughter. "We are going to the Urgent Care tomorrow. If your ribs are broken, you won't be seeing him anymore. And I don't care if you're in rumspringa." Gathering her materials, Becky left the room, trying not to cry. In their room, she and Steve talked about the situation. "Should we talk to Essie about this? She has so much going on."

Steve sighed. "Only if he continues in this way. Is she going to stop seeing him?"

"She doesn't know yet. She really likes his mamm and doesn't want to see her hurt by this."

"Her heart is too big." Steve's voice was flat. He sighed. "Well, we just keep a very close eye on the two of them, if she chooses to continue seeing him."

"And pray."

"Ya."

AFTER COMING HOME FROM THE URGENT CARE Center the next day, Kate decided to give Mike some space. X-rays had shown a small, hairline fracture of one rib, so she was wrapped up one more time and given potent painkillers. After waking from a medication-induced nap, she went downstairs and began to work on replenishing the go-bags she and her mamm used in their work. "Mamm, are you sure…?"

"Nee, no other work. Other than chopping vegetables and stirring pots for meals. I'll get my sister to help with housework."

"What about going to deliveries?"

Becky paused as she kneaded the bread dough. "I think, as long as you aren't actively exerting your upper body, you should be fine. Ya. You do every-thing else and I'll do the heavy work until your rib heals."

Kate's smile was wide. "Denki, Mamm!"

Becky hurried to the door at a signaling knock. Swinging it open, she froze, and then frowned at the person standing on the porch. "Mike."

"Missus Lapp, may I please speak to Kate?"

"That's up to her. Kate? Mike is here." Becky refused to leave her position at the front door until Kate nodded to her that she'd be all right.

"Yes, Mike?" Her voice was just as distant as Becky's had been.

"Uh… I wanted to tell you that I'm sorry. Mamm found out how you got hurt. And she laid into me right bad. So, I'm here to say I'm sorry."

Kate's eyebrow creased. "So, you're sorry only because your mamm found out? And yelled at you? You're not sorry because you knew in your soul that what you did was wrong?"

Mike's hand flew up in supplication. "Nee. That's not what I meant. I knew right away, but I figured we both needed time. And besides, you took off in such a way that I couldn't find you!" Mike's voice rose.

Kate, hearing the increased volume, forced herself to stand without backing up. She felt Becky standing right next to her. Felt her mother taking her hand. "It seems you're getting mad again, Mike. Maybe we should wait to talk until you can stay calm when we talk about difficult topics." She shut the door so Mike couldn't come in. Releasing a long sigh through pursed lips, she closed her eyes and rested her forehead against the burnished wood of the door. She jumped as she felt Mike's fist hitting the opposite side of the door.

"Kate, get over here." Becky tugged on Kate's hand, which she still held.

Kate didn't argue. She scuttled backward, guided by Becky.

"Kate! We're not done!"

"Mike, go home now!"

"Kate! I— Deacon Kopp!"

"And why are you yelling for Kate through a closed door?" The deacon knocked, keeping an eye on Mike.

"I, uh. I was trying to apologize to her for—" Mike stopped abruptly.

Becky answered the door. "Deacon, come in."

"Do you want him to come inside?"

"Nee! He needs to go back to work right away. After all, he and Essie need every penny he earns." Becky's brows rose, sending a strong signal to Mike.

He understood that message and hurried off. "I'm sorry, Kate." He mumbled the words as he ran off. Leaving in his buggy, Mike castigated himself for being so stupid.

"Missus Lapp, is there a reason you didn't want him inside?"

Becky looked at Kate.

"Deacon, Mike and I went out with other kids on Friday night for rumspringa. Miriam and I went to the girls' room to talk privately. Mike thought I was gone for too long. I told him that I'd only been gone for a few minutes. I nudged against his arm with my shoulder, something we've done before. He bumped against me, but much harder than he'd ever done before. I was pushed back into the side of our table. Miriam and Jonah brought me home, and Mamm put some salve on it. We went to urgent care this morning, and I have a hairline fracture of one rib. So, I'm not sure I should be around Mike at this point."

"Ya, Miriam told me a little of what happened. I'm glad she and Jonah had the presence of mind to get you out of there. Tell me, Kate, do you think he has the tendency toward violence? Mike, that is."

Kate gazed off into the distance as she thought. "I didn't think he did. But now? I wonder…"

"He lost his daed at a very young age. Males in his family he would normally get guidance from live at a distance from Lancaster. I should see if someone can fill that role for him. Being Miriam's daed, I don't think it's appropriate for me to do."

Kate nodded. "Denki."

"In the meantime, young lady. You do as I directed Miriam. You stay away from him. If you meet him in town, stay where others can see you. Understand?"

"Ya, and I will."

WHILE KATE'S RIB HEALED, SHE AGAIN BEGAN thinking about the possibility of leaving Lancaster and living among the Englisch. While going to the library was working out for her now, she was painfully aware of her lack of experience in chemistry and other sciences.

CHAPTER 4

After helping with the housework and cleaning up from dinner, Kate told Becky where she was headed. "I'm going to the library to see if I can find some books that will help me figure out what I can do—along with you—to help our patients when they experience problems in labor."

"Gut! See if you can bring books home so I can learn as well."

"I will. I'll be back before long."

In the library, Kate got assistance on the computer in looking for the information she needed.

"Okay, here's what you need. The books with

an asterisk are currently in the library. Some, you'll have to wait for, if you don't mind too much."

"No, that's fine. I'll just start with the ones available right now, and when the others are here, hopefully, I can check them out."

"Excellent! Let me know if you need anything else."

Kate smiled. "I may need some help. We can't use the internet, so I would need someone to help me find something, if it's not here."

"That's not a problem. If I can't, I'll get a circulation librarian to help you."

Kate found two of the books she needed. Looking at the clock, she decided she still had some time, so she sat down in one of the comfy armchairs to read. One hour later, as if she had an internal alarm clock ringing in her head, she loaded the books into her bag and left. Walking home, she was grateful for the cooler daytime temperatures.

"Kate! Hey!"

"Miriam! Hi!"

"Get over here. I saw Mike a few minutes ago. He still looks upset. I'll take you home so he doesn't spot you."

Kate gasped. "Ya, denki! Your daed told me to stay away from him."

"He's right. You don't need anyone hitting you, whether accidental or not. Why did you walk to the library, anyway? We could have gone together."

"It's such a pretty day, I thought the walk would do me gut. But not at the expense of running into Mike!"

"Are you breaking up with him?"

"I don't know." Looking around, Kate drank in the bright colors of mid-summer as she thought. "He doesn't try to understand. Although, I understand because Missus Hoffman was his cousin."

"Feeling sympathy is one thing. Allowing him in so he can intimidate you is quite another." Miriam's voice was firm.

Kate cringed. "You're right. And that's why I'm trying so hard to learn more. I don't want another Missus Hoffman, if we can help it."

"Ya, I under— Oh, no! Mike is coming that way!" Miriam signaled the horses to turn left so she could take another route to Kate's house. "You know what? We're close to my parents' place. Let's just wait there until it's safe to take you home."

"Ya, gut idea." Kate was watching the side road from the side of her eye, praying Mike wouldn't intersect them. As they pulled into the Kopp yard, she sighed with relief. After she and Miriam unhitched the team from the buggy, they ran into the house.

"Girls, why are you running? You look like a wild horse is after you!"

"Nee, not that. Mike Newman. And he didn't look happy." Miriam dropped the shopping bags on the table.

"So, Kate, you're all right with avoiding him?"

"Ya. My rib is still healing and I don't need any more confrontations."

"Gut. You need to make a decision about him, sooner or later."

"Ya, I know. I've just been preoccupied with finding ways to get more midwifery knowledge."

THE NEXT WEEK, KATE WENT TO THE LIBRARY with Becky. They had decided to stop by on a Saturday evening, before it closed. Giving her list of books to the circulation librarian, she smiled when she realized a textbook on "conditions of pregnancy" was back. "Yes, I'd like to check it out."

"Are you a midwife?"

"Both my mother and I are. Extra knowledge never hurts."

"Here you go. I'd say, 'enjoy reading,' but this is a heavy topic."

"Ya. It is, but it will only help our patients." At home that night, she read later than usual—the next day was not a Meeting Sunday, so she didn't have to be up quite as early as usual. *The body leaks protein into the kidneys as preeclampsia begins to develop. So, this is where the whole sickness process begins? Should the mamm eat more meat? Or less meat? Her body and boppli still need nutrients so the baby is strong and healthy…* Closing the book, Kate sighed, feeling frustration. She remembered vivid, isolated moments from their struggle with Mrs. Hoffman. *I need more information. And access to this information. If I left here, started living Englisch and went back to school to become a doctor, I could give so much more help to women who develop this horrid condition.*

THE FOLLOWING MONDAY, ESSIE NEWMAN, Mike's mamm and Mrs. Hoffman's auntie, was cleaning her house. As she did, she thought about Anna as she struggled with tears. *Did they do enough to save her? I remember Becky from when she first started working as a midwife. So smart! But did she or Kate have the knowledge*

or skills they needed to help Anna? Setting her mop and bucket away, Essie poured herself a cold drink of water. *This preeclampsia is something I've heard of. It is a bad sickness, one that develops silently until it becomes almost an emergency. It has to be dealt with fast. I remember seeing Anna's face and hands getting so swollen. We thought that was just the normal swelling of pregnancy.* Essie thought about Anna's three young kids, who now had no mamm. *Speaking of which, I'd better stop gathering wool and get busy with supper. It's my night to make Anna's family something to eat.* Quickly, she made beef stroganoff, along with vegetables, for the family. Separating out what she and Mike would eat, she put the rest into leftover containers so Mike could take them to his cousin's family. As he walked in the door, Essie smiled at him. "Clean up right away. I need you to take these containers to your cousin's house so the food doesn't get cold or spoil."

A few days later, Essie spotted Kate in the market. Placing her hand on the girl's arm, she asked, "Do you have a few minutes to talk, Kate?" As Kate nodded, she continued, asking her about how things were going with her family. Then, "Kate, I have a question for you. I just wonder… what else could have been done…for Anna, I mean?"

Kate sighed. She knew just how close she and her mamm were to being blamed for the unanticipated deaths. "Missus Newman, preeclampsia is so unpredictable. We don't know—even doctors don't know—what causes it or who is likely to develop this condition. It's horrible! But we do know that the mother's body begins to leak protein into her kidneys. And this starts the whole process of this sickness."

"Is there a cure available?"

"Ya. Childbirth. The mamm literally has to give birth in order for the sickness to begin reversing and going away."

Essie continued, knowing the questions were hard for both of them. "But, what if the sickness develops way before the baby is due?"

Shaking her head, Kate responded. "Bed rest. And a referral to an obstetrician so they can monitor her as closely as possible."

"So, if you know ahead of time, you can refer her out."

"Ya. Every single time."

"And…did Anna have that time?"

"Nee. She was already in labor a month early. I'm thinking she went into labor early because of the development of preeclampsia. But I don't know for sure and certain."

Knowing what she knew now, Essie was relieved. *They did everything they knew to do, once they realized how sick she was.* "Denki for being so understanding and honest."

"Missus Newman, I will always be so." Kate saw Mike approaching them and she tried to find a way of getting away without being obvious.

"Mamm, is everything okay?" Mike had spotted the two women talking together.

"Ya, it is. Kate was able to relieve a lot of my worries about Anna with her answers to my questions. They tried, Mike. They tried so hard to save her. But without a referral to a specialist, they couldn't do very much."

Mike turned to Kate. "Kate, when do our mothers get these referrals?"

"I don't know every reason why, but mainly if the mamm has had a hard pregnancy or delivery before. Or if she gets sick. If she had a health problem. And Anna's three pregnancies before were so easy. She had no problems."

"If you had a little more knowledge, Kate, would that help?" Essie was curious again.

"Definitely. Ya. We would know when to pull in an Englisch obstetrician."

Essie asked a few more questions. Feeling reassured again, she now knew that Kate and Becky had done everything they knew how to do. She released her hurt and anger toward the two midwives. Telling Mike not to be too late, she left to pay for her purchases.

Mike was now able to see and understand that Kate had been stuck in an untenable situation, one where she didn't have the needed knowledge. Licking his lips, he asked her to join him for that weekend's rumspringa activities.

Kate's expression was serious. "Nee, Mike. After what happened the last time, I don't think that's a gut idea."

"Please? I didn't understand before what kind of pressure you deal with at births. After hearing you talking with my mother, I get it now. And I know why you need more information and learning." He forgot to mention that her additional learning should be on her own time and only at the library. "Please? I really miss you."

Kate looked into Mike's blue eyes. Seeing the pain of missing her, she relented, praying she wouldn't regret it. "Okay. But if anything like that ever happens again, I won't go out with you anymore. In fact, we'll be history." Kate pressed her hand gently against her rib, which was by now, almost completely healed.

Mike, seeing the action, felt terrible. "I'm really sorry for that. I didn't realize how much strength I was using when I pushed back."

"That's fine. Just nothing like that again." She agreed to meet him for that weekend's activity. "My parents won't be too happy. So you're going to have to request their forgiveness and show them that you can and will behave better from now on."

On Friday, as Mike waited for Kate to come downstairs, he answered Steve's question with discomfort. "Sir, I was wrong to react as I did the last time we saw each other. I know that. It won't happen again."

"You're right. It won't. Does your mamm know?"

Mike nearly choked on his nervousness. "Uh, n-nee, she doesn't."

Steve sighed, a long, gusty sound. He didn't see Kate, tears in her eyes, watching him. "Okay. As long as she's willing, you can see her. But. If you *ever* do anything to hurt her or make her cry, Mike Newman, you are not going to be allowed to even ask her the time of day. Do you understand?"

"Ya. Ya, I do. Denki."

Kate quickly wiped the telltale tears from her face. Smiling at her daed and Mike, she came downstairs. "I'm ready. Daed, we'll be back later tonight."

"Okay. Be careful. And, daughter. If he does anything, you get a ride home, do you understand?"

"Ya, I do. And I will, if anything happens."

During the evening, she talked and laughed with her friends. Things between her and Mike were relaxed and easy, as they used to be. Except for one thing—when she would have easily leaned into his arm and bumped against him, now, she refrained, not feeling gut about that.

Mike didn't pick up on this. Instead, he was just relieved that he was back with Kate. He vowed that he would try to understand every single mood and question she had. *As a new midwife, she probably feels lost without some of the information and knowledge she's looking for. So just be understanding. Give her suggestions.* The evening went well and, in front of Kate's parents' house, he gave her a fleeting kiss. He wanted it to be much deeper, but just in case her daed was watching out the window, he felt it was best to be careful.

Feeling comfortable and more understood around Mike, Kate decided to resume their relationship. She felt at ease discussing some of the questions she had with Mike. If he relied too heavily on giving her advice she wasn't really seeking, she was able to overlook that.

In her work with her mamm, Kate found that she was feeling a little more comfortable. On one Friday afternoon, it became obvious that she and Mike would miss their date because the patient they were with was making slow progress. "Mamm, I'm going to go outside for just a minute. I'll be back, and then you take a break."

"Do you have a call to make?" Becky's look was wise.

"Uh, ya. I'll be right back." Placing her call, she asked for Mike at the carpentry shop. "Uh, Mike? Mamm and I are still working with a patient. It doesn't look like I'm going to make—"

"What? But I had special plans!" Mike was upset and his voice reflected this.

"Mike, I'm sorry. But you remember what we talked about when we first started dating? My patients come first if a labor goes through a Friday or weekend night. Period!"

Mike heard the fine note of steel running through Kate's voice. About to respond, he sighed and bit the hot words back. "Okay. I understand. How about tomorrow?"

Kate was silent for a few seconds. Then, "I don't know."

Running back, Kate relieved Becky for a few minutes. While she was alone with their patient, she checked her vitals. "You're doing gut, Rebecca. How are your contractions?"

"Gut...ohh, they're getting harder!"

Becky walked in. "You're going into transition. That's the hardest phase, aside from the pushing." She checked Kate's notes. It was after ten that night when Rebecca and Sam finally welcomed their first boppli. Bustling around the room, Kate was aware of a sense of wellbeing and accomplishment. *Thank you, Gott. You gave her an easy labor.* On the way home, she and Becky discussed the delivery. Then, Becky asked her question. "What did Mike say?"

"He was...*disappointed* that I couldn't go with him."

"'Disappointed?' Or more like angry?"

Kate sighed, not wanting to answer the question. "Well, ya, both. But I think—"

"Nee, daughter. Don't make excuses! If he behaved badly, call him on it. He has to know right away, so he can change his behavior."

CHAPTER 5

The next day, Mike came to the house after supper as if nothing had happened.

Kate, who had made up her mind about spending the evening with Mike, answered the door, clearly not ready to go out.

"Why aren't you ready?"

"You were pretty upset last night when Mamm and I were helping our patient to deliver her baby. By the way, we didn't get home until after ten last night. Because first babies sometimes take longer to arrive."

"So, you're upset?"

"Ya, I am! You know we talked about how you view my vocation. How seriously I take it. You expected me to drop everything—delivery included

—and go out with you as if nothing was happening."

"I thought you'd be ready by the time we made our plans for."

Kate stepped onto the porch, aware that Steve was standing just inside. This gave her a sense of security she needed. "Mike, while your carpentry work is difficult and physically challenging, the items you make don't do unexpected things at night or on the weekends. Mamm and I don't know when a patient will go into labor. When it happens, it happens. So, no, I don't want to go out tonight." She wheeled around and went back into the house, locking the door securely behind her. Looking at her daed, she saw a smile of approval on his face.

"You did gut, daughter. You stayed strong." Steven enfolded Katie's trembling body into his arms and held her securely against his chest.

Kate gulped tears back. She really cared for Mike, but she didn't want her own plans to be buried under his need to be first in her life. "Daed? Do you think Mike wants to be the first in my life? When Gott should be?"

"Ya, I do. And I am so happy to see you standing strong when he gets demanding."

I may need to stand strong if I decide to leave Lancaster

and live among the Englisch. Kate felt a peculiar sense of worry. "I think I'm going to go to bed early. I have a lot to think about."

"Okay. Sleep well, and I hope you find the answers you need."

Upstairs, Kate dressed for bed. Instead of blowing her lantern out, she got into bed and sat against her pillows, just thinking. Finally, she realized she needed answers she or her parents didn't have. *I'll visit the library Monday to see if I can find out about the classes I would need. Just in case.*

ON HER WAY HOME FROM THE LIBRARY, KATE SAW Miriam, shopping with her mamm.

"We missed you at the gathering the other night. Mike too." Miriam's eyes showed the worry she felt.

"Ya. Mamm and I were real busy attending a birth. We didn't finish until after ten that night. So, I just stayed home. I was exhausted."

"And? What did Mike do?"

"He wasn't happy. I called him from our patient's house to let him know I wasn't going to be able to see him. He came over Saturday night to pick me up. I wasn't in the mood to spend time with him. And I let him know why. He wasn't happy. I told him that I can't always predict when I'm going to be able to go out with him or not. Childbirth is not like carpentry. And he needs to realize this. So I told him 'good bye' and went back inside."

"Did you break up with him?"

"Nee! I want to spend time with him. But I am not going to allow him to make me do anything that isn't in my patients' best interests, boyfriend or not."

"I saw him glaring at you before services started yesterday."

"Ya. He's still upset, and that's why I wasn't at the Sing last night."

Mrs. Kopp joined in. "Gut. We have to respect our men. But we don't have to be their doormats. You perform a vital service, Kate. He hasn't realized that."

"So, what were you doing? Did you go to the library?"

"Ya. I got another book." Kate didn't add that she had also had the librarian print out admission and class information for her from the internet. She still wanted to keep her thoughts to herself until she had enough information to make a gut decision.

WHILE KATE AND MIKE WERE ON THE OUTS, SHE decided that it would be a gut idea to take some time to think before she went out with him. When he came by a few days later to see if she wanted to go to the upcoming Sing, she told him of her decision. "Mike, I really care about you, and I love spending time with you." Sensing him about to interrupt, she shook her head. "Please let me say what I'm thinking. Without interruption. Right now, I'm still busy learning what I need to know about being a gut midwife. Wait! When a woman goes into labor, it lasts for hours and hours. So that means that, if Mamm and I are called to someone's house at five in the morning, we may still be there at seven at night. We can't predict."

"So, what do you want to do? Just call me when you're not working?"

"Nee. And don't be sarcastic. I want to take a break from seeing each other." Kate struggled not to break down. She didn't want him to think she was weakening. "Rather than worrying that I'm not going to be able to make it to a date to see you, I am going to be studying. I want to see if I can learn some new midwifery skills. If I have more knowledge, I can be more helpful to the mothers and to my own mamm."

"This feels like a breakup." While Mike didn't sound angry, the way he growled the words from deep in his chest make Kate think that he was about to get angry.

"I have to go. Mamm needs my help in the kitchen and Daed is mighty hungry." She ran back into the house. She felt oddly *light*, as though a thousand-pound weight had been removed from her back.

"So, you look like you feel much better." Becky smiled.

"Ya, I do. Mike was just here, and I told him I want to take a break. Mostly because he refuses to understand what my work—our work—is all about. He thinks I can set a laboring mamm aside at five-thirty so I can go out with him."

"Was he still bothering you about that? We helped that mamm two weeks ago!"

"I know. What shall I work on?"

Kate accepted the apple crumple recipe and began working on the dessert. She answered Becky's questions as well. "I don't know that I'll go to Sings for a while. If Mike is there…"

"And, are you still working on your learning?"

"Ya. But some of it is so confusing. So, that's why I spend so much time at the library."

"That is fine. Just make sure you are at home around the time that we have to go assist someone."

"I will." For the next few weeks, even though Kate wasn't feeling the pressure from Mike, she still missed him. His laughter and sense of humor. How he kissed her so lightly in the buggy. Having the extra time allowed her to spend even more time at the library. She found that she had to allot herself short times at the library, so she made the most of those moments. On her way home, equipped with several pages of notes from the internet, Kate pulled into her parents' yard, only to see Becky running outside. "Thank Gott you're home! We have to go! The twins are coming!"

Kate took a few seconds to come to the present. "The twins. Oh, ya! Let me put my books away."

"Nee, no time. I have your bag. Let's go, now!"

On their way to the woman's house, Mike passed by them and tried to stop Kate.

"Nee, we don't have time! A woman's in labor!"

Becky brought Kate up to date with the details she'd need know. "Twins. We have to worry about one of the twins being in the breech position. Have you read anything on that?"

"No, I haven't found anything. Is her labor progressing normally?"

"The last time I saw her, everything looked fine."

In the family's house, aunts and sisters were taking care of the two older kinder. Becky took a moment to request that everyone stay out of the delivery room, unless the mamm requested their presence. Hurrying upstairs, she reviewed what she knew about the woman. "This is her first set of twins so this is completely new to her."

"What role will we play?"

"I'll lead, you'll be my assistant. If I see anything happening, you'll have to help me turn the situation around. Now, let's check her out."

Kate assisted Becky as she had done in many previous labors. In this labor, the mother's blood pressure was slightly elevated, but nothing that worried her or Becky.

"Things are going well, Mamm. Why don't you take a break? We could be here for quite a while."

Becky thought for a minute. "Okay. Ya, but you call me immediately if anything changes. I'll be downstairs having some tea."

"I will."

Kate oversaw the laboring mamm for several

minutes, monitoring her blood pressure and contractions. "How are you feeling?"

"Just tired. When will my babies come?"

"In their own gut time. You've had two kinder, so you know how it goes." Kate rested her hand on the pregnant abdomen and observed the tightening of the orb.

After ten minutes, Becky came back upstairs. "I feel so much better! How is mamm here?"

"Tired, but things are going well. Her contractions are still three minutes apart and she's about six centimeters dilated."

"Gut. You go downstairs and take a ten-minute break. If anything happens, I'll call you."

Kate hurried downstairs. Like her mamm, she had coffee and downed a delicious sweet roll, made by the grandmother of the coming kinder. "Denki! This is so gut!"

"You're welcome. Please enjoy. I made several, and I know you and Becky are very busy upstairs. Eat more because you're working so hard."

Kate took one more roll then, seeing that her time downstairs was just about up, she went back upstairs. "Mamm, how is she?"

"In a little more pain. Contractions are now about two minutes apart—wait! Nee, don't push!

Let us check you first." After doing so, Becky announced that it was time for her to begin pushing. "Kate, check the placement of the little ones. We need to make sure they're both properly positioned for birth."

Closing her eyes so she could envision the bodies of the twins within their mamm. "Uh, mamm?" She edged closer to Becky so she could whisper her news. "One of the babies is breech."

Becky's face paled. "Do you remember the last breech baby we delivered? Do you remember what I told you to do?"

Kate began to regret the second roll she'd eaten. Feeling her stomach sour, she swallowed hard. "Ya. Turning it around."

"We're going to have to do an external cephalic version once the first baby's been born."

"What—what's wrong?" The mother was picking up on the new somberness in the room.

Becky smiled, trying to reassure her. "We found something unusual. So you're going to give birth to your first baby. You'll have to keep from pushing until we've moved the second baby around. That one is breech."

"B-breech? You mean he's not head first?"

"Nee, but we can handle it safely. As soon as you feel the urge to push, let us know."

For the next half-hour, mamm labored. Finally, she gasped and moaned. "I have to push!"

Kate checked her and spoke. "You're ready. Follow my instructions, look at me and we'll get baby number one born!"

For the next thirty minutes, everyone worked together in a seamless ballet. Becky gave a tired laugh of relief. "And your little boy is born!" Quickly, she handed him to a waiting relative to clean up. She turned her attention back to the mother and Kate. "Kate, start applying firm pressure when you find baby's head. Start turning it toward mother's birthing canal. I'm going to check this one's vitals and his auntie can clean him up."

Swallowing hard, Kate began working to move the baby around. She apologized for the pain she was causing the mother. "I'm sorry! It'll be over soon. Just try not to push!" Finally, the baby was head-down. "Okay, push!"

Mamm pushed and stopped, pushed and stopped. Every time she stopped, Kate, then Becky checked the position of the baby's head.

"Okay, as long as this little one stays positioned correctly, we're all okay. Push!"

The second delivery took closer to an hour. By the end, mamm was sweat-soaked and almost out of energy. She gratefully accepted the apple slices Kate handed to her. Finally, almost one hour after the baby had been turned, she was born. Kate caught the child and almost cried as she announced it was a little girl. She and Becky cut the baby's cord, cleaned the baby and took care of its vitals.

Kate got mamm to feed both babies, showing her how to position pillows so she could feed both babies at once. By the time they left the house, it was dark. Kate's stomach rumbled loudly.

Becky checked the time. "We'll have something at home. I'm powerful hungry myself!"

"What time is it?" Kate was bone-tired.

"Almost ten."

Kate wasn't surprised. Looking down the road, she sighed. "It's Mike."

"Be strong, girl. Just like you were while we were working together."

"Where were you? I stopped at your house to see if we could talk." Mike was irritated.

"We just came from delivering twins, Mike. We got to their house at ten this morning."

Mike, about to speak, was caught by the length of time the delivery had taken—and by the sheer exhaustion in Kate's voice. He looked closely at her face. Seeing her sleepy eyes and the dark circles under them, he felt ashamed for yelling at her. "I'm —I'm sorry. We'll talk later."

Kate nodded her head once and signaled the team to begin moving again. Once Mike was long past, she spoke. "Or maybe we won't talk later."

"Nee, Kate. Ya, we don't like that the two of you are still dating. But you owe him the courtesy of your thoughts and feelings."

Kate sighed. "But, Mamm, I'm so tired of his attitudes."

"Ya. I dated someone like him before I met your daed."

"And? How did you deal with him?"

CHAPTER 6

Becky sighed as they pulled into their yard. "Gut. He's not following us. Let's deal with the team and put the buggy away. Inside, we'll have lemonade and butter and jelly sandwiches."

Once they'd fed the team and gotten inside, Becky put their things away as Kate pulled the bread from the pantry. She made thick sandwiches slathered with almond butter and apple jelly.

Becky poured the lemonade and set plates and napkins on the table. Drinking from her glass, she sighed. "I was your age. Your daed and I had noticed each other, but we were both dating someone else. So, at first, I thought I was happy with John. But, I was going through the same things with him that you are with Mike. He didn't want to see that we couldn't schedule deliveries between seven and five during the day. He wanted me ready to go out with him, regardless. So, I finally broke up with him. But not before I sat down with him and told him exactly why. I don't like what Mike is doing to you. He's discounting the importance of our work, like John did. It may happen because he's not secure. But it's wrong, period. You owe him that courtesy, Kate. If you decide you're not going to—" Becky's words were interrupted by a huge yawn. She shook her head. "Excuse me! If you're going to break up with him, let him know just why. This way, he may learn for future relationships."

Next, Kate yawned. "That's catching! Let's finish so we can get to bed." She took a huge bite of her sandwich.

"Ya, dawn will be here too fast."

WAKING UP THE NEXT MORNING, KATE KNEW SHE had a lot to think about, besides the possibility of leaving her home. Now, she had to consider breaking up with Mike.

Becky and Steve noticed that Kate was quieter

and more contemplative. Becky had to stop Steve from going up to Kate to ask her what she was thinking. "Nee, husband. She's thinking about her situation with midwifery and Mike. He's still giving her trouble, and she's getting right tired of it." She explained what happened on the night they delivered the twins.

"She didn't tell me. I need to know, Becky."

"Okay, but give her the room she needs to figure things out for herself." Becky explained how they bumped into Mike and his irritation at not being able to find her.

Steve growled. "It's a gut thing he works in a different shop. Or…"

Becky nodded. "She has a gut head on her shoulders. I did tell her that, whatever she decides, she needs to give him the courtesy of an explanation."

IN THE LIBRARY ONE DAY, KATE ENCOUNTERED chemical equations. Because she hadn't taken very much chemistry before she finished with school, she didn't know how to work with them. Sighing, she closed the book and sat back.

A few tables away, a handsome medical student sat, watching Kate. He'd noticed the books she was reading. He decided to sit back and just watch what happened with the pretty Amish girl for now.

Kate finally decided to study something else that didn't require working out chemical equations. Thinking of the breech birth and preeclampsia, she asked for help in finding books that dealt with those topics. After a few minutes, she returned to the study table, still unaware of the handsome, Englisch medical student who had noticed her. She quickly became absorbed in the topics she was reading about. Looking at the time, she decided to check both books out.

"Have you ever thought about going to medical school? It looks like you're trying to self-teach." The observant librarian said as she checked the books out for Kate.

"I've thought about it. But I don't know."

"Are you a midwife?"

"Ya. I apprentice with my mother. And I still have so much to learn."

Back at his table, the med student had to strain to hear. *Hmmm. Amish midwife. I can see why she wants more learning.* After Kate left, he focused on his studies again.

THAT NIGHT, KATE TOSSED ONE OF THE LIBRARY books aside, frustrated. *I need to make a decision. Soon!* A thought occurred to Kate. *I'm going to have to help mamm find a replacement if I do leave.* After falling asleep later than normal, Kate dreamed. *"I'm sorry, Missus Cade. But your body won't stop going into premature labor. We're going to have to admit you to the hospital so we can try to stop those contractions."*

"But I'm only five weeks away from giving birth!"

"And your baby can't breathe on its own this early. Almost as a bystander, Kate noticed and admired "Doctor Kate's" firmness. *"Do you want your baby to have any struggles if it's born early?"*

"Well, no. But I don't want to miss..."

"Miss what?"

The woman blushed. "Well, my family's beach vacation. It takes place in three weeks. So I wouldn't mind at all having my baby this early."

Kate sighed. "Missus Cade, if you want to have your baby early just so you can go to the beach, you're not thinking of the baby's needs. It would have to be hospitalized for several days."

Mrs. Cade was silent, and then she shot a glare at Kate. "I want to go home."

"You can go home, but not until we have given you a medication that will stop your premature contractions."

Mrs. Cade continued to glare at Kate. Then, "What's your accent? German? Jewish?"

Kate thought she was used to curiosity about her Amish heritage and way of speaking, but this shocked her. "I was Amish." She gestured toward the nurse and handed her the order for the IV medication for Mrs. Cade. "You should be able to go home before nightfall tonight. I'll be checking on you periodically."

In the end, the woman's contractions stopped and she got to go home. But she wasn't happy that her baby wouldn't be born this early.

Kate entered a note into Mrs. Cade's file. "Mrs. Cade said she wouldn't mind giving birth to her child five weeks early so she could go to her family's beach vacation no longer pregnant. I have concerns about the baby's safety and would like for him or her to be monitored once born."

Hearing the thump of her daed's feet on the wood floor, Kate roused. Before she got out of bed, she remembered her dream. *Wow! Could that really happen if I become a doctor? There are so many decisions to make, so much responsibility.*

Days would go by where Becky and Kate would have no deliveries to attend. These were the times where Kate would help her mamm, then study or go to the library.

One day, as she was on her way home from the library, Kate bumped into Mike. "Mike! I need to get home. Mamm needs help with supper."

Mike's hand shot out and he gripped Kate's upper arm firmly. "Nee. Not until we sit down and figure this out."

"Nee, Mike! I've told you time and time again that we don't know when mothers are going to go into labor. Do you know when you're going to…" Kate had to search for something that wouldn't be too offensive. "Oh, I don't know. Burp? Or does it surprise you?"

Mike laughed at the comparison. Seeing Kate with a serious look on her face, his laughter stopped, seeming to trickle off. "Uh…"

"That's all you can say? Really? Think, Mike. Do you plan your bodily functions or do they just happen? Independent of your wishes?"

Mike didn't like the feeling he was getting. As if he was in the wrong. His mouth curved down into a distinct frown as he rolled his eyes. "Ya? Well, so what? I burp when I need to and do other things when they need to happen!"

"You just made my point. It's the same with every mother we work with. Mike, this is our profession. Our vocation, if you want to hear it that way. That means I can say that I'll go with you to a social or to a Sing. But, if between the time I say 'yes,' a mamm goes into labor, well, I'm sorry. That takes precedence over spending time with you and my other friends. I will not neglect my patients just because you get mad." And, because Kate was feeling angry, she jumped into her buggy and left before Mike could react. Getting home, she took care of the horses. In the house, she thumped her bag down upstairs. Back downstairs, she washed her hands with sharp, jerky movements.

"Are you okay, Kate? You're angry."

"Ya. Mike still thinks I can set patients aside just to spend time with him."

"What did he tell you?"

"He said he wanted to talk. Fine. I asked him if he was able to control burps or other bodily functions. Or if they happened independently of his will. He laughed. I told him I was serious. He got mad. But he admitted that his bodily functions happen without him being able to control them. So, I told him that's how it is with our mothers, and that we can't just leave them because their labors and deliveries are 'inconvenient' for the plans we've made." Kate made air quotes as she spoke.

"Well, you did the right thing."

"Denki! Then, I jumped into the buggy and just got myself home before I said something I would regret."

Becky sighed. "I think I need to have a talk with Essie about this." Seeing Kate beginning to object, Becky shook her head. "Nee, Kate. She needs to know so she can teach him that his girlfriend can't just be waiting around on his pleasure or beck and call. If we don't have any deliveries, we'll go tomorrow after he's left for the shop. And yes, you are going with me."

Kate sighed. "Mamm, I don't think it'll help. She's his mother and she'll take his side."

"Nee, she won't. She's had eight kinder, remember. She knows what labor is like."

Kate, about to say something else, shut her mouth. "Well, maybe you're right. But I don't think I should go with you. It would be like asking her to take sides or something."

"Child, you are going with me. Because he's doing this to you. I heard about a community not too far away that's fighting domestic violence and sexism. They are making it clear to the men that both of those are wrong, against the Ordnung. The women of their community, along with some of the men are helping to get the message out."

Kate was silenced. "Domestic violence?" She'd heard the term, but had never seen it. "You think Mike could become violent?" Her voice was quiet. Inside, Kate felt like every organ in her body was quivering, like a bowl of Jell-O.

THE NEXT MORNING, KATE AND BECKY KNOCKED on Essie Newman's front door. Kate was scared, not knowing what to expect of Mike's mamm.

"Ya? Becky! Kate, come in! Would you like some tea or lemonade?"

"Either is fine. Essie, we have something serious to discuss with you."

"Oh?" Essie paused for a second as she tried to think of what the issue might be. She put coffee cake on the table as well. "Now, please eat up. And tell me what's going on. I…my guess it's Mike?"

Becky took the lead. "Ya, it is. He and Kate have been seeing each other for a while. He knows gut and well that she's apprenticing with me."

"Oh, no. Don't tell me that he's trying to hog your time, Kate. I am so sorry!"

"Denki. It isn't your fault, Missus Newman. I've talked to Mike about the needs of our mothers. They need us to help them birth their children. I…I hate to bring this up, but he already knows about Anna and how we tried to help her. If she had been on her own, things could have been even worse."

"How has he been causing trouble? I want to help."

"Essie, Kate has told him that, if they have plans to go out, those plans won't happen if a mother is in labor. We have to be there."

"Oh, ya, definitely."

"Missus Newman, I asked him if he's able to control his bodily functions. I used burping as an example so I wouldn't intrude on matters that aren't my business. He finally admitted that he can't control when he's going to burp. So, when I told him that it's the same with the mothers who go into labor, he didn't like it. He just wants to be with me. And, while I'm flattered, I can't do that. And I won't."

"Ya, for sure and certain. You have to be with the mothers. Do you want me to talk with him?"

Becky smiled. "It would be helpful."

"I will, then."

"Missus Newman, I also go to the library in Lancaster so I can learn more about labor and delivery. Illnesses, like preeclampsia. Breech births, conditions that make a C-section necessary. That takes time because I finished school in the eighth grade, like everyone else here. So things like chemical equations really slow me down." Kate stopped there, not wanting to verbalize what she was really thinking—about leaving the Amish so she could return to school and become an M.D.

"You know, Kate, when your grandmother helped me to deliver my kinder, she was so calm and knowledgeable. And it was so helpful. I was able to be calm, even if something happened. My twins were premature and she was just so matter-of-fact about that. And that helped me to deliver them. They were so little and they needed specialized care. So she arranged for them to go to the newborn intensive care unit at the Englisch hospital in Lancaster. Now, they're twenty-three. And married."

"That's what I want. That calm that comes from being confident that I know what I need to know to help my patients. Mamm has that."

"Kate, you keep going to the library, if it helps

you. And I will talk to my son. I know that he came home pretty upset yesterday evening."

Kate was curious. "Missus Newman, what did he say?"

Essie shook her head, sadness on her face. "He lied to me. Said he'd had a bad, difficult day at the carpentry shop." Her voice was low and slow, communicating the level of pain she felt.

This told Kate she definitely couldn't say anything about what she was thinking. *Nee, it's too early, and it'll push Mike into a position where he'll start pressuring me even more.* "Mamm, we'd better go. I have a lot to think about." Trying hard not to cry, Kate pushed the coffee cake away from her. She'd lost her appetite for the sweet treat.

In the buggy, Kate was silent and dispirited.

"Daughter? That was bad news. But maybe Gott meant you to hear that. It doesn't... what I mean to say is that Mike revealed his character."

CHAPTER 7

"**. . .** To Missus Newman when he lied. Ya. I know." For the rest of the day, Kate stayed home, helping Becky with housework and cooking. She was so upset that she decided to stay home from the library. *Besides, I'd only risk running into Mike again. I just can't face him right now.*

"Kate? Are you staying home because you're sad? Or because you're afraid you'll see Mike?"

"Both. I don't think I can face him now."

"I can't blame you. But you need to face this head-on. After supper, let's go see Miriam. Maybe she'll be able to go with you to the library."

Kate thought about that for a little while. "Ya,

but not every day. I can't monopolize her time. She has clients who need their quilts delivered on time."

"Ya, I hadn't thought about that. Are you checking books out?"

"Ya."

"Then, just study here. Go to the library only when you have to return the books and check new ones out. Maybe Miriam can do that twice a month?"

Kate looked up. "Ya, maybe she can. Can we go after supper?"

"Ya. We'll take your daed with us."

At the Kopp house, the Lapps explained everything that had happened between Mike and Kate. "So, she doesn't want to run into him. She's pretty upset."

"And rightfully so." Deacon Kopp's voice rumbled from his chest. "I cannot believe Mike Newman did that! Kate, have you decided what you're going to do about your... *friendship*?"

"Nee, not yet. All I know is that I can't talk to him or I'll do or say something bad. I wanted to ask Mariam a favor. Miriam, I still need to go the library. I know you can't go every day because of your own work. But can you go with me twice a month, when I have to return books? Please?"

Miriam's eyes were large and her hands were gripping Kate's forearm in sympathy. "Yes, I will. I can work my schedule to fit the days when you have to go to the library. And there is no way that I'll let Mike talk to you."

Deacon Kopp's eyes widened. "Daughter, how would you do that?"

"Simple. You and Mamm both tell me that I'm a complete chatterbox, right? Well, if Mike tries to stop Kate and me, I'll just keep talking so he can't get a word in. That's how!"

"Well, it would be effective, that's for sure." The deacon sighed. "Okay, but only on one provision."

Miriam raised her eyebrows.

"That you two skedaddle on out of there if Mike gets angry. Kate, do you think he could be a threat?"

Kate shivered. "I hope not. I hadn't really thought about that."

"Has he ever threatened you before?"

"Nee, just gotten frustrated and raised his voice."

The deacon sighed again, looking at Mary, his

wife. She nodded slightly. "Okay. Every two weeks. But, at the first sign of trouble, I'm going to have to pull back on my agreement. And Kate? You really should think about breaking up with him."

Kate nodded, her chin quivering. "Ya. I'm thinking about that." *And leaving here so I can be a real doctor.*

LATER IN THE WEEK, BECKY AND KATE GOT A call from a new mamm who was extremely nervous about her first pregnancy. "Ya, Missus Zook?"

"Kate! I need to speak to your mamm. It's an emergency!"

"What's going on? Is there something happening with your pregnancy?"

"I think so. I keep getting these odd, random pains."

"Well, I can help—"

"Nee. I want to talk to your mamm."

Kate handed the phone to Becky. "Missus Zook."

Becky grimaced silently.

Kate overheard Becky's side of the conversation.

"So, the pains aren't regular. Then, you're having what's called Braxton-Hicks contractions. They aren't the real thing. It's just your body practicing, if you want to call it that, for the real thing... Nee, I've been doing this for thirty years. I know what these are. Come to your house? Now? Missus Zook, it's fixing to rain." She finally rolled her eyes. "Okay, Kate and I will be there as soon as we can. Kate—"

"Nee, only you! I don't trust an apprentice!"

In the end, Becky went and, within one hour, was back at home. Her face was tinted red from the anger she was feeling.

"Mamm, what happened?" Kate set the sharp knife down that she'd been using to slice vegetables for supper.

"Oh, that woman! It's a gut thing your daed's not home yet." Becky set everything down with jerky movements. "She was sure I was wrong, that she was in labor early. Not even when I checked her dilation was she convinced. She hasn't even begun to dilate yet. It was only when I'd been there thirty minutes and her pains stopped that she believed me."

"Why didn't she want me to go?"

"That's what made me the maddest. She doesn't

trust you, even though I've trained you and you're going to take my place."

Kate's jaw fell open. She closed her mouth and opened it again. "Mamm, I began to apprentice with you well before she even got married! Who is she——? Nee, I won't think that way! What's going to happen when she really goes into labor?"

"You'll be with me. And you'll let go of every uncharitable thought going through your mind right now. Ya, I'm thinking them, too. But she will be needing our help when her time comes. And we will give her every bit of our knowledge that she needs, do you understand?"

Kate let her head fall back. She closed her eyes and breathed in deeply. "Okay. But it better be a gut, long time before she goes into labor."

As the situation unfolded, Abigail Zook went into labor five weeks later. When Becky and Kate both showed up, she shook her head. "Nee! She can't be here. She's too young and inexperienced. She's not even married!"

Becky rolled her eyes, not bothering to hide the motion from Abigail. "Abigail, shut your mouth! I told Kate what you said a few weeks ago, and she pointed out the fact that she started apprenticing with me after she finished her schooling—almost four years ago. She is a very able assistant, and she still takes the time to learn even more."

Kate wordlessly pressed Abigail's legs open and quickly checked her dilation. Telling her mother the percentage, she took Abigail's blood pressure and temperature, competently giving them to Becky to write down. Before they had arrived at the Zook home, Becky and Kate had decided that Kate would take the lead in examining Abigail and making decisions.

"Why are you doing everything?"

Kate gave a polite smile to the young woman. "Because I know what I'm doing. Would you like to stand and walk around? It'll help speed your labor."

Abigail, not knowing what to say, shut her mouth and laboriously got out of bed. With Kate and Becky's help, she walked back and forth, up and down the hall. When contractions hit her, she stopped walking, leaned against the wall, breathed and sometimes bent over. After walking for thirty minutes, she went back to bed, about to lie on her back.

Kate forestalled this action. "Nee, Missus Zook. Lying on your back isn't gut for the boppli. You need to be lying on your left side so she or he gets the best blood flow possible before being born. Laying this way also allows your blood pressure to remain at a healthy level."

More time went by. Becky answered a soft knock at the door. "Ya? She's still laboring. There's still a lot of work she has to do."

Abigail got tired during her labor. Right after she entered the transition phase, she wanted to give up. "I'm tired! I can't do anymore!" As the youngest child, Abigail had been pampered and somewhat spoiled, and this showed in her petulant, weepy voice.

"Nee, Missus Zook. That little one has to come out and begin life in the big world. Use your breathing!" Kate's voice was slightly bossy and she enjoyed giving the order to the older girl.

Abigail had never received this kind of treatment before, and she didn't know how to deal with it. Her eyes widened and she gasped. Looking into Kate's eyes, she saw a tough young woman who knew just what she was doing. Stopping the whining, she complied with Kate and began to breathe through her contractions. Now, it was too painful to walk, so she stood in place. Or she sat on the edge of the bed and bounced gently at Kate's direction. Before long, she felt the urge to push hard. Scooting back on the bed and sitting up, she followed Kate's directions to breathe. Eventually, she felt the burning below that signaled the baby's head was about to show. Screaming, Abigail tried to get away from the burning pain.

"Stop! That pain means you're making progress and your little one is about to be here. Just let me check, and I'll let you know when it's okay to push." Kate checked and, finding that Abigail was fully dilated, she nodded. "It's okay to push now. On my count, push for ten seconds. One! Two! Three and…push!"

Behind Kate, Becky got the gown ready for the baby. She hurried downstairs to warm a blanket for the baby. Once it was warmed, she hurried back up again.

"Okay, gut. Push again. The baby's shoulders will be born. Again! Nee, you can do it! Push, Missus Zook! Gut! Just a few more times and you'll have a baby in your arms." Kate was unrelenting— something she'd learned from Becky. "I know you're tired, but we need to get that baby born! Come on!" Finally, the baby was born, with Kate catching it in the warmed blanket. She handed the baby to Becky once the umbilical cord was cut. "Now, I'm going to check you, and you'll be delivering the placenta."

"Nee! I'm tired of pushing things out of me! Just let it stay inside!" Abigail, spoiled at the best of times, had become petulant.

"Oh, really? Then, I suppose you want an infection that could rob you of your ability to keep your woman parts and to have more kinder." Kate made as though to cover Abigail.

"Nee! I'm just tired, is all. I'll push."

"When I tell you, then."

Behind Kate, Becky stood, holding the baby. Her mouth had dropped open. Smiling, she attended happily to the new life, putting a diaper and gown on her, and then wrapping a blanket around her.

"Okay, push the placenta out. That'll be much faster and easier." When the placenta had emerged, Kate quickly checked it to make sure everything had come out. "Okay, we're going to clean you up, then be on our way."

Downstairs, Mister Zook had placed the envelope with the payment for Becky and Kate on the table. "So? Is my child born?"

Becky smiled. "Ya, a beautiful little girl. She's upstairs with Abigail right now."

Daed rushed upstairs to meet the baby.

In the buggy, Becky began to chuckle.

"What is it, Mamm?"

"How you were with Abigail. I have never seen you like that. So sure and certain of everything that was happening."

Kate grinned. "She needed that after what she said about my status as an apprentice midwife. I wasn't going to let that slide."

Slowly, the word got around about how firm Kate had been. Mike found out when he was talking with a friend, and he sighed.

"What's wrong?"

"Kate. She won't talk to me."

Mike's friend, Abe, looked at him. "Mike, the word has gotten out. The last time you and Kate were supposed to go out, she had a delivery. You weren't happy that she wasn't ready and waiting for you at home when our get-together started. From what my sister said, she and Missus Lapp didn't get home until after ten that night."

"Ya, so?"

"So? The baby comes when it's gut and ready!

If it's not ready to be born until midnight, after the mamm has been in labor for fifteen hours, so be it! I'm real sorry, Mike, but on this, I support Kate. You were dead wrong, and you owe Kate an apology."

Mike was silenced by the revelation. He couldn't say anything because he got the uncomfortable feeling that Abe was right. He inhaled and exhaled, hard. "So, how do I get her to listen to me?"

"Tell her you're sorry. Ask for her forgiveness, although she's probably already given that to you. Let her know you'll give her the time and room she needs to do her work, even if labors and deliveries cut into the plans you've made. Just *support* her. She doesn't do easy work."

Mike shifted. He took a sip of his beer, aware that Abe was right. Sighing, he shook his head. "You're right. How'd you get to know so much about what she does?"

"My auntie. In Ohio. She's a midwife. Many's the time that my uncle had to give up on waiting at home for them to go to a family get-together. Sometimes, she would meet him there. Other times, the labor was just a slow one or the mamm ended up having to go to the hospital."

"That's another thing. She goes to the library. A lot!"

"I wouldn't be surprised. My auntie did the same. She has to keep up with what's happening in the midwifery practice, even though she doesn't have a state license."

"So, I should be happy that she's spending so much time away from me?"

"Mike, are you jealous of her vocation? Of her sitting at a table and reading difficult Englisch textbooks about labor and delivery?"

"Well. When you put it that way…"

"Mike, one question. Does she go to the library in the evenings?"

"Nee, because she knows her daed doesn't want her out late."

"Okay, so, when she doesn't have a delivery, is she happy to be spending time with you?"

"Well, she used to be."

"'Used to be.' What do you mean?"

"Before this happened, she was gut with going out with me. Now, one of us or the other is mad during dates, and it ruins them."

"Mike, I'm going to be real honest, and I hope I'll still have a friend. It sounds to me like you're jealous of the time she spends working. What are you going to do if the two of you get married, and she gets a call in the middle of the night?"

"Ah...well..." Mike stopped because he was seeing now just what Kate and Abe saw. "I have a lot to think about."

"Here's one more thing. Figure out why Kate's vocation threatens you."

CHAPTER 8

"I'd better go. I'll see you later."

Abe sighed. "Still friends?"

Mike shook Abe's hand. "Ya. I just need to think."

DRIVING BACK, MIKE DECIDED TO GO TO A FIELD not far from home. Arriving home, he put the horses in the barn and watered them. Running upstairs, he ran into Essie in the hallway. "Mamm, I'm home. But I want to think about my situation with Kate, so I'm going to go for a walk in the field next door and figure things out. I have my key and I'll be home before long."

"Gut. She is an honest girl, Mike."

"I know. I just don't know why I get so upset that her work takes higher importance."

Essie smiled at her son. "Do this, son. Put your get-togethers, rumspringa and your times with Kate up against the effort a mamm puts into having her new baby. Bringing that new life into the world. Mike, I'm going to name the problem. If you get mad, you get mad."

Mike shifted uncomfortably. "What is it?"

"Jealousy. You're jealous of the work Kate does. Why? Who knows? But you'd better figure that out."

Essie wasn't wrong. Mike was mad, but he knew better than to blow up at her. "I-uh, I'll be outside in the field." He swung away and went downstairs to the kitchen and grabbed two cans of soda on his way out.

Essie went back into her room, where she closed her eyes and prayed silently that Mike would break through and begin understanding why he had such a strong reaction to Kate's work and vocation.

In the field, Mike tried to figure things out. He thought about what Abe had told him. *Why do I get so upset?* When he thought about him and Kate, married, with her leaving at odd times of the night or day to attend to laboring mothers, his breath grew thick in his throat. *I can't. She should stay at home. I can take care of her and any babies we have.* Mike realized that he was more comfortable thinking of Kate staying at home, not working as a midwife. He would even be happier with her working at quilting or baking. When he thought of trying to change his way of thinking about her vocation, he felt physically and emotionally uncomfortable and he consciously decided to remain in his emotional comfort zone. *I'll just make her believe that I've changed how I view her career or whatever she calls it.* Thus, Mike decided he would lie to Kate in an effort to get her to resume their relationship. He didn't try to figure out how to react to her career once they got married.

The next week, Kate and Becky had no deliveries they anticipated. Instead, Becky went to visit expecting mothers for their regular monthly visits. Kate went to the library and checked out more books.

Again, as she was reading one of her books and taking notes, Casey James, the medical student, was studying as well. Looking up, he saw the pretty, Amish girl was back for more books.

Kate felt someone's eyes on her. Looking up and around, she spotted Casey looking at her and blushed as he smiled and waved at her. She reluctantly smiled back at him, and then returned to her studying.

That night, at home, Kate was in a reflective mood. She realized she felt more confident now that she didn't have to justify the time she spent working with laboring mothers. While she hadn't made up her mind about breaking up with Mike, the thought began to come back more frequently.

At home one day, after Kate and Becky had finished their housework, Kate was studying. Again, she ran into a difficult concept. Leafing through the notes she'd taken in previous study sessions, she found something that might help her understand what she'd just encountered. But, as she tried to apply her previous studying to what she was studying now, it didn't work. She tried to look through the index for an earlier mention of the topic. Finding it, she leafed through to the correct page and read what she found. While she got some help from this, she still wasn't able to fully understand everything she needed to know. "Mamm, I'm going to go to Miriam's and see if she can go to the library with me."

"That's fine. Are you having trouble with something?"

"Ya, some. It's on something we encounter at times in our work."

"What is it?"

"Prolonged labor. I'm trying to understand how doctors determine that the mother needs a C-section. If we were to understand this, we could figure out, hopefully sooner, when to send mothers to the hospital."

"Ya, I agree. Go ahead, but be back before suppertime. I need your help with the cooking."

At a knock on the door, both women looked around. Becky's smile wreathed her face. Amelia, come in!"

"Mamm, we thought we'd come for a visit and supper. Tom had to go out of town." Amelia hugged Kate and Becky, who were playing with the kinder.

"Kate, do you still want to go to the library? Or stay and visit?"

Kate thought for a few minutes. She really wanted to stay and visit, but she felt an odd urgency to be learning. "I'd better go. I'll get Miriam and we'll be back before you start supper."

"Since Amelia is here, stay at the library for a little longer, if necessary. She can help with supper."

Kate smiled. While she was okay with chopping vegetables and stirring hot food, she didn't like to combine ingredients. "Denki! I'll be back by supper-time." She hurried out and to the barn.

AT THE LIBRARY, MIRIAM SEARCHED FOR NEW library books to check out while Kate studied. Kate wasn't aware that the medical student was there and that he'd noticed her entrance. Reading the Dewey Decimal System number the librarian had written down for her, she looked for the book. Finding it, she matched the title on the book's spine to the title she'd written down. Finding a match, she smiled and pulled the thick book down. Before opening to the section she needed, she checked the copyright date of the book.

With relief, she sighed—the book was likely to have the latest information she needed to find. Getting comfortable, she began to read the chapter and jot down notes. Eventually, slowly, she began getting the feeling that someone was staring at her. Thinking it was Miriam, she set her book down and, with a broad smile, she looked up at her friend, who was completely engrossed in her book.

Hmmm. Who could it be?

Looking around her slowly, Kate saw only one person looking directly at her. She inhaled quickly. She saw a young man in a pullover top with a short button placket. His hair was short and disorderly, as if he'd run his fingers through it repeatedly. Kate couldn't see the man's eye color, but she felt a sense of warmth and kindness from his gaze. Blushing, she looked down and tried to resume reading.

Casey James, the young man who had been watching Kate, approached her. "Hi. My name's Casey, and I've been noticing you for the past several weeks."

Kate didn't smile. "Hi."

"Uh, do you mind if I sit down across from you?"

Kate shrugged. Her voice seemed to have vanished.

Casey sat down and extended one hand to her. "Casey James. I'm in med school. From this book and your appearance, you're a midwife or one in training, correct?"

Kate's eyes widened at his ability to glean all this. "Uhh…ya."

"Like I said, I'm in med school. If you need any help with anything, just let me know. By the way, that book's the bomb."

"'The bomb?' What about a—?"

"No! Not a real bomb. That's just an expression that means that book is wonderful. Lots of information and it's easy to understand."

Kate kept her voice at a whisper. "You're going to be a doctor?" She didn't know it, but a gleam of interest brightened her eyes.

"Yup. I sure am. I plan to focus on children. Pediatrics. You know, we should go into practice together. You help the babies be born and I'll take care of them after." The smile on Casey's face was impish and friendly.

Kate gasped. How could he have…? But no, he couldn't have figured her out.

"How do you know?"

"Know what?"

Looking around, Kate assured herself that Miriam wasn't looking her way. She moistened her lips. "How do you know I want to be a doctor?"

Now, it was time for Casey's eyes to widen. "But, you left school at fourteen. You you could get your GED, and then go to college. We need more gynecologists and obstetricians. Especially for underserved areas."

"Really? I could go back to school, ya. But I would have to…"

"Leave your community. That would stink. For you and for your family."

"Ya." Kate was entranced by Casey's ability to understand her conundrum. "I'm a midwife, apprenticing with my mother. I have been for going on four years. We run into situations with the mothers. We… We lost one mamm and her baby a few months back. She had preeclampsia. And we helped with the births of twins. One of them was breech and I had to help turn the second baby."

Casey grimaced sympathetically. "Oooh. So you've already experienced some of the sad part of labor and delivery. I'm so sorry. I've been working with the obstetrician here on my breaks. Three days a week. And yes, we've seen Amish mothers come in with their husbands and midwives. Do you and your mother have a center?"

"Nee, not yet. We'd have to have more staff. Although, it looks like we're going to be pretty busy in the next few months."

"So, she also sees them in prenatal appointments. Do you help with that?"

"Some, but not very much."

"Why is it you want to go to med school? It's rough."

"Ya, I kind of figured. After those experiences we had, I just feel the lack of experience. What time is it?"

"Going on four. You need to go?"

"Ya. I do. Thank you." Kate stood.

"Before you leave, I can help you with your studying any time you're here. I go to Pennsylvania State University, and the fall term begins in late August. So I'm available to study with you at any time you can be here."

Kate smiled quickly. "Let me think about it. I'll probably be here tomorrow. Unless something happens."

"Wonderful! I'm here Monday, Wednesday and Thursday afternoons. Mornings and on Tuesday,

I'm in clinic or at the hospital with the doctor." He stuck his hand out to shake with Kate.

After making tentative arrangements with Casey, Kate hurried over to Miriam. "We have to go."

Miriam's grin was impish. "Ya. I was just waiting for you to finish with Handsome over there. What did he want? A date?"

Kate blushed. "Nee. I'm still with Mike. He's a medical student and planning to be a pediatrician. He offered to tutor me."

Miriam's jaw dropped and her eyes widened. "Nee! Are you serious?"

"Ya! He'd meet me here in the afternoons, depending on my schedule with mamm. She still doesn't have me helping during her clinics, but once a while. I only go to the deliveries."

"And? Are you accepting his offer?"

"I'm thinking about it."

"Kate! What's to think about?" By now, the girls were outside the library and Miriam's voice returned to its normal level.

Kate floundered. "Time, for one thing. Both his and mine. For another thing, will it be proper? Especially since I'm still officially Mike's girlfriend."

"Mike isn't treating you right. You should stop seeing him. Even Daed and Mamm say so."

"I don't know." Kate wasn't ready to talk about her thoughts of leaving. "I'd love the help, especially with hard-to-find information or areas that are hard to understand."

"Then, do it. It can only help you and your mamm. And your patients."

"Maybe. I want to think about it some more." Kate was quiet as they drove home.

Miriam elbowed Kate, who grunted. "Mike! To our right! Swing left, swing left!"

Kate swung the buggy to the left and sped up. "I'm not ready to speak to him yet. He still won't understand."

"He still thinks you can finish a labor by five in the afternoon to be ready to go out with him? He's mupsich!" Miriam's voice was high as she spoke over the rushing breeze. Soon, they pulled up to Miriam's house. Jumping down from the buggy, they unhitched the team and moved them into extra stalls in the Kopp barn. Inside the house, Kate waited until she was sure that Mike was out of the area. "I need to go now. Mamm wants my help with supper."

"Nee, you can't go by yourself. Let me get my

daed." Miriam hurried out to the barn, where she explained the situation.

The deacon came inside. "Kate, I'm happy to take you home. Miriam, follow me in our buggy so we can get home."

Soon, two buggies were trundling down the road. Kate kept her eyes open, looking for Mike's wagon. "There he is." Kate looked down.

"Nee, girl, look up. You've done nothing wrong. He's seen us anyway."

Mike pulled up to the deacon, Kate and Miriam. "Deacon Kopp. Kate. Miriam. Kate, where have you been? Is anyone in a labor that will keep you up half the night?"

"Mike Newman! You won't disrespect Kate Lapp this way! Apologize, right now!" The deacon's voice was a low rumble as he responded.

Mike's eyes widened. "I-uh, I'm sorry, Kate. I don't know what I was thinking."

"You're forgiven, Mike. But I won't forget this. It tells me you still don't understand the importance of my work. Or that everything goes to the wayside if a mamm needs us."

Mike didn't even take that into consideration. "What time should I pick you up on Friday?"

"Friday? Pick me up? Nee! You're sarcastic, and

you still need to learn. I'll stay home. With Mamm, Daed, my sister, brother-in-law, nieces and nephews. Deacon, please take me home." Kate was out of patience.

The two buggies pulled up in front of Kate's parents' home. Jumping down with her book bag, Kate thanked the deacon and Miriam, and then hurried to take the horses and buggy to the barn. Once she was inside the house, she told her mother and sister what had happened with Mike. "I told him I wouldn't be going out with him this weekend. And I need to chop vegetables."

Amelia smiled. "Rather than vegetables, why not knead the dough for the biscuits?"

Kate grabbed the bowl and began working. Ten minutes later, at a heavy knock on the door, Becky answered.

"Nee, you can't see her. She told me what you said, and she is angry right now. And she has every right to be."

As Becky was confronting Mike at the front door, Steve came in through the back. Hearing the argument, he hurried to the front door.

CHAPTER 9

"Becky, what's happening here?" Steve's voice was a low rumble.

"Husband, Mike says he wants to see Kate. She told me she doesn't want to see him."

"Kate, is that true?"

"It is. Mike, nee."

Steve turned to Mike, crossing his arms over his muscular chest. "She told you her wishes. Now, go."

"Mister Lapp, I-I saw her with Miriam a few minutes ago, going to Miriam's. I just need to talk to her, convince her that I'm—"

"'Convince her'...of what?" Steve seemed to grow even taller in his anger.

Seeing this, Mike cowered slightly.

"Kate, did you see him earlier?"

"Ya. On the way home from the library with Miriam. We turned down a side road. Then, Deacon Kopp brought me home. Mike tried to get the deacon to agree he could talk to me."

"What was the topic of your conversation with Mike?"

"He wanted me to go out with him Friday night. Even though I might be with someone who's giving birth. He refused to consider that, if this happens, the mamm might be in labor for several hours. Oh, and he was also sarcastic about my whereabouts at night when Mamm and I are working."

"Mike, that tells me you still don't understand Kate's situation. I'm sorry. If her wishes are not to see you, I have to respect that. Kate?"

"Nee, I don't want to see him."

Wordlessly, Steve gestured to the porch and road outside the house. "Please leave."

Mike could do nothing else. Glaring at Kate, he complied. Turning, he leapt off the porch and took off as fast as he could go.

Sighing, Steve shut the door and turned around, looking at Kate. "Good, girl. You did the right thing."

"Denki, Daed." Still, Kate was sad. "I...I'd

better help Mamm with supper." For the rest of the night, Kate was quiet, preoccupied with troubled thoughts.

Becky and Steve looked at each other after the kitchen had been cleaned. Becky shook her head and pursed her lips slightly, telling Steve they should give Kate the room she needed. In their room that night, he brought up the issue. "We need to talk to her about what she's thinking." The last few words were muffled by Steve pulling his dirty T-shirt over his head. Chucking it and his dirty clothing into the hamper, he continued. "She's confused and ferhoodled, wife."

"I know she is. She's also seventeen and well able to figure situations out on her own. That's the only way she'll grow—don't you remember telling me that about her older brothers and sisters?"

Steve remembered. Sighing, he shook his head. "Okay, if you think this is the wisest course of action. But if she's still like this in a few days, we will be talking to her."

Having gotten a small concession from Steve, Becky nodded tentatively. "Let's just see how it goes with her."

For the next few days, Kate continued to struggle with her thoughts and confusion. *I want to do more to help pregnant mothers, but I don't know if I'm supposed to stay or go. I don't want to see other families suffering. At the same time, I can't let anyone else here know what I'm thinking, or I'll be thrown out even before baptism.* Grabbing a stiff stick, Kate ran it hard up and down the tree, creating a scraping noise. She stopped as she saw a small, Japanese-model car driving up the road. Turning fast, she tried to get away from the road so tourists wouldn't take her picture against her will.

"Kate. Kate!"

The voice sounded familiar, reminding Kate of her studies in the library. Slowly, she turned her head, looking at the Englischman. "Mister James! What are you doing here?"

"Just driving around, getting familiar with this area. Now I know where you live."

Kate gasped. "Nee, you can't!" She looked around, praying her parents wouldn't see her talking to an Englischman.

"I don't think anyone's around. Now that I've seen you, I just wondered if you're going to go to the library this week."

Kate sighed. "I don't know. I'm thinking too much of leaving here, and I think studying medicine at the library is just putting ideas into my head. Ideas that—"

"Ideas you shouldn't worry about having. Have you ever thought that maybe God wants you living and working in the English world? And still able to spend time with your family and friends? No, don't answer me. Not yet. Think about it and pray. You look like you're tormented by this. One thing I would like you to do though—please go to the library and study with me. Hopefully, you'll be able to make the right decision."

Kate sighed. "I'll go to the library. But don't put any pressure on me. I need to figure this out with Gott's help only."

Casey raised one hand in a pledge-type of response, nodding slightly. "I won't pressure you on your situation. I'll be praying for you as well."

Looking at Casey and trying to determine his motivation for offering to help her, she finally nodded. After he left, Kate sat under a tree, thankful for the cooling temperatures. *He has to be a Christian, otherwise, why would he have said he'd pray for me? Why would he say that Gott might want me to leave here, although that goes against everything I've ever been taught? He is right. I'm feeling tormented by all of this.* She decided to do as Casey had suggested.

She'd pray and see what she heard from Gott.

One afternoon, after Becky had come home from checking on mothers who were expecting babies, she called Kate into the kitchen. "Daughter, what's going on with you? I don't think it's Mike. He's been staying away, yet you're still so quiet."

Kate sighed. "It is Mike, Mamm. I'm beginning to think that he's going to try and control me if I continue to see him. And, Mamm, even though we're supposed to keep our dating activities private, I'm glad that I've been able to talk to you about it. Because he scares me."

"Has he ever tried to hit you or force you physically to do something you didn't want to do?" Becky's concern had just shot up.

"Nee, he hasn't, Mamm. All he wants is for me to drop whatever I'm doing by five, five-thirty to go out with him. As though I can just put a laboring mother to the side and tell her I'll see her bright and early Monday morning. And I'd never do that."

"I know, and that's why I'm so proud of you. Are you having any more success learning more about pregnancy and labor?"

"Some. Although some days are still hard. And the topics!"

"Such as?"

"Chemistry. I almost feel like I should get tutoring or something." Kate had said this as a sort of test. If her mother was accepting of additional learning, she would know that, in time, she would be able to tell her about her thoughts of leaving Lancaster.

Becky turned her coffee cup around and around. She thought as she gazed into Kate's troubled eyes. "Daughter, you know what the Ordnung states and why. Formal education ends at fourteen, with kinder beginning to learn their chosen vocations. Although some communities do allow their teens to go on to a vocational program, I don't know if midwifery would apply to this. If it did, would you consider that?"

Kate was stunned. She exhaled as she thought about her mother's offer. "I don't know. Would such a program teach me chemistry and the equations I would need as a midwife? Teach me about preeclampsia, eclampsia, conditions that require a C-section, breech babies and issues like that?"

Becky was in the position of knowing whether these topics could potentially be covered in a vocational program. She sighed, regret evident in the small sound. "Nee, Kate. I don't think so. Is your studying getting that hard?"

Kate made a fast decision, praying it wasn't the wrong one. "Ya, it is. But... I met a medical student at the library a few months ago. He's been helping me out and he's offered to tutor me formally."

"Oh. *He*. He might be romantically interested in you, Kate. And you know that can't happen. I like that you have this offer. But I would prefer that it came from a female student instead. Have you said anything to him yet?"

"Only that I'd think about it, and that I don't want him pressuring me about anything, if I say yes."

"Hold off for now. Continue going to study. I want to talk to your daed first. Whatever we decide will be final, do you understand?"

Kate nodded quickly, not even daring to hope. She was just scared. "I do."

Kate began to wait through hours that seemed to stretch into weeks as she and Becky cleaned out and refilled their medical bags. Once they were done with this, they began working on supper. Kate had to force her meal down her throat. Even though she drank copiously of her hot tea, she felt as though her throat had transformed itself into a dry, totally arid desert. Once she had eaten, she felt as though it would soon come back up. Therefore, after supper ended and she finished with the cleaning, she retreated to her room. Downstairs, she heard the drone of her parents' voices as they discussed Kate's situation and Casey's offer.

"So, what do you think?" Becky secretly wanted Kate to get permission to accept tutoring from the medical student. She rubbed her hands together, squeezing the fingers repeatedly with her opposite hand.

"He's Englisch? What would the bishop say? And he's a man! I don't want him getting ideas of courting our daughter. I don't know…"

"Steve, you know that your own daed's mother left the Amish in Ohio. She met your daadi after living among the Englisch for years. Did she say anything that would lead you to think that the Englisch have bad intentions toward us?"

"Nee, Becky, and that's not fair. Bringing my mammi up—"

"Steve, I only did so to remind you that your grandmother wasn't badly affected by her stay in their world. She maintained her faith. When she got engaged to your grandfather, she lived with a family here and wore Plain dress. Why, it's almost impossible to pick up that she hasn't lived Plain for every day of her life!"

Steve had to admit that Becky was right. "Call Kate down."

Kate came downstairs, praying her meal wouldn't come up. Her throat was scratchy and dry, and she felt hot all over. "Ya?" She swallowed—her voice was raspy.

"We talked, daughter." Steve sighed deeply. "You know my grandmother lived away from the Amish for several years before coming back to marry my grandfather. She managed to retain her faith and modesty. Ya. You can be tutored by this young man. But—" Steve's finger shot into the air next to his head. "The instant he tries to make a move on you, the tutoring arrangement is ended. Do you understand?"

Kate nodded. "Ya, I do. Mamm, I don't feel very w—" Feeling the strong need to vomit, she rushed into the bathroom closest to their living room, where she lost her supper.

Becky rushed in, hearing Kate retching. "Oh, daughter!" Feeling her forehead, she gasped. "You're burning up!" Grabbing a washcloth, she wet it in cool water and after wringing the excess water out she placed it at the back of Kate's neck. She and Kate were in the bathroom for several minutes, until Kate was finally over the paroxysms of sickness. "Get upstairs and into bed. I don't know what you have. But you have a fever. What else is wrong?"

"My throat is scratchy, it hurts and it's dry. My muscles ache." Kate felt miserable, though slightly better since she had thrown up.

"You may have strep. If it's still early enough, we can go to the urgent care center in town. If it is strep, you need medication right away."

"Wife, what's wrong with her?" Steve stayed well out of the bathroom; he'd never been good with illness.

"Fever and sore throat. It may be strep. What time is it?"

Looking at the wall clock, he nodded. "Not yet seven-thirty. Kate, you and your mamm get into the buggy. We're getting you checked out."

Kate, holding a bucket, sat in the back, praying she wouldn't get sick again.

AT THE URGENT CARE IN LANCASTER, KATE listened to the physician's assistant standing before her.

"Kate, you do have strep. I'm sending you home

with a sample of antibiotics, along with a prescription. At home, alternate between acetaminophen and ibuprofen. Rinse your throat three times a day with salt water. Drink plenty of fluids. And, in one or two days, you'll begin feeling better. Also, don't stop taking the medication just because you do feel better, okay? We want to kill that bug inside your body."

Kate nodded. "Ya, I understand." She could barely be understood through the scratchiness and hoarseness of her voice.

"Kate, don't talk." Becky put a hand out toward Kate. "We'll talk for you."

Kate nodded.

THE NEXT DAY, KATE WOKE UP WELL AFTER THE sun had come up. Her head still hurt and her throat was still really sore. She moaned. Sitting up, she held onto the side of her bed until her dizziness stopped. Downstairs, she poured water into a glass and sipped it, not wanting a return of the vomiting.

"Kate, would you like to eat? Maybe some broth."

Kate shook her head. "Maybe later."

"You need to eat to take your antibiotic, or you'll be sick all over again."

Kate sighed. "Okay. Broth, please." In the end, she was only able to get down about half of the broth. When her mother set a bowl of rice pudding in front of her, Kate sighed. "No appetite, Mamm."

"Just do your best. And take these." Becky set a large antibiotic capsule and two ibuprofen tablets in front of Kate.

Now that her tea wasn't burning hot, Kate was able to swallow some with her medications. After eating, she moved slowly to the living room, where she collapsed onto the sofa. Her heartbeat reverberated through her body and she still felt hot. As someone banged on the door, she groaned.

"Ya? Mike, she can't see you."

"Why not? Your buggy's still in the lean-to, so she's not working."

"Mike, she has strep throat. She's still very contagious."

Kate was too weak to muster up the glare she wanted to send to Mike, so she just shut her eyes and prayed he'd leave.

CHAPTER 10

Becky's words got the result she wanted.

"I-I'm sorry. Kate, I hope you feel better!" Wheeling around and holding his breath, Mike nearly rocketed off the porch and toward his wagon.

Seeing Mike acting in such a cowardly manner, Becky suppressed a loud laugh. Closing the door firmly behind her, she rested a hand on Kate's forehead. "Still feverish. I'm bringing more hot tea and a big glass of water. Get these down you so you begin to feel a bit better."

Kate barely nodded. She wanted to die. Wetting her lips, she tried to speak. "I just hope nobody goes into labor today or tomorrow."

"Ya, because you are highly contagious. If

anyone does, I'll get Missus Hoffstetter to cover. Or we can go out together."

Kate sent a confused look to Becky. "Mamm, you can't. You've been exposed to me. Germs all over you and your clothing. You'll expose the mamm and baby." Wincing, she drank some water, forgetting her fear of vomiting again.

Becky growled. "I forgot about that. I wonder where you could have gotten that."

"I think it's going around. One of the Mast kinder was sick when we went to see if her mamm was in labor. The little one looked just as bad as I feel."

"No wonder. It's going around, then. I'll call the bishop. For sure and certain, you are staying home from services this Sunday."

Kate was stunned. "But I won't be contagious then." Now, she took a big sip of the hot tea. "Ow! Hurts!"

Rushing to the sideboard, Becky pulled out a bag of throat lozenges. "No more than four in a full day."

Gratefully, Kate popped one in her mouth. She closed her eyes in relief. By the end of the day, she changed her mind. She just might live. Sitting at the supper table, she ate a little bit of the meatloaf Becky had prepared.

By Monday, Becky was sick. Telling Steve to get to work, Becky said that Kate could take her to their doctor. Back home after getting the prescription for Becky, Kate walked out to the phone house to listen to their messages. *Gut. No calls from anyone in labor.* Reading through Becky's appointment book, she called the women who had prenatal appointments for that week. She informed each patient that Becky was sick and would see them the following week. In the house, she looked at the recipe for chicken potpie. Telling herself she could make a palatable meal, she put the chicken into the stockpot and started to boil it. Next, she peeled and chopped potatoes and carrots and opened a can of peas. After checking the chicken, she made the crust for the potpie, relieved when it came out looking gut.

After checking the doneness of the meat, she peeled the skin off and chopped the chicken. She carefully made the gravy for the pie, tasting it to make sure it wasn't too salty. She was finally able to assemble the pie and slip it into the oven.

Becky came downstairs painfully. "Did you get the potpie into the oven?"

"Ya, just a minute ago. You should be in bed."

"Just want to check on you." Becky gasped at the pain in her throat.

Kate poured a glass of water and started the teakettle. "Drink. We still have leftover soup from last night. That's your supper."

Becky nodded.

FINALLY, TWO WEEKS LATER, KATE AND BECKY were completely healthy. One evening, a call came in as Kate was studying the assignment Casey had given to her.

Becky came running into the house. "Kate, get your bag! Missus Troyer just went into labor!"

Kate's mouth fell open. "But she's not due for another six or eight weeks!"

"Eight. We'll help her deliver, and then take her and the baby to the hospital. If the little one manages to make it."

AT THE TROYER'S HOME, KATE AND BECKY readied themselves for a long night. It turned out that Eliza Troyer had tried to deny to herself that she was truly in labor. If she had called several hours earlier, she could have been taken to the hospital, where the doctor could have stopped her premature labor.

"Kate, go warm the blankets and gown. Eliza is ready to push." Becky's voice was terse as she tried to quell the frustration she felt at her patient.

Downstairs, Kate forestalled the inevitable questions. "She's doing well and we're going to take her and the baby to the hospital after she's delivered. Mister Troyer, if you'd like, you can come upstairs. Your wife needs your support."

Daniel Troyer hurried up with Kate and, sitting behind Eliza on the bed, he supported her back.

"Eliza, give me a gut push! One, two, three…" Becky counted to ten, signaling that Eliza could relax. "Take a cleansing breath. And push again." After thirty minutes of focused pushing, Eliza gave birth to a tiny little girl. Becky and Kate hurried to clean her, clear out her breathing passages and cut her cord. "Daniel, get your wife downstairs. We're taking them to the hospital right now!"

On the ride, which seemed to last a lifetime, Kate had to stimulate the baby to continue breathing. At one point, very close to the hospital, she resuscitated the tiny infant. "Come on, little one! Breathe! You can do it!" Gently, Kate massaged the tiny chest and breathed in gentle, quick breaths from her own lungs. Jumping out of the buggy, she hurried in with her tiny bundle. "Eight weeks early. I've had to stimulate her breathing twice already." The emergency room nurse snatched the preemie away, set her into an Isolette and hurried to the NICU. Pacing, she watched as Eliza Troyer was examined, then checked into the labor and delivery floor.

"Kate and I are going home." Becky's eyes were scratchy with tiredness and she was sure Kate felt the same. "We'll be checking with the hospital—the NICU has already said we can check on baby's progress."

Slowly, word got out about the premature birth and the Lapp midwives' role in the delivery. Mike heard the story. Coming to the Lapp home, he pleaded with Steve to let him talk to Kate.

"That's up to her. Kate! Do you want to talk to Mike?"

Setting down the cleaning items in her hands, Kate sighed. "I may as well, Daed. Mike, we'll talk on the porch."

"Daughter, I'll be listening. Leave the door open." Steve's voice made it clear to Kate that his directive was not negotiable.

Kate nodded, leaving the front door open. Sitting on one of the porch chairs, she indicated to Mike that he could speak.

"I...I heard about the baby you and your mamm helped with. Mister and Missus Troyer—are they okay?"

"Ya." Kate didn't offer anything more.

Mike sighed, thinking that Kate was going to make it as difficult for him as possible. "Kate, I see what you were saying before. I understand now that it's really hard for you and your mother."

"Ya, it is. Can you get to your point? I need to get to my studying."

Mike grimaced at Kate's distant voice. "Girl, you don't make this easy! I'm asking if we can start seeing each other again. I won't be so tough on you."

Kate sighed. "Mike, I don't know if you'll want

to after you hear what I'm going to tell you. There's a medical student who uses the library to study his assignments. He saw me—"

"Wait! *He* saw you? And what? He wants to go out with you? He's Englisch, if he's a medical student." Mike's voice slowly rose.

"Michael Newman, shut your mouth! And listen. He saw me trying to work on something that I didn't know much about. Chemistry. He helped me to understand it. And he suggested that he could tutor me. So I have more knowledge when Mamm and I have a hard delivery to attend. That's all!" Kate made to rise and go back inside.

Mike shot his hand out and stopped her, putting one hand on her shoulder. "Wait. I stepped in it again, and I'm sorry. Okay, I understand that as well. You can get tutoring from this medical student. But if he makes a single move on you!" Mike seemed to be giving his permission.

Kate let out a growl of exasperation. "I can't give you an answer now. Check with me tomorrow or the day after." She got up and, before Mike could react, she slipped into the house.

Steve nodded with approval at Kate. "Gut for you."

Kate sighed, nodding with a smile at her daed.

"Denki." She finished the dusting and moved on to gathering dirty laundry for the next washday. As she worked, her troubled thoughts swirled through her mind.

AT A FROLIC THE FOLLOWING THURSDAY, ONE OF Kate's friends, Ursula Mast, accosted Kate.

Kate felt herself dragged into a quiet, more private area of the farm. "Ursula! What are you doing?" She freed her arm and brushed wrinkles out of the sleeve of her dress.

"Is it true? Tell me!"

"What? Is *what* true?"

Ursula had the grace to blush. "Well…I…" Then, she remembered the topic she wanted to discuss and she straightened out, trying to intimidate Kate. "I heard from someone that you are getting instruction from an Englisch professional. About your midwife work. So? Is it true?"

Kate nodded. "Ya, it is. Why is that important for you to know?"

"Really, Kate? From someone who's Englisch?" Ursula managed to make it sound like someone with three heads was helping Kate.

Kate failed to see the humor. Sighing, she threw her hands in the air and let them drop. "Why does that concern you? And how?"

Ursula took herself a little too seriously. "Kate. You don't want to be corrupted!"

Kate was stunned. "How? How could a medical student corrupt me in the library, of all places?" She remembered to keep her voice low. "He's teaching me concepts about pregnancy and delivery that I don't know yet. I'm checking books out and studying at home. But you remember. When did we ever learn advanced chemistry equations?"

Ursula suddenly didn't seem very sure of the rightness of her position. She took a step back. "Uh, well, I just want to make sure that you know what you're doing. That's all."

Again, Kate sighed. She felt a headache coming on. "That's what my parents are for. And the elders, who haven't come by our house. If you'll excuse me, I need to go take something for this headache." Wheeling around, Kate made a beeline for the host family's kitchen, where she asked for some ibuprofen. Drinking it down with a glass of water, she was thinking. *I need to make a decision. Soon. Then, I need to tell Mamm and Daed what I'm thinking of.*

AT MIRIAM'S, THE TWO GIRLS GIGGLED AS THEY baked. Kate slowly grew more serious. "Miriam? If I tell you something, will you try to understand?

"Ya, sure. Is it that you don't care for Mike anymore? I'd completely understand that."

"Nee, although my feelings about him are changing. This is about something different. I've been feeling like I don't have enough information to really help our pregnant mothers. You know I've been studying. But, Miriam, it's deeper than that." Kate slowly told her, the feelings and thoughts she'd experienced for the past few months, finally coming out.

For several long seconds, Miriam was quiet, just sitting in stunned silence. "Kate! Wow! You mean, you really feel the need— Shhh, Mamm is coming in." Her voice coming back to its normal tone, Miriam checked the last batch of cookies. "These are looking gut, but they aren't ready to be boxed up. Do you want to go to my room so we can talk?"

"Ya! Let's go! Hi, Missus Kopp!" Kate waved, with a smile on her face.

"Girls, you look happy! Miriam, I'll be needing your help with supper. Kate's going to have to go home soon. Kate, do you need my husband to take you home? Or follow you?"

"Ya. That would be gut. Denki!" She followed Miriam to her room.

"Talk. Now." Miriam waggled her fingers as though she was asking for a fistful of dollars.

Kate sighed. "Miriam, I just feel like, if I become a doctor, I could do so much more for pregnant women and their babies."

"You…wow, when you want to make a change, you go about it in a big way!" Miriam's eyes were round in her face. "But I understand. You were always one of the smartest in our class. You understood math and science so fast, while the rest of us really had to work at it."

Kate's smile was small. "Denki. I've really had to work at this level of chemistry. Remember that medical student? The one tutoring me?"

Miriam was quiet for a few minutes. "Wait. When I went with you to the library, I saw this guy, this young man, talking to you. Was that him? What does he look like?"

"Hmmm. Brown hair and eyes. Tall and sort of muscular."

"Ya, I think I remember that's who was talking

to you. So, he supports you going to medical school?"

"Ya. He suggested I pray about whether to stay or go. He knows about the Amish, Miriam. He's Christian and he said he'd pray for me."

Miriam didn't think she could be surprised again. "Wow. Wow! I don't know, Kate, but I think Gott is speaking to you. I can't say what you should do. But you really should listen to what He's saying. Maybe that's what you're supposed to do, although I'd really miss you something terrible. I saw Ursula grab you the other day. Like she wanted to talk to you. Did she…?" Miriam's finger wagged between the two of them, indicating their discussion.

"Ya. I got mad at her. I don't care who she thinks she is. She takes herself way too seriously. She heard, from Mike, that I'm studying at the library and getting the tutoring. And she thought she could make something big out of it. I told her that I had my parents' permission."

"Oh! Ursula will talk! I think you'd better tell your parents right away. Or they're going to find out, probably from Ursula or her daed."

Kate frowned. "Ya, I know. That's why I told you. So, do you understand why I've been so odd lately? Off in the clouds, thinking?"

"Ya. I do. You know, when teens like us leave our communities, it's mainly so we can just live without the restrictions we face here. Go out, use electronics, dance, drink, use electricity... But you, Kate, you want to help others! That's all! So I don't see how anyone could be mad at you, even the elders. You're not even baptized yet!"

At home that night, Kate came downstairs with her heart pounding. "Mamm, Daed? Can we talk?"

CHAPTER 11

Kate's heart pounded as she beheld her parents' faces. "I...uh. Well, I need to say something."

"Daughter, if this is about your studies and future plans, you shouldn't fear telling us what's in your mind and heart." Becky's voice was tender.

"I've been thinking... Mamm, you know I've been worried that I don't know enough when it comes to complex deliveries. My studying has helped. A lot. But, I'm wondering if I should take my learning all the way and..."

"And *what*, Kate?" Steve's voice was low and his eyes showed the amazement he was beginning to feel.

Kate's voice faltered. Clearing her throat, she

forced herself to speak. *Come on, girl. Out with it!*
"Daed, I've been thinking of returning to school. So
I can become a medical doctor and help pregnant
mothers. After seeing what Anna Hoffman went
through, I—"

"You would leave Lancaster? Our community?"

"Ya, Daed. I would. I'd live among the Englisch.
Go to school and hopefully, earn a medical degree."

Steve was silent—he couldn't speak at all, for
his shock.

"Daughter, are you that unsure of your
midwifery abilities? Or of my training?" Becky was
hurt and her emotions showed in her voice
and eyes.

"Nee, Mamm! Never! I just…oh, I'm messing
this up so badly! Mamm, it's because I've gotten
such gut training from you that I feel like Gott is
telling me I have to do this. When I think about it, it
feels…*right*, somehow. I would be living in the
Englisch world, but I wouldn't be leaving to experience things that are forbidden here. I want to do
gut, Daed. That's all."

"Does anyone else know of your thoughts?"

"Just Miriam."

"And what does she say?" Steve folded his arms
in a defensive gesture.

"She thinks I need to continue praying about it. But she also says that, because of how well I did with math, science and chemistry in school, that I should think about it." She decided now wasn't the time to bring up Casey James, the medical student who had been tutoring her.

Steve was silent except for a long, sibilant sigh. Finally, he spoke. "I need to think and pray about this, Kate. For now, you don't breathe a word of this to anyone other than me, your mamm and Miriam. Not even Mike. And what are you going to do about him?"

Kate now sighed, echoing Steve. "I haven't decided. He's just so stubborn about not accepting the reality of my work—that I should be ready and waiting for him when we've made plans."

Here Becky rolled her eyes. "That boy is selfish. And seeing how his mamm and daed raised him just like his older brothers and sisters, I am ferhoodled."

"Ya. He'd better never take a fist or open hand to you." Steve's eyebrows lowered as he thought of the big teen hitting his slender daughter.

"Nee. He hasn't, Daed. But we have gotten into some big arguments. He wants me to go out with him tonight. But, if—"

"…Someone goes into labor…' Becky shook her head.

"Exactly. I didn't say ya or nee."

"Get in the barn so we can hitch the team to the buggy. We're going to the Newman home so you can tell Mike nee. Unless you want to go out with him."

"Nee. I don't. I'm getting tired of his attitude that he 'owns' me. Nobody does."

AT THE NEWMAN'S HOUSE, KATE PACED BACK AND forth on the porch as she argued with Mike. "Nee, I can't! What if someone goes into labor while we're out?"

"So, that's more important than my time with you."

Kate gazed at Mike in amazement. Then, she heard a tiny voice. *Take him with you to study. He needs to see that it's more than just standing alongside a woman, guiding the baby out.*

"Mike, I'm not going to respond to that. Instead, I want to invite you to go to the library with me. Now, if that's okay with you, Daed."

Steve blinked as he tried to keep up with Kate's

thinking. "Daughter, why are you inviting him to watch you study?"

"Because, if he sees the words on the page, along with pictures, he might begin to understand that it's hard work."

"If Mike is agreeable, then ya, go. But, I'm going to be behind you and in the library, as well."

Kate nodded, knowing where Steve was coming from.

Mike wasn't as happy about this wrinkle in their time together. He nearly refused the opportunity. Then, he decided to accept it, after all. *Let her see how easy it is for her to do her job. After all, how can being a midwife compare to* my *work? I make beautiful pieces of furniture and work with dangerous equipment every day.* "Okay. I'll go." Mike followed Kate and Steve to the Lancaster public library. After Kate had run her library card through the card reader, she moved straight to the medical texts section, where she seemed to be looking for a specific book. Finding it, she nodded once and leafed through the pages. She was looking for one of the most difficult things that obstetricians and midwives faced in deliveries— placenta previa, when the placenta completely or partially blocked the cervix. She also wanted to show him information about preeclampsia.

Marking the two sections with bookmarks, she turned to Mike. "Sit and we'll talk about my work."

Mike sat, sure he'd be able to show Kate the error of her thinking—then his eyes fell on the bloody image of a laboring mother bleeding out. He gagged. "What is this?"

"This is a mamm who's bleeding out, Mike. When she gets pregnant, her body creates a life-giving device in her body. It's called the placenta and it helps to deliver blood and nutrition to the boppli. But, if that placenta is covering the opening from her uterus to her vagina, problems develop. One of them being...look at this, Mike. One of them being almost uncontrollable bleeding."

Mike's face was greenish-white. He pulled his eyes away from the gory image. "I—" He swallowed convulsively several times, forcing his nausea back down."

Kate was implacable. Now, she flipped the pages of the large textbook over to the section on preeclampsia. "Read that."

Quietly, Mike did so. "Mei Gott. Is this what happened to my cousin?"

"Exactly. The only way to cure this condition is to deliver the child. But, if the mother develops seizures, her condition has become much more dangerous. She now has eclampsia and it can kill her. She can suffer liver or kidney damage. Have a stroke." Quietly, she turned the page to show an image of a mother with preeclampsia. "See how swollen her face, feet and hands are? That's because of the protein building up in her kidneys. Her body is poisoning itself."

"Why?"

"We don't—we, meaning obstetricians or midwives—don't know yet. Research is being done. But until the day when we know the cause or causes of this condition, we have to work fast."

"So, why couldn't you save Anna?"

"Amish midwives can't insert IVs. You know about Epsom salts. You've probably used them if you've gotten a sprained ankle. Doctors and nurses use this to help stop the mother from going into convulsions." Again, she flipped the page, showing a picture of a mother in convulsions, with staff working over her. "All we can do is try to get that baby born as fast as possible."

Again, Mike saw the image, which was graphic. Now, he couldn't avoid the inevitable. "Bathroom, please!"

Kate quickly pointed out the restrooms just a short distance away.

Mike flew to the men's room, where he was sick.

In the reading area, Kate just waited. She wished Mike hadn't gotten sick, of course. But if he was going to understand the seriousness of her work, he had to understand that labor and delivery weren't easy on anyone, especially if something went wrong. She turned as she heard her boyfriend's shaky sigh. He dropped down into the chair next to her, rubbing his hands over his face. Putting on a show of bravado, he chuckled, trying to make it a strong sound. "Well, my work is still much more difficult. Measuring lumber, cutting it on a dangerous saw, trying not to chop off a finger or an arm." He hiccupped, almost regretting talking about the loss of limbs. He swallowed hard. "Other than Anna, I don't see what's so hard about helping mothers giving birth."

Kate's shoulders slumped. Now, she knew what she had to do. "Mike, it's obvious to me that you *still* don't understand. You're going to keep on getting angry with me when I can't get away from a delivery 'on time.' So, I'm going to have to stop seeing you." Standing, she left the book where it was. "Daed, I'm ready to go home. I believe one of our patients might soon be in need of our help."

Steve, who had heard the whole exchange, just

nodded. In the buggy, he gave Kate a few minutes to herself. "Are you all right, Kate?"

"Sad. But, oddly, I feel like I no longer have a big weight on my shoulders."

"You're not going to see him anymore?"

"Nee."

"I'm glad. He wanted to hold you back, Kate."

"More than that. I think he wanted to make me stop my midwifery. Bake or quilt to earn money. But he doesn't know how bad I am with needle, thread and fabric. And that following a recipe is one of the hardest things for me." Kate began giggling.

"What?" Steve was confused.

"Kate stopped laughing. "Oh, I was just thinking that if I'd allowed our relationship to continue, we'd have gotten married. And he would not have been happy about my inability to cook."

"Well, you're going to have to learn sometime." Steve chuckled. He'd experienced one of Kate's less-tasty baking attempts.

"I know. Depending on what decision I make about…you know." Kate lowered her voice slightly, having seen the judgmental daed of Ursula Mast.

"Ya, hello, Abraham! How are you today?"

"Gut." Mr. Mast sent a searching look toward Kate, seeming to want to see within her mind.

Kate, not knowing what to think, tilted her head in confusion. "Is there something wrong, Mister Mast?"

"Oh. Nee, I was just wondering why you were coming from the library again."

Kate's mouth dropped open. "What? I was studying."

CHAPTER 12

"A gain? At this rate, you're going to be a doctor before long." Now, the man's eyes sharpened even more.

Kate sighed, resisting the urge to roll her eyes. *Mustn't be disrespectful.* "I'm still learning, sir. My parents are just fine with my studies. I made sure they knew about it before I began to come to the library, and all I want to be is a midwife. Help other women."

Now, Mr. Mast's look focused on Kate's face, seeming to look for evidence of lying as though Kate would have snakes crawling out of her eyes. "Well, okay."

"Abraham, why would this matter to you, anyway? You aren't an elder."

Abraham Mast colored deeply. He'd secretly been sure that, by now, he would have been selected by Gott as an elder. "Well, nee, I'm not. But we can't relax our vigilance over our kinder. They can get up to bad faster than you would even believe!"

Steve reared back, stunned. "Are you saying that Kate is up to bad by studying? You mean, just like your oldest girl? Who left, became Englisch, and is today involved in the party scene?"

Mr. Mast colored deeply. "She's not involved in that! She's a writer!"

"Okay, then. If she's a writer, she's earning an honest living. My daughter is earning one as well, as a midwife motivated to learn as much as possible. Now, do you see how harmful careless words can be? If you had spoken to anyone about Kate's studying, you would have had her dancing among the Englisch every night!"

Again, Mr. Mast flushed, uneven mottling staining his face. Without a word, he signaled for his team to resume walking.

Kate sighed deeply. "Thank you, Daed. Did I tell you that Ursula cornered me with similar questions the other day?"

"Nee, you didn't. And, given what you're thinking about, you need to be highly discreet. Your mamm and I are thinking about our response to your future. While it's clear to me that you want to do gut in the Englisch world, others won't see it that way."

Kate took the warning, as Steve intended. "Ya, Daed. I will. I won't talk about this with anyone else."

"Not even Miriam."

"Daed? May I say something?"

"Speak." Steve was in a thoughtful mood.

Kate was careful to find only respectful words and have a respectful attitude. "Miriam won't say anything. She knows to keep this between the two of us."

"Of that, I have no doubt. But, Kate, have you ever heard the saying that the more people know a secret, the better chance there is that it will get out?"

Kate opened her mouth, ready continue speaking her piece. Hearing what her father said made the words die out in her mind. "I...oh! I see what you mean. So, the less I share with Miriam, the better."

Steve sighed. "Ya. I'll tell you what. If you limit your secret-sharing to Miriam and nobody else, you can continue to tell her what is happening."

Kate smiled at Steve, relieved. "Ya, because now that she knows, she wouldn't like it if I stopped talking with her about it."

"One question. Why did you start with Miriam?" Steve wanted to make sure the answer wouldn't hurt him or Becky.

"Because. Her daed's a deacon. If she's able to accept what I'm thinking about without getting angry or accusing me of thinking I'm more special, then it's more likely that others here will think the same way."

"Except for people like the Masts. First, they would spread what they consider your 'shame' throughout the community. Second, they would shame you for even thinking of leaving. Just…take your time in making this decision."

Kate's eyes filled with tears. Sniffling, she spoke. "Ya, I will. I want to be with you and Mamm as long as possible. And I want to be sure I'm making the right decision."

"Don't forget to pray about it."

Kate nodded.

AT HOME, KATE HAD TIME TO HELP WITH MAKING

supper. As she worked, she told Becky what happened at the library. "I showed Mike the book with the graphic photos. He turned green, Mamm. Then I showed him another set of pictures, of a woman with preeclampsia. He got sick. He still doesn't understand what midwifery means. I broke up with him." Kate delivered this last sentence so quietly, Becky wasn't sure she'd heard right at first.

"You broke up with him?"

"Ya. I was fed up to here with his assumptions and demands."

"Well, wunderbaar! " As Becky exulted, and the timer dinged, the outside phone rang. "You get that, Kate. I'm going to move the meat to the table and get everything dished up."

In the phone house, Kate spoke to the husband of a woman about to give birth. "Mister Hamm? Ya, do you know how far apart her pains are? Three minutes! We should have been called when they were five minutes apart! You have four older kinder."

"Ya, I know. But her mamm is here. She's keeping things under control."

"And the kinder? Where are they?"

"Under my and my father-in-law's supervision."

"Okay, we'll be there just as quickly as possible."

"Denki."

Kate hurried back into the house. "Mamm, Missus Hamm is in labor! Three minutes apart!"

Becky gasped. "Is Missus Hoffstetter there again?"

"Ya, why?"

"Every time she is there when Barbara goes into labor, she makes poor David wait until almost the last minute to call us. Grab your bag and let's go!" In the barn, Becky explained the late call to her husband.

Steve re-hitched the horses to the buggy and helped Kate and Becky in. "Be careful! I'll put the food away."

COMING INTO THE YARD, MIKE SLOWLY CLIMBED down from the buggy and led the horses into the barn. Brushing them down, he thought. A small voice told him his behavior toward Kate had been shameful. *You just wanted to control what she did and even the work she did. It's no wonder she broke up with you.*

Entering the house, Essie took one look at him. "Mike? What's wrong?

Mike shrugged. "Kate broke up with me. At the library."

"Did you try this trip so you could learn to understand the work she does?"

"Ya, I did. I saw some pretty terrible pictures. Got sick."

"Childbirth isn't pretty or sanitary. Nor is it an easy field to enter. Becky and Kate are both brave and very giving to enter midwifery. They give up meals, sleep and time with family and friends to attend all the women here. And I heard that we need another midwife to help take some of the pressure off."

"Well, Kate better finish her apprenticeship."

"Mike. Stop your nonsense. That's exactly what she's been doing, studying and attending all these births. And you kept trying to take her away from the women she assists." Essie sighed. "You're my son and I love you. But you made a bad mistake. And I'm glad that she broke up with you. Don't get me wrong. I like her. But you were trying to control her work hours versus her recreational hours. You leave her alone and figure out where you went wrong. You aren't supposed to control a woman's work."

Arriving at the Hamm home, Kate and Becky hurried into the large kitchen, finding David Hamm pacing back and forth, looking helpless.

"David! Where's your mother-in-law?" Becky was amazed.

"She won't let me support my own wife. As though I don't know how babies are born!"

Becky said nothing. Everyone was familiar with Mrs. Hoffstetter's overbearing personality. "Did you get everything together?"

"Ya, it's all over here." David indicated the large towels and basin of still-steaming water that Becky and Kate would use to sterilize instruments. He took the water while Kate and Becky grabbed the rest.

"He needs to get out of here!" Mrs. Hoffstetter snapped as the door opened.

Becky, long used to the bossy ways of Barbara's mother, shook her head. With a calm voice, she spoke. "Nee. If Barbara wants him in here, I'm agreeing with that." She looked at Barbara, who was between intensifying pains.

Damp with sweat, Barbara nodded as she

breathed in and out. "I want him in here—OWWWWW!"

David plopped the steaming water onto the chair and hurried over to his wife's side. Grabbing one hand, he pressed his lips on the back. "It's okay, Barbara." He helped her ride out the pain. Experienced with her labors, as well as the labors of his livestock, David remained calm. Slowly, he gained Barbara's attention and, gazing with love into her eyes, he helped her with the familiar breathing patterns.

"Kate, you get Missus Hamm's vitals. I'm going to talk to Missus Hoffstetter." Beckoning to the older woman, Becky indicated the hallway with a sharp motion of her head.

"Missus Lapp, if you're going to kick me out…!"

"David told Kate that you made him wait to call us. You *know* we like to be called when the mamm is at five minutes apart!"

"Becky, this is her fifth child. Her body knows the process and my daughter knows her body."

"Did she want us here earlier?"

Silence. Mrs. Hoffstetter had the grace to blush. "Er, well…ya. She did. But I convinced her…"

Becky got mad. "And that's how baby number

three suffered that birth injury. If you had called us much earlier, we could have given her oxygen. And your granddaughter wouldn't be developmentally delayed. Downstairs, now." Becky didn't bother to see if the other woman was following.

Mrs. Hoffstetter was glowering by the time she got to the first floor. "What?"

"I want you to leave. Because, the last time we were here helping Barbara and David, you kept interfering. 'Well, that's not the way we did it when *I* was giving birth!' Things change, Missus Hoffstetter. Things aren't done the way they were thirty years and more ago. Now, go! I'm going to see how that young woman is doing."

Becky made as if to go back upstairs. Instead, she stopped a little past the wall separating the kitchen from the living room. Tiptoeing over, she observed Mrs. Hoffstetter breathing deeply, clenching and unclenching her hands. Becky held her breath until she saw the woman whirl around and grab her cape and handbag. She closed her eyes, not relaxing until she heard the door lock behind her. Hurrying upstairs, she looked into Kate's eyes. "Well?"

"Pressure and respirations are normal. She's two minutes apart and says her water broke early this morning. She's actively in transition." All of this was reported quietly and professionally.

"Gut. Missus Hamm, I'm checking your dilation now. As you know, you have to be at 10 centimeters to—"

"Did you make her leave?"

Becky was caught off guard. "Ya, we did."

Barbara's eyes closed in relief. "Thank you! I've forgiven her for what happened to Annie, but I will never forget it. I'm just grateful David didn't listen and called you already."

Becky and Kate nodded, looking at each other. The child who'd suffered a birth injury was on their minds. Becky spoke. "Well, we're just going to make sure that this boppli is as healthy as possible."

"Gut— OH!" Barbara made as if to sit up on the bed. She raised her knees in anticipation of the next wave of pressure. "Got to push!"

Becky quickly checked Barbara "Gut. Push on my count! One, two, three…" At the count of ten, she had Barbara stop pushing. This process continued for almost 45 minutes. At the end, Kate caught the baby, a little girl, with relief. She cleaned her off, put a diaper on her, and then wrapped her in a warmed blanket. "It's a girl!"

David's eyes welled over with tears. He'd wanted a girl so badly.

Barbara let out an exhausted laugh. "This one is Theresa."

After finishing and cleaning up, Kate and Becky went home. By now, it was close to eleven at night. At home, they ate sandwiches, and then tumbled into their beds.

The next morning, Becky was finishing the breakfast dishes. Steve had just left for the carpentry shop. Looking toward the living room at an insistent pattern of knocks, she indicated that Kate should take over the dishes. Answering the front door, she saw Mrs. Hoffstetter. "May I help you?"

"You can start with why you kicked me out of my daughter's labor and the birth of my granddaughter!"

Becky opted for honesty. "I'm the midwife; Kate is my apprentice, and you don't have the education, skills or training to know when it's time to call us. You waited too long with the third baby. Now she has a permanent brain injury and her family will have to take care of her all her life."

"Posh! She can learn a trade. All she needs is to give in to my will, and she'll be normal."

Becky felt her breath leave her body in a fast

huff. "Wha'? What? 'Give in to YOUR will? Be normal?' She was deprived of oxygen for over six minutes! And the only One whose will we are supposed to give in to is Gott!"

Mrs. Hoffstetter realized her mistake much too late. She gasped. "I…" Without saying a word more, she turned her hefty body and bustled back out the door.

Becky was left to try and make sense of what had just happened.

"Mamm? Was that Missus Hoffstetter? I heard what you were saying to her."

"Ya, and you won't believe it. She had the nerve to say that, if little Annie would just give in to 'her will' and focus on getting better, she would begin to learn normally."

Kate gasped, just as her mother had. "Mei Gott!"

Becky shook her head. "This isn't charitable and I know it. But I feel sorry for Barbara, David and their kinder."

"If that's a sin, I just committed it as well."

"We'll keep an eye on her attitude. If it continues, or if she becomes a problem for David and Barbara, we'll go talk to the elders."

Kate gave a slow, troubled nod. She didn't like that they might have to do that.

That afternoon, Miriam came to her house. "Hi! Are you ready to go study? Hi, Missus Lapp!"

"Ya, I am. I need to return this book and check out another one."

"Daed is taking us. He needs to do some work in town, and then he'll pick us up before four this afternoon."

"That works really well. I want to see if I can find anything on prematurity."

The two girls chatted all the way to the library.

"Remember, I'll be here before four. Kate, should I go in?" The deacon was ready to stay or go.

Kate thought for a few seconds. "Nee, that won't be necessary. I broke up with Mike, and it's been quiet."

"I'll be here at four, then."

CHAPTER 13

Essie caught Mike glowering on the couch after supper. "What is it?"

"Nothing... well, I'm thinking of how Kate broke up with me. I... I might have said something to Mister Lapp that I shouldn't have." Mike's voice was slow and hesitant.

"Michael Newman. Look at me straight in the eyes and tell me what you said. Now!"

Mike was long familiar with Essie's ability to worm things out of him. He sighed, trying to delay the inevitable. "I've suspected it for a long time. I think Kate is getting ready to leave here."

"And that's what you told her daed? Do you know why she's thinking this way?"

"You mean to get away from me? She says she wants to be a better midwife. But, I don't know."

Essie's fast mind began to put things together. *The midwife apprentice is studying at the library to learn more about her vocation. Maybe, instead of working as a midwife, she feels she can be more effective as a...doctor.* She pinched Mike's upper arm.

"Ow!" Now, he was touchier than before.

"Michael, you don't see what's under your nose. Kate and Becky both take their work seriously. Kate was very upset about Anna. She didn't say it, but I saw it in her expression when we talked. Mike, did you ever stop to think past your own wishes? Because I think she's thinking of leaving here—so she can go back to school and become an obstetrician."

Mike was silent for a long time. He shook his head with a sudden, sharp motion. "You mean live among the Englisch, go to the university, graduate and begin working as a doctor."

Essie nodded. "While I hate to see our youth leave here. But, for Kate to progress even beyond what her mamm has accomplished, she might have to do so."

The house was quiet as Mike thought about

everything he had discussed with his mamm. "I'm going to bed."

"Good night. Just keep one thing in mind. I know you haven't gone around her since she broke up with you. Keep that up. No matter what she decides, she doesn't need the pressure you can exert on her. I believe that it could be the best thing for our community, especially if she practices here in Lancaster."

Mike nodded unhappily. *I goofed up terribly. And I lost her.*

THE NEXT MORNING WAS A QUIET ONE FOR KATE and Becky. They spent the time catching up on cleaning they hadn't been able to do while assisting at the most recent deliveries. Becky looked at Kate as she stopped mopping. "Daughter, I had an idea. Before I tell you what that is, understand that I don't know yet what your daed and I will decide. It's just an idea. If you still want to leave here and go back to school, we could open a midwifery/obstetrics center here in our community. That way…"

Kate's jaw dropped. She gasped. "If you and

Daed give me the permission… Ya! Because I don't want to practice in the big cities."

"If you got our permission, would you return to Plain traditions?"

"Like the clothes and other practices? I would expect that I would do so, ya."

Becky nodded, looking a little more reassured. "You're serious about that?"

Kate was adamant. "There are many conveniences in the Englisch world. Living in a big city means everything is just right there, around the corner. But I'm used to rural, simple living." Kate paused to bend over and start putting rugs on the now-dry floor. "It scares me, living among so many people."

"Do you know where you're thinking of going?"

"Probably Pennsylvania State University." *Like Casey.*

THAT NIGHT, AFTER KATE HAD GONE TO HER room, Becky told Steve what they had discussed. "And she actually wants to come back here. We could open a midwifery clinic away from home, somewhere here in town!"

"Really?" Steve did some mental calculations. "Kids go to college at about eighteen, I believe. If Kate does the same, if we give her that permission, she would go before she's baptized, which is gut." Steve fell silent, worrying his lower lip with his fingers.

Becky had seen Steve go into deep thought in the same way before. She simply waited for him to come back to the present.

"It's gut because she won't be banned. She could easily come back and start living and working here again. Except for those who believe that, even without being baptized, she sinned in leaving, she would be welcome."

Following Steve's words and thoughts, Becky nodded quietly. "We still need to think about this before we make our decision. And that's what I told her."

Steve sighed. "Wife, I don't think a decision will come for a gut, long time. But it needs to be before she's baptized."

"A little more than a year. She'll be eighteen in a few months."

LIFE CONTINUED IN LANCASTER. KATE continued studying and working with her mamm. She grew a little more confident about her knowledge and ability to help Becky.

Mike did as Essie had told him. He stayed away from Kate, even when he saw her in town.

Kate continued to learn with Casey James.

Propping his head on one hand, Casey smiled at Kate. "Do your parents know that you're thinking about med school?"

"Actually, they do."

Casey's eyes widened in surprise. "And?"

"They're thinking about it. Mamm and I were talking the other day. Mamm told me that, if I do get permission to go back to school and become a medical doctor, once I graduate, I could come back home and we could open a midwifery/obstetric clinic in our community."

"Well, what about the banning problem?"

"I've been thinking about that. If I leave before I turn nineteen and get baptized, I could come back without hurting them."

"Does this mean you'd be baptized later?"

"Ya. If I do everything this way, I'll still be in good standing."

"Ah, got that." Casey went quiet. "You never

got a high school diploma because you left school at fourteen, in the eighth grade. Which means you'll have to take the GED and pass that with the highest scores you can muster. Then start the application process at Pennsylvania State. I can help you with all that."

Kate smiled, feeling grateful. She also felt something more—a sneaking attraction for this Englischman. Turning to her book, she silently indicated they should study. For the next hour-and-a-half, they discussed how and why babies were premature. By the end of the study session, Kate felt like she could discuss this with Becky.

"Take this home and read these chapters. When do you want to meet again?" Casey looked at Kate, who was organizing notes, her new library book, and her pen.

"Well, I don't know when we'll get a call. And I think Mamm told me we're going to have a lot of deliveries coming up."

Casey's eyes widened. "Okay, then why don't we plan for this Saturday, about ten in the morning? If you're not here by ten minutes after ten, I'll know you're working."

"Ya, that works."

"Okay. I'll be praying for you, and for you and

your parents to make a decision."

"Denki." Miriam and Kate rode home with the deacon, chatting the whole way. Miriam spotted Mike, who had seen them. "Shall we run for it?"

Kate looked at Mike for a long time. "Nee. He's not coming here and it's clear he saw me."

Deacon Kopp kept a close eye on Mike the whole time they were driving past him.

AT SERVICES THE NEXT SUNDAY, KATE FELT disapproval coming off in waves from Ursula and other, more conservative community members. Shifting uncomfortably, Kate looked at Becky. "They're mad at me." She mouthed the words, trying to keep those staring at her from reading her lips.

"Pay them no never mind. I wonder who told?"

Kate had an excellent idea. While serving hot and cold beverages, she edged around to the Mast table. "Missus Mast, would you like some hot tea? It's getting cold again."

"Nee. Don't want to talk to you."

Kate's mouth fell wide open.

Becky, seeing the interaction, rushed to Kate's

side. "Daughter, what happened?"

Kate opened and closed her mouth. She didn't want to drag... *Wait a minute! Someone's gossiping!*

"Here. Let me take over and you move desserts to the dessert table." She turned swiftly to Mrs. Mast. "What is this I heard a minute ago?" She was direct and probing.

Mrs. Mast sniffed. "If you must know, we heard tell that Kate is leaving."

Becky was silent for a minute. *Forgive me, Gott.* "Nee, she isn't. She works with me. She goes to the library and studies hard to learn material she needs to know. As a midwife, there's quite a bit I'm showing her. And more that I plan on introducing as she gets more experienced." Angrily, Becky poured steaming-hot coffee into Mrs. Mast's coffee cup. The hot stream nearly missed the mug, causing Mrs. Mast to push her chair back quickly.

At home that evening, Kate spoke with her parents. "Somebody's gossiping about my work and studies. Mamm, when she told you that she heard that I was leaving, what did you tell her?"

Becky sighed. "I asked for Gott's forgiveness, and lied. I told her that you're spending time at the library, deepening your knowledge of midwifery and of everything that can happen in pregnancy and labor. I also told her that I'm showing you everything I know and have plans to show you even more, as you're ready for the new material." She looked sadly at Steve. "Husband, I'm sorry. But Missus Mast is too big for her britches. She thinks she knows what's right and wrong for everyone. And I was angry this afternoon. I nearly spilled hot coffee all over the table—and her—and I would have been glad." Becky's face now had a definite flush to it.

"Becky, we're going to be confronting situations like this for a while. It's best that we learn how to keep it from upsetting us too much. Now, you handled that situation as well as you could, even lying to protect Kate here. Kate, you might want to start telling your friends that you're not leaving any time soon. Even though your mother and I are still thinking about your proposal, it's best that it not be common knowledge just yet."

"Ya, I can see that. I'll start with Miriam and, if it comes up with other friends, I'll 'correct' that information."

"Gut." Shortly after, while Kate, Becky and Steve were reading, someone knocked at the front door. Steve answered, opening the door to Deacon Kopp.

"Deacon! Come in! I hope there's nothing wrong." Steve had a good idea of what had brought the deacon over.

"Denki. I'm gut. But gossip is going around about Kate and her studying."

"Coffee, Deacon?"

"Ya, please."

Everyone sat down at the kitchen table, where Becky poured steaming cups of coffee and cut slices of coffee cake. "Please tell us what you heard."

The deacon sighed, stirring milk and sugar into his coffee. "It was Missus Mast. After lunch ended and most people had left, she approached me. I can only thank Gott that she didn't go to the ministers or the bishop. She told me that Kate's going to leave and join the Englisch. 'She's probably going to learn how to use those fancy computers and pads. Use a cellphone. Electricity. And live as wild as the Englisch live.' Kate, what's going on?"

Kate sighed. *Here it is.* "Deacon Kopp, when Mamm and I lost Anna Hoffman and her baby, I—we—felt that deeply. I felt as though I still don't know enough. And I asked my parents if I could add to my knowledge of pregnancy and childbirth by checking out library books on these topics. If I could study at the library, so I can easily find additional resources. And the librarians have been very nice, looking things up online for me.

"Only, now I'm beginning to think that, maybe I can be of more benefit to the women here and outside our community if I earn my medical degree. I'd have to leave here, enroll in a GED program, and then go to college and medical school. Mamm and I have even been talking. If this does happen, I could come back home and we could open a midwifery clinic that also offers obstetric and gynecological services. This way, our mothers won't have to find an Englisch doctor if they have a problem with their pregnancies." Kate picked up her coffee mug with a shaking hand. Steadying it with her other hand, she took a sip of the hot brew.

The deacon was quiet for a few minutes, just thinking. "Are you sure you don't want to indulge in some of the excesses that our youth sometimes find?"

"Nee. I'm sure I'll be tempted, but my only goal is to learn what I need to learn so I can help the women in our community. And, if I do leave and go to school, it would have to be before I begin baptismal instruction and get baptized. I do want to return. I can't see myself living in a big city away from my family for too long." Kate made herself stop talking. *Stop your babbling, girl!*

Now, the deacon sighed. "Well, your goals are commendable, Kate. Does Miriam know?"

"Ya. And I did ask her to keep this confidential."

"Gut. Because, as you experienced this morning, Missus Mast and others are all assuming the worst."

Kate cringed. "Has my reputation been ruined, just because I want to be of more help?" Her voice quavered as she tried to hold tears back.

"Not ruined. Just…dinged a little bit. Here's my suggestion. Starting with Miriam and your other friends, start passing around a corrective piece of gossip. Like: 'She's at the library so much because she's studying. Her parents know and approve.' Say nothing about your thoughts of leaving here to go to college, ya?" The deacon's green eyes sparkled as he smiled. "One more thing. I heard from Miriam that you broke up with Mike Newman. Gut! I have been seeing him looking sad."

Kate nodded. "Mamm, Daed and I already decided I'm going to be telling my friends that I'm staying. There's no need to stir up trouble."

CHAPTER 14

K ate sighed. "I'm sorry for how he feels, but he knows what he needed to do so I would have stayed with him. He refused to understand the demands on my time. I refuse to neglect our patients just because Mike wanted our dates to be uninterrupted or interfered with. Childbirth is a miracle."

"Ya, it is. Becky, Steve, it's clear to me that you raised all your kinder right."

Another knock came at the front door. Then Millie Kopp, John, her husband, and their three kinder all tumbled into the living room.

"Millie! Come and join us. Kinder, you go on upstairs and play there. We're having grownup conversation here." Becky's face was beaming with a bright smile.

"Deacon! I hope everything's all right." John was nonplussed. Taking Millie's cape, he hung it over the coat tree in the corner of the living room, and then joined her at the kitchen table.

"It is gut, John. I hope all of you are healthy."

"We are. So, is it okay to ask why you're speaking to my in-laws?"

The deacon looked at the Lapps. Getting nods from each of them, he nodded himself. "Ya. Simply put, Kate is feeling deeply her lack of knowledge when it comes to complications of pregnancy. She has been studying at the library and gaining new knowledge. Sometime in that process, she began to think that, if she left here, returned to school and earned her medical degree, she would be of much more valuable service to our pregnant mothers. And to the Englisch women in this area who also need her services."

"Kate! Leave the Amish?" Millie's bright blue eyes were wide.

"Ya, but just for the time it would take me to learn, earn my degree, and do anything else the state requires of its doctors. Like testing or certification. Mamm and I were talking a little bit about maybe opening a clinic once I come back—*if* I go at all. She'd offer our midwifery services and I would be available for issues she refers to the doctors in Lancaster."

Millie grinned. "Well, I think it's wunderbaar. While my pregnancies have all been easy ones—to date, anyway—I do know there are women here who have one problem or another. Do it. Please."

John nodded his head slightly. "Millie is right. If Anna Hoffman had been able to get to a doctor faster, would she still be alive?"

"Possibly. They can offer treatments that we can't. We don't know how to start IVs, for example. Anna would have benefited from an IV solution of magnesium sulfate to stop her condition from worsening." Becky sighed as the grief swept over her again.

"But, John, Millie, for Kate's sake, we aren't saying anything to anyone at this point. Besides you, me, Kate and her parents, Miriam is the only other one who knows. Did you see the scene at lunch this afternoon? The one between Missus Mast and Kate?"

"Ya, I saw glimpses. I was sitting with one of my friends and overheard a few words here and there. Kate, unless you correct peoples' impressions of you and your plans, you're going to be as gut as banned."

Kate nodded. "Ya, I know. I was stunned when Missus Mast said what she did."

The deacon entered the conversation again. "Kate, Missus Mast is a big pain in our...*bodies*. She thinks she knows everything about the Ordnung and our bishop has visited her more than once to remind her she isn't to give her opinions to other people. That's our role. In fact, I think you'll have to alert the bishop before long."

This statement scared Kate and she got up to start walking around. Pausing in front of the darkened kitchen window, she sighed. "Ya. I know. Would it be better to do so sooner or later?"

"As soon as you can. He'll understand. He's not as conservative as the Masts. And I think you'll find him understanding." He finished the last of his coffee and cake, and then rose from the table. "Well, I had better get on home. Steve, please let me know if anyone else gives Kate, Becky or you any trouble. I'll get the elders together and we'll go talk to them."

"Ya. We will."

After the deacon had left, Millie laughed. "I am so excited for you! You always liked the science in school. And the math! You were the best scholar in your class there."

Kate smiled, her heart pounding. "Ya, but now, I struggle. I wish I could find someone to help me." She didn't think it was the right time to reveal to others that an Englisch medical student had been training her. *After all, I just appealed to the deacon for permission to consider this.*

The rest of the evening flew by, as Millie peppered Kate with questions. Kate and, if needed, Becky answered them. "Well, Kate, I approve. After Missus Mast did what she did, I was so upset! I couldn't eat anything else."

"I saw what happened as well. I was talking with another carpenter and saw Kate going back into the kitchen. Becky, you did the right thing, that's clear to me. You made Missus Mast stop! And that's not an easy thing to do."

Everyone chuckled. John was right. Mrs. Mast was a force of nature, all on her own.

"She made me so stinking mad! I told her why Kate's going to the library and how it's helped us both. Frankly, if she does go to medical school, it will benefit the entire community."

Kate heard the implicit approval of her idea in

Becky's voice. She gasped. "Mamm! Do you approve of my idea?"

Becky realized what she'd said. Opening and closing her mouth twice, she nodded. "Ya. I do. But it's not my decision alone."

EARLY THE NEXT MORNING, KATE FINISHED UP the week's shopping for Becky. Conscious that they had a patient due to go into labor, she wanted to hurry home.

"Kate? Do you have just a minute?" Essie Newman approached the younger woman.

"Ya, but just a moment. What is it?" Kate stuffed her wallet back into her purse.

"Let's go outside. We can talk privately in my buggy."

Kate was ferhoodled. "Okay. But I need to put my groceries…"

"I'll be happy to help."

After they had loaded the groceries into the rear seat of the buggy, Essie and Kate went to Essie's buggy, not far away. Essie sighed and smiled at Kate. "First, even though Mike is my son, you did the right thing in breaking up with him. I never—*we* never—raised him to think like that."

"I know. He seems to have picked up some rather old thinking when it comes to my work. And it was just too much of a distraction."

"I understand. Completely. Now, I overheard Missus Mast on Sunday afternoon—what she said about you leaving. And I heard your mother's response. Kate, is it true? Are you leaving?"

Kate felt close to Essie, so she decided to be honest. "Ya. I'm—we're—thinking about it. I just think I could do so much better if I can learn what the doctors know, become a doctor myself, and come back here. So leaving the community would only be for a few years, until I earn my degree and complete everything, which I still need to look into and decide."

"What do your parents say?"

"Daed is worried. But he understands. Mamm is really supportive, because we're talking very tentatively about opening a midwifery clinic that also offers a medical doctor's—my—services to those women who need them. Also, I would accept Englisch patients."

Essie gasped. "So, this means you could possibly

help mothers like Anna. So they don't become disabled or even die."

"Ya, exactly." Kate's smile was tentative.

Essie grinned now. "I like it! And, if anyone, like Missus Mast or anyone else, gives you any trouble, just let me know. I'll help you. Who else is helping you?"

Kate smiled again. "My parents, Miriam and Deacon and Missus Kopp. Hopefully, the bishop and ministers, eventually."

"Ach, wunderbaar! I'd better let you go. You have perishables in your buggy."

"Ya! Thank you so much, Missus Newman!" Kate jumped out of Essie's buggy and ran to her own.

"MAMM, YOU AREN'T GOING TO BELIEVE THIS."

"Tell me. You look very happy." Becky's smile rivaled Kate's.

"I ran into Missus Newman while I was leaving the store. She asked if she could talk to me and we talked about what happened on Sunday afternoon. She asked if I was leaving. I told her that you, Daed and I are talking about it. And that it's only in the talking stage. I also told her that we're talking about opening a combination midwifery-obstetrics and gynecology clinic. She loves it." Kate sobered. "Because of Anna."

Becky's smile dimmed. "Ya. It's too bad that gut change often comes from tragedy. I do have to say, Kate, that I'm proud of what you are doing. You're going to sacrifice years of your time, just to become a doctor. But first, we have to talk to the other elders." Becky waved her hands in the air, willing tears back.

KATE CONTINUED HER STUDIES WITH CASEY James. Even as she was learning more than she'd hoped for, Kate fought a sneaking attraction to the medical student.

"So, how do you 'cure' preeclampsia?" Casey tested her.

"Delivery only. Englisch doctors can administer IVs with magnesium sulfate in them. To slow or stop any seizures the mamm may get."

"And we deliver the baby just as quickly as we can. Then, monitor mom for her blood pressure, damage to her kidneys and liver. And we make sure she doesn't develop any infections."

Nodding, Kate scribbled Casey's words down. "Okay, got that. Now, I have a question about premature labor. Can that be stopped, if the baby's too small to survive outside the womb?"

"Yes, it can. Again, as a midwife, you wouldn't be able to order the medications needed to stop the progress of labor."

"Again, the limitations." Kate sighed. "What are the meds?"

"Antibiotics, just in case of infection. Corticosteroids, delivered through the mother's bloodstream so they get to the fetus and make its lungs a little readier for delivery. Finally, we give mom tocolytic medications that can stop preterm labor. These are terbutaline, nifedipine and indomethacin. And, if the baby is less than 32 weeks, we can give magnesium sulfate to the mother. It helps, somehow, to prevent brain damage in the baby that leads to cerebral palsy."

After scribbling all this information, Kate set her pen down and shook her head. "Wow. I have so much to learn." She dropped her head onto her hands, which were resting on the table.

"Kate, look at me." Casey's voice was soft, yet commanding.

Kate, hearing the firm tone, raised her head and looked into his kind face. "Ya?"

"Yes, you do have a lot to learn. But you're really intelligent, and you pick new concepts up fast. Plus, we're working on increasing your knowledge. I'll tell you what, if you do get into med school at Penn State—"

Kate was confused. "Wait a minute. You're going to Pennsylvania State University, right?"

"I am. Oh, I see, Penn State is a nickname for the university."

Kate nodded, relieved. "Oh. Denki."

"We've been at this for a while. Do you have something to do?"

"Ya. Mamm has prenatal visits to make. She's not taking me today, so I'm going to do things around the house and study."

"Give yourself and your brain a break today. I threw a lot at you. Just let it simmer in there. You'll be much better off retaining that material if you do."

"Really? I thought I had to start studying as soon as I learn the material."

"Not this kind of material. Do your chores.

And, at the most, try to relate today's lesson to the labors you've attended. It'll be so much easier to remember that way."

Kate smiled. "Okay, denki! I'd better go."

"See you next week? Say, Tuesday?"

Opening her small planner, Kate checked the upcoming week. "Ya. That'll work." She jotted the appointment down as Casey entered it into his smartphone's calendar.

THAT NIGHT, KATE AND BECKY WERE AT A LABOR. Kate took the mother's blood pressure and, alerted by the high numbers, she checked feet, hands and face. "Mamm, we need to talk." In the hallway, she quietly told Becky, "I think she's developing preeclampsia. Her blood pressure is elevated and she's swollen."

"We're taking her to the hospital right now. I'll tell her husband. You help her into their buggy." Becky hurried downstairs as Kate went in to let the mother know she had to go into the hospital.

Ten minutes later, as the buggy trundled down the road, Kate and Becky monitored their patient's condition, helping her through contractions. "We're almost there!" Ten minutes later, they pulled into the hospital's parking lot. "Stop at the emergency entrance and we'll get her admission started."

Inside, a nurse conferred with Becky. "Suspected preeclampsia?"

Becky showed her the numbers Kate had recorded. "We lost a mamm a few months ago to preeclampsia. Kate picked up on her symptoms and we left right away."

"Good. We'll get her admitted, and I'll get the doctor on-call to speak with you. Do you mind if I make a copy of your records?"

Becky quietly handed them over. "Kate, we'll wait to talk to the doctor, and I just realized, we need a ride back home."

"I'll call Daed." As Kate spun around to use a pay phone, she heard her name. And stopped, chilled with fear.

"Kate! Over here." Casey was walking toward Kate and Becky.

"Oh, hi. We brought a mother in. She's pretty sick, so we didn't want to take the chance."

"Good. Is this your mother? Missus Lapp, my name's Casey James. I've been tutoring your daughter, and I have to tell you that she is very smart. And dedicated."

Becky's jaw dropped, and she looked at Kate for a few seconds. Redirecting her attention to Casey, she spoke. "Are you the medical student she's spoken of?"

"Yes, I am. Please, let me explain. The first time I saw Kate, she was trying to get the librarian to print educational information she needed, but the librarian refused. So, I offered my services. Kate was having trouble with one piece of what she was studying—. I believe it was a chemical equation—so I helped her. As we've worked together, I've learned about her dream of becoming an obstetrician. And I support her in that."

"Ach, ya." Becky's words were slow. "I am grateful to you, Mister James. Kate, call your daed so he can pick us up, please."

Kate turned to make the call.

CHAPTER 15

"Wait, Missus Lapp, I can take the two of you home. I've finished my shift already; although, I might come back to look in on your patient."

Becky had no choice but to accept. On the short ride home, she was impressed at the depth of Casey's knowledge of pregnancy and its possible complications. *He knows so much. Not only about medicine and pregnancy, but also about the Amish.* "Mister James, how is it that you know so much about the Amish?"

"I've lived here all my life, right here in Lancaster. Over the years, I've gotten to know some pretty wonderful, faith-filled people. And that's only helped me on my own faith journey. Your daughter, for instance. She doesn't let anything stop her. And I can see that her faith sustains her during rough times."

Becky nodded thoughtfully. "Do you want to keep tutoring Kate?"

"I would. She shows a lot of promise."

"I'm glad. Kate, I want you to remember that your arrangement is only for tutoring. Nothing else."

Kate blushed, wishing her mamm hadn't spoken so openly in front of Casey. She sighed. "Ya, Mamm, I know."

The next day, Becky and Kate worked on deep cleaning the house, along with Becky's other daughters. The next Meeting Sunday was coming up, and they were hosting the church, lunch and Sing.

Outside, Steve and his sons worked on cleaning the barn so the benches could all be fitted inside. Stopping, the men all wiped their sweaty faces with big handkerchiefs and guzzled ice water. Steve was unaware of the conversation taking place in his home.

"Kate, have you gotten closer to a decision about school? I think your daed is wondering, and a little worried."

Kate expelled a long breath through pursed

lips. "I'm still praying about it. It's such a big decision. And I know some here will be angered and think I'm only doing it for myself, for more freedom. Ya, I am thinking about the additional freedom, but only so I can eventually come back and be a real help to the mothers who need our help."

Becky smiled. She wasn't a very demonstrative person, but on this day, a physical expression of her feelings was all that was appropriate. She smoothed her hand over Kate's cheek. "I know. You have never had a selfish impulse, ever in your life."

Kate blushed. Not used to the rare praise, she shuffled her feet and didn't know what to do with her hands. Shrugging, she spoke. "I have the best example with you and Daed."

Becky pulled Kate into a long hug. "I love you, daughter. Make the right decision, you hear?"

"I do." Kate's voice wavered slightly. She and Becky were both close to tears. "Whew! We'd better get started with dinner."

"Ya, we had. I'm thinking chicken stew with loaded baked potatoes. It'll be so much faster with everyone here." She, Kate and the rest of her daughters got started on the big meal.

At lunch, Caleb, Kate's oldest brother, spoke up.

"Hey, what's this I hear about you being tutored by some Englisch student?"

Kate glanced at Steve, who nodded. "Mamm and I lost a patient several months ago. I've been feeling the lack of knowledge on several topics, so I went to the library and began to study. Well, one day when I asked the librarian to get some information for me from the internet and she refused, the medical student overheard. He came to my table, introduced himself, and told me he's a medical student and that he plans to become a pediatrician. He offered to help me out. Mamm and I had to take a patient to the hospital this weekend. He was there, just finishing up some practice hours, so he introduced himself to Mamm and offered us a ride home. It was getting late, so we accepted. Daed, should I...?"

"I think it would help, ya." Steve sat back, finishing the last of his stew and biscuits, just listening.

Kate sighed. *This is the hard part.* She looked around at her brothers, sisters, nieces and nephews. "Because of what happened to our patient and to a few other women, I began to think that, maybe, I could do better for them—give them and their babies a better chance—if I just go ahead, go back to school and get my medical degree. It would mean leaving here for the time being, earning my GED, then going to college. Then, hopefully, being accepted into medical school. Because…" Kate gulped. "I want to come back here and open a clinic with Mamm. This way, any of her patients who get sick or have any other problems that put their babies at risk will have immediate help without having to go all the way into town, to the hospital."

Silence. The quiet stretched, like a rubber band being pulled to its fullest length. Then, Caleb spoke. "Go for it. The same thing happened to Sandy's best friend. She lost the boppli. All because of the weather and distance from a gut hospital."

Everyone else nodded and tossed in their agreement.

"Everyone, listen." Steve's voice was low, gravelly and commanding. "Kate is still thinking and praying about her decision. No matter what she decides, she's likely to face resistance, gossip and downright despicable behavior."

Millie shifted in her chair. "Kate, did I hear right when Mamm told me you broke up with your boyfriend?"

"Ya. He said he understood what I was going through. But he still insisted that I leave any pregnant mamm in labor at the end of the workday on Fridays and weekends. No matter what. He wanted my time and attention and resented it when I had to stay working through our planned times together. I finally told him that, if he wasn't going to stop, we'd have to stop seeing each other. So, I stopped seeing him."

Millie's jaw dropped as she gazed at Kate. "So strong! I don't know if I would have been able to do that, if I had faced the same situation."

Kate flushed. "Ah, ya, you would have, Millie. You know that, when work has to be done, you need to finish everything. And follow up, any time that's needed."

Millie, who was a quilter, agreed. "Ya. But my work doesn't have such life-altering consequences. Yours does. You have my support anytime anyone speaks against you." She looked around at the rest of their brothers and sisters, who all nodded.

Steve nodded in appreciation. "Gut. Because she will face resistance. It's my understanding that Missus Mast has already expressed her disapproval. Along with Ursula, her daughter."

Kate nodded unhappily. "Ya. I'm sure there will be others. Lancaster is a big Amish community."

Millie remembered what Kate had told her about Missus Mast. She nodded slowly.

"Daughter, when it happens, we'll support you. Just speak up."

Kate didn't know it, but that would happen soon. Mrs. Mast, along with Ursula and a few other community members who thought more conservatively, went to the bishop with their complaints. Mrs. Mast was the spokesperson. "Bishop, have you heard about what Kate Lapp is doing?"

"Nee, what?" The bishop would soon come to regret that innocent question.

"She is going to the library in town. To *study*, she says. But I just know she's up to no gut! I spoke to her mamm, who said she's given Kate her permission to *study* at the library." Missus Mast's voice took on a heavy, sarcastic tone. "That she is *increasing her knowledge* of childbirth matters. Is there anything you can do? Ban her? Make her stop?"

This was the first he'd heard of Kate's educational activities. "Now, Missus Mast, everyone, I'm sure Kate has a perfectly gut reason for doing what she's doing. She has always been a gut, devout girl, looking out for others and helping them. She has never—"

"Bishop! She is in rumspringa! She is experimenting with Englisch practices. And maybe she's already started using that evil, infernal internet!" Mrs. Mast inhaled, trying to keep her considerable ire under control.

The bishop had had enough. Smacking the table with an open hand, he startled every one of his visitors, who were really up to no good. "Stop! I have heard no complaints from her parents or from her patients. And they are the ones most responsible for her behaviors and actions. Now, I'm going to go and talk to them. And you are *not* allowed to do or say anything to *anyone*. Do you understand?' His face was dark with disapproval and anger.

Mrs. Mast clearly had not expected this reaction. She had truly thought that, if she involved the bishop, he would go immediately to the Lapp's home, talk to Kate and her parents, thereby making Kate resume walking on the narrow, approved path of the Amish. "But…the…the Ordn…"

"STOP! She is not violating anything! Now, go!" After the group had left, the bishop poured another cup of coffee, wondering just what had prompted this visit. He knew that Mrs. Mast and her circle of friends were conservative and very…*nosy*, truth be told. He had tried to ignore it in the past because the subjects of their past intrusions had not been harmed. But now, Kate Lapp could be badly hurt by their conjecture and gossip. "Make this a part of the next sermon, which, if I'm not mistaken, takes place at the Lapp's home."

"Husband, what were you saying?" Mrs. Troyer came into the kitchen, ready to start supper.

"I'm reminding myself to include the harm that gossip can do. Those *visitors*? Missus Mast and her crew." The bishop's face contorted into an expression of distaste.

"Oh, no, what are they doing now?"

"Sit. They are asking me to discipline Kate Lapp or even ban her because she's studying at the Englisch library!"

"Nee! I know just why."

"Educate me, please. I'm going to have to go and talk to the Lapps, and the more I know, the better."

Sarah sighed and explained. "Kate is going to the library so she can learn more of pregnancy and childbirth. After Anna Hoffman died, she was very upset by what happened. She blamed herself, her lack of experience. And, I've heard from other mothers that she is now more confident during childbirths. So, clearly, it's helping her."

"As I thought. She's doing something to improve

herself for the good of others. And the Mast crew wants to stop all that good."

Sarah frowned. "Go and talk to them. Tomorrow, if you can."

"Oh, ya. I plan to do so. First thing." The couple ate their supper in near-silence, wondering what the Mast group had on its mind.

ON THE WAY HOME, THE MAST GROUP CONFERRED about what to do. "Bess, the bishop didn't like what we were saying about Kate Lapp. Can't we—?"

"We will continue, Amos. That girl is up to something. And it can't be anything gut. She shames our community. We will go to the Lapp's house tomorrow morning."

Thus, a showdown was set into action—one that would roil the community for weeks.

The next morning, as Kate was hurrying to help Becky with housework so Becky could go see patients and she could study, the bishop knocked at the door. "Bishop! I...is everything okay?"

The bishop's smile was small. "Nee. I need to know if your mamm is here."

"Ya, but daed left just a few minutes ago."

"Nee, he's on his way back. I caught him as he was turning toward the shop."

"Oh. Come in and I'll get Mamm." Kate hurried into the kitchen, where Becky was verifying she had all the equipment she needed. "Mamm, the bishop is here. And Daed will be inside in a minute."

Becky's mouth dropped open. "Bishop, come in. Coffee?"

"Ya, please."

Becky and Kate pulled four cups down, pouring the coffee and putting a platter of coffee cake on the table.

Steve walked in with a worried look on his face. "Bishop, what's wrong?"

"Everyone sit." Bishop Troyer waited until everyone was focused on him. "I got a very...*interesting* visit yesterday. From Bess Mast, her husband and some of their likeminded friends."

Kate gasped. "Oh, no. Bishop, I know what this is about. She refused my offer of coffee at the last Meeting lunch, and then accused me of being ready to leave and join the Englisch."

"Ya. That's exactly it. I understand you're spending a lot of your time at the library, studying about pregnancy and childbirth, ya?"

"Ya. I'm also being tutored by a medical student. On one of my visits, the librarian refused to look up information I needed, so Mister James offered to teach me. Mamm and Daed know about the tutoring." Kate didn't say anything about her thoughts of leaving the Lancaster community to go to medical school. She knew this wasn't the time.

"Gut. They know and they approve. Because Missus Mast made it sound like you were doing something bad. Forbidden."

"Nee! Never, bishop!" Kate was about to continue when a thumping knock interrupted her.

"Wait, Kate. I'll answer." Steve hurried to the door. "Mast! What are you doing here?"

"Why aren't you at work? We need to talk to you and your wife, about your daughter and her activities."

"Ya, well, we know. Come in." Steve said nothing about the bishop being there.

When the Masts and their friends saw the bishop glaring at them, they halted. Then, in a babble of loud voices, "She's sinning! She's up to no gut! She lies! Her *studies* are a cover!"

"QUIET NOW!" The bishop's baritone voice rang out, reverberating through the large kitchen.

The Mast group gasped as one.

Kate stood, ready to defend her actions.

"Kate, explain to them what you've been doing." The bishop was not in a mood to tolerate disobedience.

Knowing this, Kate obeyed. "Ya." She turned her attention to the intruders. "I have been going to the library to study. After a patient died, I felt sorely the lack of knowledge and decided to go and learn so this wouldn't happen again. Once I began to feel somewhat comfortable with my learning, I told my parents what I was doing. They approve. I told Miriam and her parents. Deacon Kopp approves. And I am much more comfortable with my work in delivering babies now." Kate stopped there, knowing now wasn't the time to mention her thoughts of leaving the community, even temporarily.

"And you have no thought of doing anything other than helping expectant mothers, ya?"

"Nee. Only for the mothers and babies."

Looking at the intruding group, Bishop Troyer pointed firmly at the front door. "Leave. Now." It wasn't until the front door had been closed that he spoke again. "Kate, there's something you're not saying. Out with it."

CHAPTER 16

K ate swallowed convulsively, regretting the coffee cake. "A-along with studying, I'm being tutored by an Englisch medical student. Mamm and Daed know. And, as long as my interaction is limited to studying and learning, they are fine with it. He also gets information for me from the internet. I think he called it *downloading*? Or loaded down? Whatever it is, he's been able to help me get the most recent information on pregnancy and childbirth, so that I feel so much more comfortable when we're confronted with a difficult situation."

"And? I get the feeling there's more." The bishop sat and waited, not expecting what was to come.

Kate exhaled loudly and looked at her parents. *I'll do this.* "Mamm and I have long been talking about opening a clinic for our mothers here, so we could offer prenatal visits and, when it's time, help them to give birth to their babies. After…after Anna Hoffman died, that's when I really felt my, well, my *newness* in midwifery. Also, if we had known that Anna's condition had started so suddenly and would become so severe, we could have gotten her to the hospital in time. As it was…"

"That didn't happen. Ya, I understand. What are you thinking, Kate?"

Kate squeezed her eyes shut as she worked her courage to its highest-ever level. "I-I've been thinking of becoming a medical doctor." She rushed these words so they seemed to run together. Swallowing hard, she continued. "Mamm and I talked about it. If I become an obstetrician, we can work as a team. If she has a patient who develops something like preeclampsia, she can get me involved. And, with the medical training and access to treatments I'd have, our mothers would have a better chance of a happy outcome. I'd also be able to use treatments that Mamm and I can't use now." Heart hammering, Kate slowly raised her eyes to the bishop.

Bishop Troyer was silent for several long, creeping seconds. *Mei Gott! I never knew this. What she says is right. They could offer a full set of services.* Coming back to the Lapp's kitchen, he roused himself. "Well. You wouldn't want to leave here or the Amish permanently, would you?"

"Nee! I want to come back, once I have completed my education and my training, whatever that might require. I plan to ask Mister James what exactly I'll have to do. This way, I can make a better decision."

"So, you're still not sure?"

"Nee. I still have a lot of thinking to do. I need to learn what I'll have to do."

Steve entered the conversation. "First, you'll have to get your GED, Kate. Then, unless I'm much mistaken, apply to a college. Do you have one in mind?"

"Ya. I think it's Pennsylvania State University."

Steve and Bishop Troyer winced. "That's over two hours away—by car. You'd have to stay in the dormitories. That's a lot of exposure to the Englisch."

Now, Kate winced. *A dormitory? Why can't I just ride home every day?* "I hadn't thought about that."

"Can you find a school closer to Lancaster?"

Now, she sighed. "I'll start checking."

"Because, unless you find one that will allow you to attend classes without having to stay in residence, I don't know that we elders could give you our permission."

Kate's wide eyes flew up to the bishop's serious face. She opened her mouth to protest, then thought better of her impulse. She sighed. "I'll ask Mister James the next time we meet."

"Gut. In the meantime, I advise you to pray so you can make the best decision. Honestly, this is probably the first time that I've heard anyone express a wish to leave, get an education beyond eighth grade and come back, so she can be of service to our mothers here. And that is the only reason that I'm inclined to give you permission. But…"

"Look into colleges that are closer to home. Ya, I understand." Secretly, Kate was relieved—she didn't want to have to live with the Englisch, even though they would also be pursuing their own educations.

AT HER NEXT MEETING WITH CASEY JAMES, KATE

brought up the events of the past week. "Mamm and Daed are thinking of allowing me to leave for a while, get an education in medical school and come back, so I can become partners with Mamm."

Casey's eyes rounded as he heard Kate's news. "Wow! That's terrific! What about going to Penn State?"

Kate shook her head. "No, not that far away. The bishop also knows. Bishop Troyer is strict, but he's understanding. He is going to talk to the elders about my wishes. He doesn't think they'll say no, provided I find a school that's within closer driving distance. They don't want me to have to stay overnight in the dormitories."

At first, Casey was disappointed. "Well, I do know of three colleges that are nearby." He paused, thinking. I don't think that Pennsylvania at Lancaster Center or the Central Pennsylvania College at Lancaster Center offer medical programs. The only one, and it's one you'd be real comfortable with, is Eastern Mennonite University at Lancaster. That has a pre-med program." *And it's two hours away from my school.* A part of Casey felt like sinking under the table to sulk, and then he remembered that Kate had already accomplished so much. He smiled. "Our tutoring arrangement would have to end once you start school. That's about two hours away from my own school." He looked closely at Kate for her reaction. He wasn't disappointed.

Kate's eyes dimmed slightly in disappointment. Then they brightened again. "There is a school? And it's a Mennonite school? Hmmm. That might make them feel a little better."

"*Might*? Care to explain?"

Kate smiled. "It's simple. The Mennonites are more willing to accept technologies that we, as Amish, can't accept because of our Ordnung—our rules. I won't make it any more complex with explanations of the different levels of conservative versus not-conservative. But many of the Amish aren't comfortable with the Mennonites' acceptance of technologies, such as electricity, cars and even using computers and the internet."

"Shhhh!"

Kate and Casey both jumped and turned around. They saw a middle-aged Englisch woman glaring at them. She mouthed the words, "Be quiet!" to them and emphatically held her finger against her closed lips.

Casey nodded, his face serious. He turned to Kate and signaled to drop their voice levels.

Kate whispered. "Anyway, Mamm and Daed may give me some pressure. The elders might as well."

"Shall we move? Over toward those private study rooms over there?" Casey pointed toward several small rooms, some occupied, some empty.

After moving to another table, they began to study, with Casey whispering. When they finished covering what he'd planned on, Casey invited Kate to have coffee at the coffee shop next door. "We can talk without being shushed."

Kate chewed at her lower lip. "I'm only saying yes so I can find out more information. I don't want people thinking I'm dating someone from outside the community."

"Got that completely." And Casey did get it. Even though hearing the words had the effect of a punch to the gut. In the shop, he gave his and Kate's order to the barista behind the counter.

To avoid the stares around her, Kate focused on one of her textbooks, jotting down notes.

"Here you go. I also got us a couple of lemon bars. Now, what kinds of questions did you have?"

Kate took a delicious bite of her snack. "So gut! Thank you. I was wondering, will a GED be good enough for me to get in? Or will I have to go to a regular high school?"

"A GED should do it. I'll test you on the math, science and chemistry, just to be sure."

Kate nodded. "And how much does it cost?"

"If you go through the community college here in Lancaster, it's free. The testing, too."

Kate realized something about what Casey had said. "Casey, you said that the Mennonite University offers pre-med. It doesn't offer medical school?"

"No. I'm sorry. You'll have to apply to an in-state school that does. I can help you and your parents narrow one down when it's time. It's best that you have all of this information ahead of time so you can discuss it with them."

Kate sighed. "That scares me. My parents are loving, but strict."

"What about your elders?"

"Strict. But understanding."

"Then, pray that they will understand your motivation for wanting to progress this way. Once you get used to the Mennonite lifestyle, you'll be better able to adjust to the...*English?* lifestyle."

"Ya, Englisch. I just want to be able to live in that environment without having to have all of the conveniences."

"Question. If you use a computer or the internet for assignments and papers, what will that do to your standing?"

Kate sighed. "They won't be happy. But because I would be doing so to achieve my goal, they might allow it."

"Once you graduate, complete your residency and come back here, would you stop using those conveniences?"

That question stumped Kate. "I-I don't know. It would be hard to do surgery by lantern light. Keep up with current events in obstetrics without a computer or internet."

Casey nodded. "Write all of that down. Because, when you're defending your decision to the elders and to your parents, you're going to have to have the answers they'll have to hear. They might not like hearing them. But, if you are going to become a partner with your mother, you need to be able to have access to all of them. Right?"

Kate's smile trembled a bit at the edges of her mouth. "Ya. I'd better get home. It looks like it's getting late."

"Okay, then. I want you to think about all of this and what your answers would be. When you make those decisions, try to make them from a place of knowing what you want and why you want it. Okay?"

"Ya. Thank you." Kate smiled at Casey, who was going to stay and study. By the time Kate got home, she was dripping wet with sweat. Walking into the house, she sighed heavily.

"You're home! Get water, because it is horrible-hot out there."

Kate groaned as the first sips of water hit her throat. "That feels so gut!"

"How was your study session with Mister James?"

"It was gut. We went over a lot of stuff."

"So, you have a lot of studying to do?"

"Ya. I'll help you with supper and cleaning up."

"If there are no calls tonight, study."

"Denki." After supper, Kate settled down in the kitchen with her books and notebook. After she finished an assignment, she wrote down several questions related to what she and Casey had talked about. By then, it was already close to bedtime. Putting her books away, she made sure the house was securely locked. Blowing out the downstairs lanterns, she went upstairs, with a huge yawn catching her by surprise. *When do I talk to Mamm, Daed and the elders? They might be okay with me going to*

Eastern Mennonite University. That night, she dreamed.

Kate was at Eastern Mennonite University, not far from her family's home. She was easily able to take the buggy every time she had classes. She met her classmates, who were mostly Mennonite—although she had four or five Amish classmates as well.

"Kate! Do you want to study before you go home?" Tabitha came running up to her.

"Ya, thank you! That math is hard!"

"I agree!" Tabitha laughed. "But we can put our heads together." In the library, the two new friends sat down at a corner table and began working on the calculus problems. Two hours later, they emerged, having tackled the five questions assigned to them. "Let's go eat something. I'm famished!"

A few weeks later, Kate was sitting in chemistry lab, carefully following the instructions the teacher's assistant had handed out. Adding the final chemical, she held her breath. When the compound did everything it was supposed to do, she sighed in relief and began packing all of her things back into her bag. Looking around, she saw that a good eight students remained, working on their assignment. After washing her equipment, Kate jotted down her notes so she could produce a clean report on her computer.

Several weeks later, Kate emerged from a classroom. She

had just taken a test. One of the Mennonite boys in her class was just behind her.

"Hey, Kate, was that a hard test or what?"

"Terribly so! I'm just glad I studied for it. Because I don't want to lose my place here."

"Bah. You won't lose it. You are a natural for this. Are you going to med school?"

Kate, walking out with Sam, nodded. "Yes. I'm going to go to med school and become an obstetrician."

Sam, a Mennonite, stopped. "No! How did you get your elders to give you permission?"

"Honesty. I had an Englisch tutor before I studied for my GED. He told me all that I would need to discuss with my parents and the elders. One of the elders wasn't too happy. 'It should be enough for you to be a midwife like your mamm.' It wasn't until I explained my mother's and my plans with him that he understood. I had to tell him about how one of the mothers died of eclampsia, and that, if we'd had fast access to an Englisch obstetrician, she would have lived."

"So, you're a midwife."

"I am. Or I was. Now, I'm just a pre-med student with plans."

"What did your community say?"

"I got lots of support." Kate rolled her eyes. "There was one group that insisted I was going to just go out, drink and party, and that I should be banned."

"Were you baptized then?"

"No. I'm waiting until I get back, after my residency. That way, I won't violate any part of the Ordnung."

"Wow. You are giving up so much! But I really think you have it in you to make it. I hope you stick with it."

Kate smiled. "Now, I have to. If I am going to show those Doubting Thomases to be wrong, I need to successfully finish every phase of my schooling."

Kate woke up. She saw a thin edge of brightening on the horizon, so she stretched and got out of bed. Getting dressed and combing her hair, she decided that she would talk to her parents that weekend. Having made that decision, she felt much lighter.

As it turned out, she and Becky had three childbirths, almost back-to-back. By the time they dragged back into the house very early on Sunday morning, Kate was grateful that this Sunday was a non-meeting Sunday. "I'm going straight to bed. I'm hungry, but I'm so much more tired."

CHAPTER 17

"Ya. Me, too. It's midnight already, so try to be awake at the usual time, so we can feed your daed."

"Ya. Good night." Kate barely restrained a jaw-cracking yawn. Immediately after putting on her gown and brushing her teeth, she decided not to take her braid out. She just unpinned it from the back of her head and left it alone. Falling into bed, she was asleep even before her head touched her pillow.

VERY EARLY THE NEXT MORNING, KATE GROANED as she heard her mamm knocking at her door. "I'm up." Forcing herself to sit up, she stretched. Feeling her braid, she slowly remembered that she hadn't unbraided her hair. *Gut. Less tangles.* Getting dressed, she combed her hair, brushed her teeth and washed her face. Putting a clean prayer cap on, she went downstairs, still feeling the sleepiness in her eyes. When she looked at her mamm, she saw that Becky was as sleepy as she felt. "Gut morning. Or is it still midnight?"

Becky's laugh was slow and tinged with her need for more sleep. "It feels like that, for sure and certain." She exhaled and yawned. Shaking her head hard, she moved for the coffee pot. "Coffee. You make the eggs—scrambled— and bacon. I'm making cinnamon rolls."

Kate's eyes widened. "But you have to let the dough rise!"

"Already done. It had its two risings yesterday by the time we left for the first birth." Becky, still trying to wake up, got busy with her baking.

Kate, behind her, worked on scrambling several eggs as the bacon popped and sizzled in the cast-iron pan. After several minutes, she poured the fluffy, bacon-flavored eggs into a large bowl.

"Gut job! The cinnamon rolls should be out in a minute. Becky quickly mixed confectioner's sugar and milk in a small bowl, preparing the glaze for the rolls. Just as she finished glazing the rolls, Steve walked in.

"Mmmmm! This all smells so gut! Thanks to Gott, we can sit down and enjoy our breakfast. How many deliveries did you have yesterday?"

"Three. We were in just after midnight." Becky stifled another yawn, and then took a large gulp of her hot coffee. "Owwww! Still too hot."

"Will you two rest sometime today?"

"Ya. If there are no deliveries. I know we have a few patients who are near their times."

Kate shook her head. "I'd better get used to this if I decide to become an obstetrician."

"Yes, you had. And it may be that you'll always be really busy—like last night."

Kate sighed now. "I have a lot to think about."

"You do. I do have one question. If you do decide to go to medical school, you'll be much older than the usual age that our girls here marry. Will you marry someone from here or...?" Becky waited to hear Kate's response.

Kate gave herself extra time by taking a large drink of her coffee. "I don't know. There may not be any young men of my age when I come back— if I decide to go. I would have to marry someone who, like me, waited to marry. Or a widower." She chose not to mention the third option.

Steve cleared his throat after downing most of his eggs and bacon. "These are right gut. Kate, you may also meet an Englischer. Would you marry him?"

So she wouldn't choke, Kate put her loaded fork back onto her plate. "I… only if he agreed to become Amish and was baptized into our faith."

"So, your thing with Mike is definitely over."

"Oh, ya. When I made the decision to break off our relationship, it felt right. I felt so much lighter than I had before."

"Because I saw him with little Sophia Bontrager."

Kate waited to feel the sense of betrayal. When it didn't come, she smiled sincerely. "She's the right girl for him. She's a baker's assistant, so her hours are well defined. Something he should appreciate, I hope. I pray that they have a gut relationship and that they truly love one another."

THE NEXT TUESDAY, KATE RUSHED TO FINISH shopping for her mamm. She needed to be done before mid-morning, so she could meet with Casey James. Hurrying into the house with several canvas bags, she raised them with difficulty. "Here you go. And here's your change." She reached into her apron pocket and pulled a ten-dollar bill and some loose change out.

"Denki! You'd better hurry if you're going to get to the library on time."

"Ya. I'll be back, probably right before dinner."

"I'll be here. If Widow Miller doesn't go into labor."

Kate paused. "Should I reschedule? Mister James will understand."

"Nee. Missus Miller has had six children already, so her body knows exactly what to do. All of her prenatals have been very normal, so there should be no problems."

"Okay." Kate, feeling a little guilty, waved to Becky, then slung her canvas book bag over one shoulder.

ARRIVING AT THE LIBRARY, KATE CHECKED THE simple flip phone her daed had just gotten her. Given how many deliveries they were attending, the family had gotten permission from the elders to carry the little phones. Seeing no messages from Becky, she hurried into the library.

At a distance, Mrs. Mast squinted and frowned. "Did she pull a cellphone out of her pocket? That is directly against the Ordnung!"

"Ya, it looks like she was checking for messages. Or those fancy-schmancy *text* messages."

"Let's go. The bishop has to agree with us now." Laboriously, Mrs. Mast turned her buggy around, in the direction of the bishop's farm.

Sitting in the large kitchen, Mrs. Mast and her companion confronted the bishop. "She pulled a small object out of her apron pocket, bishop. She looked at it, and then hurried into that library. I tell you, she's gotten a cellphone. Now, you have to get her on violating our Ordnung." She sat back with satisfaction.

Bishop Troyer sat back, not bothering to disguise his impatience and disgust. "Ya. It is a cellphone. And it's not one of those that connects to the internet, either. It's just a small flip phone. Her daed and mamm came to all of us—all four elders

—to request permission for this technology so they can more efficiently do their work."

Mrs. Mast's face radiated anger and dismay. "But-but…!"

"'But' nothing. Are you aware that last Saturday they went straight from one delivery to the next until they had delivered babies for three families? How could they have done that without the phones? How would they have known to go to patients' homes?"

Silence. Mrs. Mast opened and closed her mouth several times, trying to find something to pin on Kate, at the least.

Finally, the bishop ran out of his famous patience. "Missus Mast. Would you like to take over in my role as bishop? Because, if it weren't for Gott having chosen me, I would sure love to get rid of this responsibility." His voice bore a strong note of sarcasm.

A deep red, mottled color now stained Mrs. Mast's face. She knew she was being disciplined. Yet, more was coming.

"You and your…*group* have been hassling and harassing the Lapp midwives now for months. All for nothing. In fact, Kate is doing everything she can to be of even more service to our mothers-in-waiting. She and her mother have been looking for ways that they can be available as needed for them. And you dare to come to me with this! Expect to hear from all of us, very shortly. All of you. Now go. Get out of my house before I *really* lose my temper."

Mrs. Mast and her friend skedaddled.

After they had left, the bishop sat, trying to calm down. Gulping the last of his water down, he made up his mind. Going into the first-floor bedroom where Elizabeth, his wife was, he let her know where he was going. "I'll be going to each elder's house. Missus Mast has gone too far now."

"I overheard. On the cellphones they have to use?"

"Exactly."

"Unbelievable! Why do they hold such a grudge?"

"I wish I knew! I'll be back in time to take care of the livestock and for supper."

IN HER DIM, THOUGH SCRUPULOUSLY CLEAN home, Mrs. Mast sat, rocking, at her kitchen table. *Why am I in so much trouble? I do everything I can to live by the Ordnung. And I try so hard to make sure that everyone*

here is doing the same thing. As she rocked away, she also munched, with workmanlike efficiency, at the shoofly pie she'd made the night before. From half a pan, she slowly reduced its size to less than one slice remaining. After swallowing the last bite, she grimaced, feeling her stomach sour at the high load of sweetness she'd shoved into it. *There's nothing for it. All I can do is wait for their visit.* Instead of going to her compatriots, in ensuring compliance with the Ordnung, she chose to let the rest of them find out without warning that they were in trouble. *How can I repent of something that I didn't do? It's up to all of us to watch over our friends and loved ones, isn't it?*

That night, after supper, Mrs. Mast started at a solid knock at the door.

"Wife, who is that so late?" Mr. Mast was perplexed.

"I... it's the elders, I think." Mrs. Mast was uncharacteristically cowed.

"*The elders?*" Abraham was angered. Growling at Bess, his wife, he stalked to the door, snatching it open. "Yes?"

"Abraham, we're here to speak to Bess. Is she to hand?"

"Ya, she is. And I would like to sit in on this meeting. It's the first I've heard of anything."

"You may." Stepping into the dimly lit room, Bishop Troyer looked around. Spotting Mrs. Mast, his face settled into an unaccustomed frown. "You know just why we are here."

"In-in here, please. Coffee? Snacks?"

"Nee. Nothing. This isn't social." The four ministers silently sat down in a row across from Mr. and Mrs. Mast. Bishop Troyer cleared his throat. He never liked doing these. "Mister Mast, you asked to be present for our talk with your wife. Are you aware that she and several of her friends have set themselves up as the arbiters of what is or is not a violation of the Ordnung?"

Abraham, stunned at his wife's audacity, just sat there, his mouth wide open. "N-nee. All she told me was that she was going to see some friends. And pray. The prayer excuse…" He glared at Bess. "The prayer excuse was new. Who have they been after… Miss Lapp and her mamm?"

"Ya. How did you know?" Deacon Kopp was puzzled.

"She has been moaning and accusing them of acting as though they were special. She took off this morning, after chores here, saying she was going to go *help* a friend of hers."

"Did you tell her anything?"

"Just that it was up to all of you to keep us on the straight path. What else could I have done?"

"Nothing. You did the right thing. Your wife, on the other hand, has been endangering the positions of the Lapp women, who are just doing the best they can with difficult work. This morning, she and her friend came to me, sure that, now, they had caught Kate Lapp in a blatant violation of the Ordnung. Kate went to the library for a study session with her tutor. From what your wife so eagerly told me this morning, Kate had violated the Ordnung even more by possessing a cellphone. A cellphone, I might add, that she and her parents requested our permission to own. For work purposes only."

Bess felt her insides squeeze hard and drop toward her feet. Shifting uncomfortably, she stared off into the distance.

"Ach. Let me guess...so that, if they are away from their home, they can still be reached by patients who need their attention?"

"That would be right." Bishop Troyer leaned back, arms crossed. "As we speak, Missus Lapp is attending the birth of Missus Miller's seventh child. Kate had gone to the library to keep her appointment, at her mother's direction. Once she finished, she went home and found her mother's note and hurried to the Miller home. Where, by now, Missus Miller and her other six kinder are hopefully welcoming a healthy baby."

Bess flushed. She knew just what was coming.

"Missus Mast, in your *zeal* to monitor and outright *snoop* on others, all to catch them in wrongdoing, you have committed the greatest wrong. You *know* it is a sin to gossip and create conjecture where there is nothing, just to create doubt in the minds of others. Now, tell me, if Kate and her mamm are not at home to hear the phone in the phone house ring, how are they to know that someone is in labor or trouble?" He clearly expected an answer.

Bess huffed. "Well, couldn't someone just call where they are so they know?"

"How do they know where their midwives are? By magic? Extra-sensory perception, whatever that is?"

Bess knew she'd been caught. She didn't try to say anything else.

"Missus Mast, you know what's coming next. We are asking you to repent of your sins. If you do, you remain a member in good standing. If not, we will be having a meeting that includes the entire community, which will all come forward with stories of their own about your...*activities*."

"Which will it be, Missus Mast?" Deacon Kopp leaned forward, the fingers of both hands linked together.

"How can I repent when I didn't sin? I was simply looking out of the souls of those that I love." Mrs. Mast's voice took on a tone of what she thought was piety.

"So, this is your final choice? You won't repent?" The bishop's face bore a look of disappointment.

"Ya. It is. I was only looking out for them."

"Wife! You know just as well as I that—"

"Husband, I was only ensuring that they are comp—"

The bishop interrupted Bess as she was trying to convince her husband of what she had been doing. "We will be letting you know about the day and time of your meeting. It may be at the next Sunday Meeting. Be ready."

THE NEXT MORNING, THE BISHOP AND DEACON

arrived early at the Lapp home. "Steve, are your wife and daughter here?"

"Ya, what's wrong?" Steve was confused.

"A development regarding the Masts. Missus Mast to be more precise."

"Ach. Come in, then. Wife! The bishop and deacon have to talk to all of us. Kate, you as well." Steve strode alongside the elders into the kitchen. "Coffee?"

"Ya. Denki."

Kate put snickerdoodles onto a large plate as Becky poured coffee into four mugs.

CHAPTER 18

"Ah, thank you. Missus Mast came to my house late yesterday morning, all in a tizzy. Kate, she had seen you at the library, getting ready to go inside. She saw you pull something from your pocket and check it."

"My cellphone. Ya, I was checking to see if Mamm needed me, after all. We were expecting Widow Miller to go into labor, which she did."

"Exactly. And, since your phone isn't one of those fancy smartphones, you can't connect to the internet on it, can you?"

"Nee!"

"Exactly. You were using it for midwifery purposes only. As we had all agreed upon when you came to us, requesting permission to buy simple phones that would not connect to that worldwide web thingie. Anyway, she was certain that she had caught you in an offense that would require discipline. But I told her that you had come to us to ask to be allowed to buy these phones. And, I told her that all of the elders would be to her house by the end of the day to discuss her wrongdoing with her. She refused to repent. She's positive that she is doing the Lord's work in her snooping."

Kate shook her head, feeling truly sad. "So, there's to be a meeting." Her voice was flat. "Everyone here knows that, even though she has been such a…a pain, I don't want to see her position here endangered."

"Ya. I agree. While she has tried to hold us back in our work, even though she was sure she was doing gut, I don't want to see her being harmed by her actions."

THE NEXT FEW WEEKS PASSED IN A BLUR FOR Kate. She helped with several deliveries, and because she was considering going to medical school, she began assisting more during prenatal appointments. As busy as she was, she appreciated this new addition to her midwifery duties. "Mamm, I feel like seeing the mothers during their appointments gives me a fuller picture. Then, I'll be ready for any developments during deliveries."

"That's exactly why I started having you take part in these appointments. Brrr! It's getting cold! We'll have a snowstorm before long." Becky pulled her heavy cloak around her, wishing she had a heavy coat on instead.

"Why didn't you bring your coat?"

"I thought this would suffice. Let's hurry home. Some hot tea is in order."

The next Meeting Sunday dawned, cloudy and cold. Kate, looking outside, thought that, if the weather were any indicator of the outcome of the community-wide meeting, Mrs. Mast would soon be banned. "Daed, we'll need to hurry to the deacon's for meeting. It's cold!"

Steve, blowing on his icy-cold hands, nodded in agreement. "Ya. Once we get everything done here today—ah, that feels gut!" He had stuck his hands under a stream of lukewarm water. "We'll hurry to the Kopp's. Bundle up before we leave!"

ARRIVING AT THE KOPP'S, KATE QUICKLY PULLED the sliced roast beef out of the buggy and hurried inside with it. She stuck it into the heated oven along with all the other warming dishes.

After the three-hour meeting finally ended, the women bustled around, serving lunch. The community was so big that everyone ate in shifts. Finally, she, Becky and the rest of the girls and women sat down to eat. Kate looked up at a slight nudge from Becky, who pointed with her head toward Mrs. Mast.

Mrs. Mast was sitting almost by herself, looking downcast, yet defiant. She hadn't eaten much of what was on her plate. Raising her head, she glared at Kate and Becky.

Finally, lunch was over and, again, the rooms were rearranged. Now, the benches were all placed in two rows, so the community could sit to listen to the elders and Mrs. Mast. A lonely chair sat in the middle of the room, facing the still-empty benches.

After everyone had taken a seat, Bishop Troyer ordered Mrs. Mast to sit down. He launched quietly into the recitation of her offenses. "Missus Mast, how do you respond? Will you repent?"

"Nee, I will not repent. Not if I was simply watching out, with love, for an errant girl. She has been gallivanting all over town, meeting with an Englischman in town at the library and carrying a forbidden cellphone! I don't buy the *reasoning* that she and her mother need those phones. I think they have been coveting after items of decadence, and now Kate can get onto that internet or whatever it's called. She's the one who's sinning!" After going on like this for several minutes more, she finally wound herself down, sitting stick-straight in her chair. Silence ensued as skeptical or sad faces watched her.

"Miss Lapp, did you and your mamm come to us a few weeks ago, to request that you be allowed to buy and use simple flip phones so patients can reach you when it's their time?" Deacon Kopp's voice was loud.

"Ya, we did. It happened just after we had three deliveries in less than thirty-six hours. My daed had to take the calls, and then hope we were still at another patient's house, rather than coming home. He knows that time is vital when a woman is laboring."

"So, you did not get those phones without our permission?"

"Nee."

"Do those phones allow you to access the

internet?"

"Nee. All we can do is make calls, receive them and send text messages. Mamm and I don't know how to do the last."

"Why are you going to the library every week?"

"Because, after the death of Anna Hoffman, I began to feel my lack of knowledge. I wanted to learn more so that I can help the mothers who are giving birth so that, if something goes wrong, we can detect it more quickly. That way, we can give treatment right away. Or, if we can't give the treatment, we can get the mamm to the hospital. So that she and her boppli might live."

At this a soft, sibilant whoosh went through the room. The gazes confronting Mrs. Mast now began to look more accusatory.

"Denki, Miss Lapp. Missus Lapp, I have just a few questions for you. Has your midwifery work here always run smoothly?"

"Ya, when pregnancies and deliveries have been normal."

"How about facing resistance from certain members of the community?"

"When it comes to resistance, my work has been slowed down. I have long, long wanted to open a clinic so that Kate and I, along with other midwives or assistants, can offer a full slate of services. Every time I have tried to start this clinic, I have been stopped by Mrs. Mast and her group of friends."

"How is it that you carry out your prenatal visits?"

"I go from house to house, with two heavy bags."

"Has your daughter begun to accompany you?"

"Ya, she has. And a better assistant, I could not ask for."

"This may be hypothetical. But, if you had had a clinic available, say two years ago, would Missus Hoffman still be alive today?"

"It is hypothetical. We midwives may not have very much warning that something is going wrong. That was the case with Missus Hoffman. She went into labor a few weeks early, because she was developing preeclampsia. While we were checking her vital signs, we realized she was sick and getting sicker. The weather wouldn't have allowed us to transport her to the Englisch hospital. There, she could have received an intravenous solution of magnesium sulfate—Epsom salts—which would have prevented the seizures that presage eclampsia. She suffered a fatal heart attack and her baby died as well."

"Please educate us on the medical services that you are *not* licensed to provide."

"IVs. Caesarian sections. Ultrasounds. Prescribe drugs. Carry oxygen. Give injections to mothers and babies. You see, in the state of Pennsylvania, only a nurse-midwife can be licensed to practice midwifery. We operate by keeping our heads low, learning everything we can and making an effort to do everything we can correctly. But sometimes nature, and Gott, have something else in mind."

Kate, hearing the direction of the deacon's questions, was quivering inside. *Please don't let him ask about my possible plans!*

"This means that you and Kate have a lot of hurdles in your work."

"Ya. We do. But we just do our best and rely heavily on Gott."

The bishop rose. "I have one question and I want every mamm here to raise her hand if you agree: how many of you would choose to work with Missus Lapp and her daughter?" Every hand in the room went up. "If you had a medical emergency, would you go to the hospital?" This time, about half of the women in the room raised their hands, some doing so reluctantly.

The bishop and deacon nodded. Now, the ministers joined them.

"Missus Mast, it's time for us to discuss your case and make up our minds. I'm giving you one final opportunity to repent."

Obstinately, Mrs. Mast shook her head. She rose and stolidly walked to the waiting room and closed the door.

A quiet, but troubled discussion ensued. It took nearly half an hour, but finally everyone agreed that Mrs. Mast had attempted to interfere with the Lapp's work. "Bishop, their work is hard enough." Steve Lapp was standing and speaking. "That weekend that they went to three straight deliveries, they were exhausted halfway through. All of us were praying that they would have easy deliveries to attend. And that nothing would go wrong. I was having a terrible time trying to find them when the calls kept coming in."

"Mister Lapp, are you saying that what Missus Mast—and her compatriots—did interfered with their work?"

"That's exactly what I'm saying. It was by Gott's grace that I was able to intercept them, after the phone calls I got, to let them know to go to those homes. If I hadn't been able to find them…"

Steve's voice trailed away, allowing others to fill in the rest of his thought.

The community voted. It was no surprise to the elders that Mrs. Mast's friends all voted to allow her to remain in Lancaster. "Okay, we have the results of our conversation. Wife, please let Missus Mast know we're ready."

Now, Mrs. Mast was scared. Her steps were small as she tried to delay the inevitable. Her head was downcast as she looked stubbornly at the floor.

"Missus Mast, we discussed every matter at hand. Mister Lapp let us know the potential impact of your actions, should you have been successful in having Miss Lapp restricted in her studies. The community has voted—to ban you. Your ban begins immediately."

A few cries of dismay rose from Mrs. Mast and her friends. Her husband, knowing what was about to happen, just closed his eyes and rocked backward slightly as he took the blow. The community, now knowing what was going to happen, studiously faced away from Mrs. Mast, ignoring her as they left the large room. Slowly, after families had gathered coats, kinder and their dishes, they filed out of the house, talking in low voices.

The elders joined the Lapps, surrounding them, just in case the Masts chose to respond to the ban.

Mr. and Mrs. Mast, effectively shut out, walked out as fast as their overweight forms would allow. On the way home, Mr. Mast directed only a few quiet words to his wife. "Set up the side table in a different room in the house. You know the Ordnung."

"You…you won't leave with me?" Mrs. Mast was fearful now, realizing that she was essentially friendless.

"Nee! Why? I'm not the one who acted wrongly. I'm not banned."

After the Masts left, the elders released their pent-up breaths and broke the protective circle they'd formed around the Lapp family. "Let us know if she continues to give you trouble. Kate, I think you should give the ministers a short update, so they know what the deacon and I already know."

Kate sent a nervous glance to her parents.

"We'll support you. Speak." Steve's voice was soft, though commanding.

Kate let out a long, quivering breath. "I have been thinking about…about more than just studying so I can be of more help to the women here. I believe that, if I go to school and become a medical doctor, Mamm and I can work together as a team to offer a full list of services to the pregnant women here. If they need more care than Mamm can offer, I would be able to provide that. Mamm gave a full list of the services that we, as midwives, can't provide."

"That means you would have to leave Lancaster and live among the Englisch. Have you found a school?"

"I would go to school and work among them. Yes. But not live. I don't want to live in the dormitories. So, my tutor found a short list of colleges that have a pre-med program. There's one less than thirty minutes away by buggy. Eastern Mennonite University at Lancaster. I could stay here and go to school. The only thing is, I would have to go farther away to medical school. There, I would probably be able to find housing and come back most weekends, unless I have studying, tests or an internship at a hospital. Then, once I graduate and get my license to practice, I can come back here full-time." Not sure she should say any more, Kate's rush of words stuttered to a slow stop.

The ministers looked at each other. The younger—and more modern one—spoke. "Well! This is a surprise. So, you don't want to go so you can live a typical Englisch life? Just to get more knowledge—which, as you know, is not something that we typically agree to?"

"Ya. Missus Hoffman is the perfect example of why I want to do this."

"Ach. My cousin, yes." The minister nodded. "We need to pray about this and discuss it before we give you a decision. Expect us to visit you soon with an answer."

Kate nodded, not daring to say anything more. Putting her coat on and buttoning it securely, she made sure her black bonnet was on. Picking up one of the platters they had brought, she followed her parents out to their buggy.

Outside, the weather had grown much colder, causing the three to close their eyes and gasp. "Buggy! Hurry! I don't know for sure, but I think a storm is coming." Steve spoke over the low moan of the wind in the trees. At home, Kate put the dishes away and reluctantly took her coat off. Grabbing a shawl, she wrapped it around her shoulders. At the window, she sighed. "Daed, there is a storm. It's starting to snow."

"Quick, put your coat on. We'll tie ropes between the kitchen and barn."

CHAPTER 19

By the time Kate and Steve had finished tying a guide rope between the house and barn, the snow had started falling hard. Because the ground was already near-frozen, the snow quickly began to stick. Stomping their snowy shoes on the porch, the two came in, shivering.

"Here, drink some coffee. Did you already take care of the livestock?" Becky was hurrying, pouring mugs of coffee for Kate and Steve.

"Ya. We took care of them early. This way, what they have will get them through the night."

IN THE MAST HOME, MR. MAST CAME IN

silently. He sat down by himself at the large table and began to eat methodically. A few feet away and facing away from him, his wife sat, struggling to eat her own meal.

"Husband, will you talk to me?"

Silence. Then, "You know I can't. And why."

Bess Mast set her soupspoon down with a clatter. "You took part, just as I did!"

"But I didn't take rumors to the bishop. You did. You heard them. They have very busy periods and you tried to take a tool away that helps them to stay in touch with patients. Now, quiet!"

Bess fumed. *I will get back at him!* But she stopped trying to engage her husband in conversation. Later that week, once the blizzard had ended, she left the house. In the buggy, she steadfastly ignored anyone who passed her—just as they ignored her. At the bishop's house, she refused to leave.

"Missus Mast, you know we can't communicate with you. You're effectively excommunicated. Now, please leave."

Bess stomped her foot. "I won't! Not until you listen. You don't have to talk, just listen." She paused until she was sure she had his attention. "Now." She arranged her heavy shawl, which she wore over her black coat. "I think you should know that my husband was just as involved as I was in telling you about Kate Lapp's activities and ownership of a cellphone." She gave him the names of her remaining compatriots as well. Standing still, Bess waited.

Instead of speaking, the bishop gave her one stiff nod.

Satisfied, Bess went back home. The atmosphere in the home had never been very easy, what with Bess' difficult temperament. Now, it was downright cold and silent. Mr. Mast wondered, every night, how long he would have to contend with her.

Three days later, the elders stopped at the Mast home to speak with Mr. Mast. Because nobody could interact with her or even accept a simple cup of coffee from Mrs. Mast, it fell to Abraham to offer coffee.

"Nee. This is business." The bishop launched into the explanation of what he had learned. He listed the other people involved, but didn't reveal who gave him the names.

Gaping like a fish, Mr. Mast stared at the elders. "I-I…" Sighing, he gave up. "Ya, I did. But she was wrong to do so. She's putting herself above everyone else." Stiffly he nodded.

"Do you repent?"

He thought about it for a few minutes. "Nee. I can't."

Sighing, the elders left. Stopping in a warm diner, the four elders drank hot, strong coffee and talked quietly. "Well, she has to stay banned. She refused to repent. Yet, she gave us the names of four other conspirators. None of whom have repented. We've been told what we have to do, gentlemen. We have to set up another community meeting. Weather permitting, it will be the weekend after next." After they finished their coffee, they braved the elements and went home.

TWO WEEKS LATER, THE WEATHER WAS SUNNY, but very cold. It was the Sunday before Christmas; while people were feeling festive, in the backs of their minds, they were aware that, after lunch, another community meeting would be held.

After lunch had ended, the remaining four conspirators sat and gave their testimony. Again, everyone listened to the discussion. And, again, the community voted to ban the remaining four conspirators. They all looked at each other; sure it had been Bess who had spoken up.

IN HER SILENT KITCHEN, BESS DRANK COFFEE, enjoying the prospect that her husband would now serve the same punishment she was. Hearing the front door opening, she slurped the rest of her coffee down and washed her cup.

Glaring at Bess, her husband growled at her. "Did you have anything to do with this?"

"Shhh. We're not allowed to talk to each other." Bess went upstairs and into her new bedroom. The only positive, for her, was not having to share a bedroom with her husband, who snored loudly.

KATE READ SLEEPILY ONE SUNDAY AFTERNOON just after Christmas when Becky's cellphone chirped.

"Ya, this is Becky Lapp. Ah-huh. Ya. She's not due until after the first of February. Okay, we're on the way."

Kate, hearing this, was no longer sleepy. Instead, she rocketed off the sofa and shoved her feet back into her heavy shoes. "Mamm, is it Emily?"

"Ya. Her daed says her heart is pounding and racing."

Kate's expression was confused. "She's not in labor?"

"Nee. I think we should both go. This sounds like her pregnancy is straining her heart."

"Has anyone called Nicholas?"

"Nee. He's at his parent's house."

"I'll call."

"Wait. Let's see what Emily's parents say." Emily and Nicholas weren't married. Instead, they had been sexually active after leaving school and beginning rumspringa. Emily had been caught in her activities when she had to reveal her pregnancy to her family. She had never really had a very strong heart.

"Okay, but I think he should know. He's shown himself to be invested in her pregnancy and in the baby's impending birth."

"I know. But Emily is still in the custody of her parents, so it's up to them." Arriving at the house, Becky quickly checked Emily out. Not liking what she saw, she sighed. "I think you should call Nicholas' parents. All of them need to be here."

Mr. and Mrs. King looked at each other. "You mean...it's that bad?"

"I'm not a doctor. I have no medical training. But I don't like what her heart is doing. It sounds like it's straining to get blood through her body. I think we should take her to the hospital right now."

Mrs. King let out a small cry. Mr. King nodded. "Call them."

Kate pulled her phone out of her pocket and immediately called the Fisher house. "Mister Fisher? This is Kate Lapp. I'm sorry to call you on such a nasty day, but it looks like we're going to have to take Emily to the hospital. Her pregnancy may be doing something to her heart. She wants him to be there and we agree. You'll meet us there?" Getting a confirmation of this, Kate hung up and shoved the phone back into her apron pocket. She swung into helping Becky and Mr. King get Emily into the family's buggy. She carried two heavy blankets and trailed behind them, handing the blankets to Mrs. King, who placed them tenderly around Emily's swollen body.

Kate didn't like the look of Emily's face. She was pale and looked like she was about to faint. She and Becky both catapulted themselves into the back seat, surrounding Emily so they could continue to monitor her condition. Kate checked Emily's pulse periodically and encouraged her to get as much oxygen as she could into her. "I know it's hard. We'll have you in the hospital before long."

Becky listened to Emily's heartbeat and lungs. When Emily closed her eyes for a few seconds, she looked at Kate and shook her head. "How much longer, Mr. King?"

"Maybe twenty minutes, Miss Lapp. How is she?"

"Still struggling." As it happened, a passing law enforcement vehicle saw them hurrying. They took Emily and Becky. Mrs. and Mr. King, along with Kate, stayed in the buggy and hurried the rest of the way to the hospital. Arriving fifteen minutes later, they rushed inside, finding Emily and Becky in a cubicle.

"The doctor has already listened to her heart. They're getting ready to take her to have a CT scan of her heart. That way, we'll get a better idea of what's happening."

The doctor hurried into the cubicle.

"Doctor, is this CT scan safe for her pregnancy?"

"The risk is minimal. We'll do everything we can to make sure the baby gets the smallest dose of radiation possible." He and a nurse pushed the gurney out of the cubicle. "We'll be back here just as soon as possible."

Kate, Becky, the family and, when they arrived, the Fisher family waited until the gurney bearing a sleeping Emily returned. The doctor was just behind. He was holding an iPad in one hand, touching and swiping it up, down and from side to side. "Mom, dad, has your daughter always had heart trouble?"

"Ya, ever since she was born. We were told just to monitor how she's doing. This is the first time in years that anything has happened."

"Okay, is it congenital? That is, is it a family issue?"

Mrs. Fisher sighed. "My grandma on my daed's side had the same thing. She could only have two kinder because the doctor said it was too much for her. We realized Emily had the same problem when she was about two."

"Okay. We have a few treatment options. But first, we're going to have you make sure she doesn't suddenly gain weight from one day to the next. Now, we can give her several medications that are safe for pregnant mothers. Do you know if she plans to breastfeed?"

Nicholas blushed, as did his daed and Mr. King.

Mrs. King nodded. "Ya, she wants to do so."

"Okay. We can give her these medications. Something called an ACE inhibitor, which helps her heart to work more efficiently. I can prescribe beta-blockers. These slow her heart rate down so that a little recovery time between beats is possible. I can give her medications that will make her urinate more frequently so she has less fluid retention. Or she could take digitalis, which comes from the foxglove plant. This makes her heart beat a little more strongly. And this is the one that I am the most reluctant to use. Anticoagulants thin the blood, which could cause her to bleed excessively during delivery. I'm not too inclined to prescribe this because her heart is still pushing blood around acceptably well. I'm going to start with the ACE inhibitor. We'll see how she's doing. Now, I understand you're her midwife?" The doctor's eyebrows rose with his question.

"Ya. My daughter and me, we are monitoring her condition every month."

"Okay, I'm glad to see she has prenatal care. Do you plan to see her weekly?"

"Ya, now that she's a month away from delivery."

"Excellent. Okay, I'm going to give you some literature. I'll give the both of you the same literature. It tells you what effect the medication should have and what to watch out for. Missus…"

"Lapp."

"Missus Lapp, I want you to monitor her symptoms. You don't have access to the internet or electricity, so you're going to have to phone me every week with what your exams reveal. If she doesn't improve, she'll have to come back and have a C-section, so she and the little one both have a chance."

At this, Nicholas gasped. He was young, but ready to become a daed. He had loved Emily for a few years now, and they were just waiting for baptism so they could be full members and get married. "Is the baby ready to be born?"

"It's about thirty-five weeks along, so almost there, Nicholas." Becky was reassuring and empathetic. "We just need to get her heart working better so she can keep this pregnancy going for as long as possible. The longer Emily can hold on, the stronger the baby's lungs will be."

"You'll…you'll help her?" Nicholas swallowed

so he could quell the threatening tears.

"Ya, we will."

After discharging Emily, everyone went home. Becky told the Kings to expect her and Kate several times a week.

Now, the Kings were more willing to accept Nicholas into their home. It had become clear to them just how much he loved Emily. And, when Emily woke and saw Nicholas at her bedside, they saw how happy she was to have him at her side.

BACK IN THE KING HOME, BECKY AND KATE created a schedule of appointments for Emily. "We will come out to see her, as we have been doing. Do everything that Doctor Scott said. Less salt, more fluids and weigh Emily daily. She's still supposed to gain a pound a week—any more than that means that she's getting a dangerous buildup of fluids. And don't hesitate to call us if something goes wrong. We'll be right back here to get her to the hospital. In fact, you might want to start asking family members to help you with the hospital bill, just in case. I spoke to the Fishers and they're doing the same."

From that day on, Becky and Kate were at the King home every other day. On the last day they were there, they saw that Emily was again gasping for breath. Checking her feet, face and hands, they saw she was retaining fluid again. And she had gained six pounds since their visit two days before. Becky sighed. "Kate, call Doctor Scott and the hospital. Their numbers are in Emily's notes. Mrs. King, we need to take her to the hospital right away. Where's Mr. King?"

"He's at the carpentry shop."

"I'm calling him and the Fisher family. Start getting Emily ready to leave, please." Fifteen minutes later, they were on their way again. As they arrived, the Fishers also arrived.

Because Kate had called ahead, the hospital's labor and delivery ward were ready for them. After Emily's vitals were taken, she was rushed into the delivery room and prepped for her C-section.

While Emily was having the baby, everyone waited in the L&D waiting room. Seeing Doctor Scott hurrying into the small room, everyone stood.

"She has a small, but healthy little girl. And, I strongly advise that this should be her only child. She was very close to complete heart failure. It's going to take her a while to regain her strength."

CHAPTER 20

At home that night, Kate stood at the kitchen window, just watching snowflakes drifting lazily down. She felt a sense of calm and rightness.

"You're just watching it snow?" Becky wrapped her shawl around her shoulders.

"Ya. And thinking. Gott blessed me with the opportunity to take part in the birth of Emily's little one. While we weren't there, helping her, we did get to take part in monitoring her health. I learned so much about heart failure related to pregnancy. And I think it'll help me once I start pre-med and medical school."

Becky was silent for a long time. "So, you've decided."

"Ya. While I know next to nothing about the heart, this experience showed me that there's so much more to monitoring a healthy pregnancy than just the pregnancy itself. There's a whole list of organs involved."

Becky was silent again. "When do you want to start? Because I'm going to need to show you as much as I know between now and then. And train another assistant."

Kate sighed. "This fall. I'll be eighteen. If I pass the GED, then I can start at the Mennonite college."

Becky nodded. Her eyes were bright with tears. "I am so proud of you. I know we don't normally say that, but you really want to do the best you can for our patients."

"Who do you have in mind to take my place?"

"I was thinking of Katherine Ernest. She's fifteen, so a little younger than you are. She has a gut mind."

"Katherine." Kate closed her eyes, thinking. "Ya, she's a gut choice. She is really gut with math and people."

"Ya. But I'll still miss you, daughter. And we need to tell the elders."

Kate swallowed hard. "Ya."

Two days later, the elders came over. Drinking coffee they gave the Lapps their decision. "It's only because she has stated her plans to return—and that she isn't leaving to take part in the wild side of Englisch life that we are saying 'yes.' Kate, we are going to ask you for a verbal agreement that, if you are accepted into these schools, you'll come back. You'll work here, helping our mothers who are pregnant."

Kate smiled widely. Her heart was thumping. "Ya, I will! Thank you!"

THAT WEEK, WHEN SHE MET WITH CASEY JAMES, she gave him the good news. "The elders said yes! They said, only because I wanted to go away and learn so that I could do gut when I come back." Kate gasped, her excitement building.

Casey, forgetting himself, enfolded Kate into a tight hug. Then, he realized what he was doing and released her. "Oh, I'm so sorry! I was just so excited and happy for you."

Kate was laughing and secretly thrilled that he'd held her. "Nee, it's okay. It's a celebration!"

Casey closed his eyes and got control of his

emotions. He sighed, thinking. "Okay, first things first. Study for your GED. All subjects. I'll tutor you on that. Then, once you pass—and you will—work on your admission to Eastern Mennonite University at Lancaster. Has your mother thought of someone to take your place?"

"Ya. She's come up with a gut girl, very smart."

"Excellent." By the end of their tutoring session, he was really struggling with his feelings for her.

As Kate was for him. She was really excited about the new vistas that were opening up in front of her. And scared about the feelings she was developing for Casey.

"Ah, Kate, would you mind coming to the coffee shop with me? I really need to tell you something."

Kate looked at Casey, her mouth slightly open. "Sure. Okay, but only for a little while." Trying to conceal the shaking of her hands, she put her books and binder away in her carryall bag. Sitting in his car, she became aware of an excitement she'd never experienced before. Her level of tension shot up.

At the shop, Casey placed their coffee orders as Kate sat at a small table away from the shop's front window.

Bringing their coffees to the table, Casey sat

down and slowly added creamer to his cup. He sighed, thinking. After stirring his coffee, he wrapped both hands around his cup, leaning his weight on both elbows. "Kate, I've been tutoring you for several months now and I've enjoyed it thoroughly. Too thoroughly."

"Oh?" Kate didn't know what to say. "I hope we can continue. I've learned so much from you." She decided to play it safe.

"And teaching you has helped me to understand difficult concepts and procedures. Although, actual practice is a better learning tool than all the reading in the world. But..." Casey fell into a silence that soon stretched like taffy, between the two of them. He felt the tension level between the two of them, as though it were a tangible being sitting at the table.

Kate waited, trying to think of something to say. She felt like she was going to break up and fly apart into millions of tiny pieces if nothing was said or done. She shrugged carefully. "Well, if you'd like, I can find a different tutor." She pushed her mug away from her, ready to grab her carryall and leave.

Casey grew alarmed, certain she'd misunderstood his drift. "Wait! I didn't mean that."

Kate stopped, allowing her bag to go to the

floor again. Feeling totally confused, she sat back down. "What is it you want to talk about, then?"

Casey had always been shy around girls. Feeling that this was too important to allow his shyness to prevail, he gathered his courage. "Kate, I...that is, I don't know if you can date someone who isn't Amish. If not, well, I would be pretty disappointed. But, is there any way you can?"

Kate was grateful she was already sitting down. Otherwise, she would have fallen in her shock. Closing her eyes, she pulled her thoughts together. *I have to be honest.* "Casey, I broke up with my boyfriend, Mike, a few months ago. He's Amish, but he didn't understand my commitment to being the best midwife I can be." She sighed, a long, sad sound. "After Mamm and I attended that birth where the mother had preeclampsia and died, I just felt so...*inadequate.* We were so scared. That's why I started going to the library. Now that I have permission from my parents *and* the elders to go to pre-med at the Mennonite University, I feel like I have the direction that Gott has intended for me to have. So I can really help our mothers. But..."

Silence. Casey waited, feeling apprehensive. "What?" Continuing to wait, he tipped his head and took Kate's hand in his.

Kate liked how her hand felt in Casey's finely shaped, strong hand. She left it there. She realized that having him hold her hand felt totally different from when Mike used to hold her hand. "Casey, I haven't been baptized yet. So, with the permission from the elders, I can still live at home and communicate with my family and friends."

"How would that affect us dating, if we decide to do so?"

Kate looked into the distance, just thinking. "The Amish don't want to mingle that much with the Englisch because we don't want to lose our identity. We choose to stay off to ourselves. We choose to live simple, plain lives with no conveniences as the Englisch have. We rely completely on Gott for everything we get."

"So, how would that affect you when you go to medical school—once you've graduated from the Mennonite University? And dating?"

"I'm still working out the living away from Lancaster part. And on...on dating, that would be frowned on. Unless..."

"Unless, what?"

"Well, there is a way. But it would mean that you have to give up so much. Living Amish is a true sacrifice, in every way."

"I'm listening. And remember, I am Christian."

Kate whooshed out a long sigh. "I could date you if you were to go through baptismal instruction…and become Amish."

Even though, in the furthest reaches of his mind, Casey had expected this, it still surprised him. However, he was even more surprised that the idea didn't seem strange or impossible to achieve. "I was expecting this. And I am willing to think about it. Because, getting to know you over the past several months, I have come to see that you are an exceptional young woman. And… I…I do have feelings for you."

Kate had just picked up her coffee mug, which was still half-full of coffee. She set the mug down hard and the coffee sloshed, wetting her hand and the table. She gasped. Her eyes and facial expression said everything. Her smile was wide and gave an incandescent glow to her face. Then, "But, Casey. You would have to give up your car. You couldn't use a computer, except at the hospital."

Casey smiled. Clearly, he had another idea in mind. "What if…what if we joined the Mennonite faith? They still rely very heavily on God's will and benevolence. You'd still be very close to your Amish faith. But, once you graduate and become a doctor, you could still live here and, instead of having to find a driver to hire in an emergency, you could use your own car."

Now, Kate began to feel overwhelmed. "Stop, stop. Please, wait. I'm not saying no. But I have a lot to think about. A lot to do. I need to find somewhere to begin studying for my GED. Take the test, and then get into the university. And I want to do this by the time school starts in the fall."

Casey backed off. "Okay. I'm sorry. Let's just take care of things in the right order. I'll help you get into that GED program and tutor you on that. In fact, let's hold off on the childbirth topics until you've passed the test. Then, get you admitted to the university. Then, we can start the medical tutoring again. And...*maybe* go out on a few dates?"

Kate propped her chin in her hand, just thinking. "Wow. So much to do. Casey, we're going to be spending so much time together."

"I do have one question. Do your parents know about me?"

"Ya, and so do the elders."

Now, Casey was the one feeling overwhelmed. "Ah, as in, minister, deacon and bishop?"

"Ya." Kate giggled. Then, thinking about the Masts and their co-conspirators, she sobered. "We had a couple of community meetings just a few weeks ago. One woman and, as it turned out, her husband and a few of their friends, well, they were trying to get me in some big trouble. Because of my meeting with you for tutoring." She reached into her apron pocket, removing her little flip phone. "And because of this. After Mamm and I had three deliveries back to back, we went to the elders and explained that we needed a way of communicating with Daed and patients. Daed was hard-pressed, trying to find us that night so he could give us messages from other families needing our help. Anyway, Missus Mast saw me checking for messages from Mamm. She went to the elders and told them. But she didn't know that they had already given us their permission. So, *they* were the ones banned because of what they did."

"Wow. So, because they were trying to do what the elders are responsible for, they were excommunicated?"

"And for gossiping about Mamm and me."

Casey whistled a low, tuneless sound. His eyes were wide in shock. "They don't mess around, those elders."

"Nee. If someone is banned, they soon remember they have no excuses for their actions.

So, your idea about going to the Mennonite church is actually a gut one. Because, no matter how I try to rationalize it, the use of a car, electricity or a computer would *never* be allowed in our community."

After this long conversation, Kate began working on her GED instruction. While Casey had to tutor her on several subjects that she hadn't had much exposure to in school, she did well. On her GED testing date, she woke with the feeling that nervous snakes were squirming around in her stomach.

"Kate, you need to eat. I know you're nervous. But if you don't eat, you won't do well."

Kate groaned. "Don't say 'won't do well,' Mamm." She gripped her stomach.

"Coffee or tea? Toast? Or oatmeal?"

Kate contemplated her choices. Sighing, she decided to have the coffee and oatmeal. "I'll make the oatmeal. I need something to do with my hands. Because Casey told me not to study any more than I already did."

Becky and Steve were stunned. "Really? Why?"

"If I study too much, I won't be able to remember the materials. And I'll have to take the test again." She poured her hot cereal into a bowl, trying not to spill it.

COMING OUT OF THE TESTING CENTER WITH HER test results in one hand, Kate jumped and pranced around. She was giggling. "I passed!"

Casey, who had been sitting in the lobby, joined her, jumping as well. "Let's get coffee to celebrate! It's spring, but the temperatures would say otherwise."

IN THE COFFEE SHOP, KATE MUNCHED ON A cinnamon roll and drank her coffee. Now, her stomach was settled and she was so hungry. "Now, what's next?"

"Well, first, a celebratory date. You could tell your parents that your tutor is just taking you to eat as a gesture of friendliness and support. Nothing about dating or, um, romance. So you don't get in trouble."

"They would be suspicious."

"I'll tell you what. I'll wear a suit and just act like…well, like a teacher acts toward his students."

Kate decided to risk it. "Okay. But I do have to dress Plain, like I am now."

"Did anyone react in the testing room?"

"I got some stares, but I'm used to those. I sat next to a Mennonite girl."

"Let's see, the one with the pink dress that had the tiny green flowers and leaves?"

"Ya, her."

"How does your community view the Mennonites?"

"Here, more positively than in other communities. We're not as conservative, so the fact that they use electricity, cars and computers doesn't bother us as much."

CHAPTER 21

Almost as soon as Kate got home, she began looking at everything she had to do. Sitting at the table, looking at an application form and scanning through the notes she had taken when Casey had run through it all with her, she sighed, a gusty sound that got Becky's attention.

"Is everything okay? You sound like you have the weight of the world holding you down."

"That's a gut way of putting it. I'm looking at everything I have to do to apply and get into the university next fall." She looked up as someone knocked on the door. "I'll get that." She was eager to get away from the overwhelming paperwork. "Mister James! I... How may I help you?" Kate was nervous, not wanting Becky to figure out that she liked her tutor.

"Kate, I just wanted to offer my congratulations to you. You accomplished something big and I'd like to take you to dinner, as your tutor."

Becky's eyes rounded. She looked closely at Kate. Seeing that her neck was tense, she hurried to the front door. "Mister James, did I hear you say you want to take my daughter out?"

"Yes. I want to offer my congratulations to her. She just took a big step forward in reaching her goal. I tutored her for a few months, and I can tell you, Missus Lapp, she is intelligent and wants to meet her goal. Which, from our discussions, means you'll also be able to realize a long-time dream of your own, right?"

Becky had to admit that Mr. James was right. "Ya... but taking her out?"

Casey had seen all the papers covering the kitchen table. "I can help her with all of her application materials. I'm pretty experienced with it, actually."

Kate nodded slowly. "Ya, you could. "Looking at Becky, she folded her hands in front of her. "Please? Ask Daed, if you need to. I understand. I... filling out all that paperwork gives me the heebie-jeebies. If Mister Casey can help me and I can get it in sooner, then I can do other work we need to do here."

Becky couldn't argue against that. She sighed. "Let me talk to him. Mister Casey, did you have a day you wanted to take her out?"

"Yes. I was thinking about this Friday."

"I'll talk to Steve. But, you understand, she'll have to wear Plain dress, ya?"

"I understand and that's fine. I don't want to make her do anything that goes against your practices."

"Gut. I'll have Kate let you know by tomorrow."

"Thank you. Kate, put all that paperwork away. It intimidates you because you just spent a lot of mental effort studying and taking your test. Just rest. Or help your mother out."

Kate smiled, feeling grateful. "Denki, I will. I thought I should just get started on it right away."

"That's not necessary. You still have a lot of time between today and the admission deadline."

Kate sighed, feeling relief sweep through her. "I'll just help Mamm then. I'm so used to it that I don't need to put too much brain power into it."

"I'll check back tomorrow to see what your dad says."

"What about tutoring?"

"Take a break. Seriously. You've been working so hard. Don't worry. You'll be where you need to be, knowledge-wise." Casey left before he wore his welcome out.

That night, after Kate had gone to bed, completely exhausted, Becky sat down next to Steve. "Husband, Mister James came by today. He congratulated Kate on passing her GED test, and he wants to take her out on Friday evening. To celebrate."

"Celebrate? I don't know... He's Englisch, she's not."

"He's also the one who found that Mennonite University. He seems to understand how difficult it is for an Amish girl like Kate to break out of what she's expected by her community to do. Steve, I know that we are already doing a lot to help her. Mister James said he would help her with her papers to get into the college. They're going to continue tutoring..."

"Is he interested in her? As more than just a scholar?"

"I don't think so. He's always been appropriate and never trying to push any boundaries."

Steve sighed, letting his head fall back to rest against the soft back of their sofa. "She is so helpful to you. But why does it seem that we are making so many more concessions to her?"

"Because, if she becomes a doctor, she can back my midwife work up."

"Ya. That's true. Well, I suppose it won't hurt to allow her to go to this celebratory dinner."

"What will we do if he wants to date her?"

"Have a strict talk with both of them."

Becky sighed. "You know, if something does begin to develop between the two of them, there is a solution."

"Ya, there is. But is he even a Christian?"

"We can find that out."

Steve stood, waving his hands around, as though waving gnats away from his face. "Why are we even talking like this? Let's just let her go with him. This time. And, if they express any interest beyond this week, we'll address it then."

"Okay." Becky was oddly pleased, although she didn't know why. "I'll let her know tomorrow morning."

THE NEXT MORNING, KATE WAS THRILLED WHEN Becky gave her Steve's decision. She hid the intensity of her feelings, just smiling slightly and thanking Becky for intervening. Her heart began to thump slightly as she anticipated her evening out with Casey. After helping to clean the kitchen, Kate quietly told Becky, "I'll be upstairs. I want to check my bag and make sure that I have everything I need. After being away for my tutoring and testing, I don't remember what's in there and what needs replacing."

"Okay. I think we may have a delivery later today. I do know that we have some prenatal visits to make, so don't take too long." As it happened, on their third prenatal visit, they arrived to find the mother seriously ill. "Faith, what's wrong?"

"I don't know. I feel *horrible*. I took my blood sugar and it was too high. I took my insulin, and then ate, but I started feeling worse and worse. Like I am totally fatigued. I have blurred vision and a terrible headache and I'm so thirsty!"

Kate intervened. "Faith, are you going to the bathroom more than usual? To urinate?"

Faith looked at Kate as though she couldn't understand what she was saying. "Uh, ya, I am."

"Mamm, I covered this in my tutoring sessions. I think it's her blood sugar. It's too high. Faith, where are your testing strips and monitor?"

Faith gestured vaguely toward the kitchen.

Kate raced to get the equipment and tested Faith's blood sugar. "Gah, Mamm! It's 193! We have to get her to the hospital now!"

"Ya, this means her baby could be much bigger than normal. And she is tiny." Becky quickly wrapped Faith in her cape and a heavy blanket; it was still cold, though it was officially spring. In their buggy, she urged the horses to hurry. At the hospital, she quickly explained the situation to an ER nurse.

Suddenly, the crowded ER exploded into action. Another nurse brought a gurney, on which Faith was placed. "Are you her midwife?"

"Both of us are. My daughter figured it out. She's been doing some extra studying."

"That's good news. We're taking her up to the L&D ward. She has to have an immediate C-section."

Kate filled in what the nurse didn't have to say. "Her boppli is going to be big, isn't it?"

"Yes. How far along is she? So we know what measures we need to take for the baby."

Becky showed her notes to the nurse.

The nurse paled. "Seven months! Amy, call Doctor Midland. He's on-call and needs to see her stat." The two nurses rushed off, pushing the gurney holding Faith.

Kate and Becky hurried along behind the nurses. Slipping into the elevator, they pressed themselves against the wall as the nurses talked in low voices. Arriving on the L&D floor, they faced the obstetrician, who peppered them with questions. "Did she have diabetes before she got pregnant?"

"Yes, she has. I put her onto a diet right away. Fresh fruits, vegetables, lean proteins and low in sugars and carbohydrates. Plus, told her she needed to stay in close contact with her doctor about her blood sugar and A1C readings. I've been monitoring her monthly. We went to her house and found her like this."

"Missus Stoltzfus, how long have you been like this?" The doctor rubbed Faith's sternum hard, rousing her.

"Since before breakfast. I did everything Missus Becky and my doctor said, but it didn't help."

"Okay. You need immediate treatment, but we need to strengthen your baby's lungs first. You'll be holding your baby within forty-eight hours."

Faith's smile was ephemeral, disappearing almost as soon as it appeared.

Doctor Midland looked at the midwives. "Stay here for a while, if you would. I'll need to read your notes to see if there's anything else we can do."

Becky handed them over. "Can you make copies? I try to keep copies for each mother we treat."

"Sure." The doctor handed the notebook to a waiting nurse. "So, which one of you figured out what's wrong with Missus Stoltzfus?"

"My daughter. She's going to get into the pre-med program this fall."

The doctor's eyes widened. "But...how? I didn't know..."

"Normally, no. But after something happened to another patient, she began to feel her lack of knowledge. I've been training her as fast as I can. So she has a tutor and, now, she plans to become a doctor herself. We'll be opening a clinic at home."

"Excellent for your mothers." The doctor accepted the notebook and began reading through it. "Okay, I see that you addressed her condition right away. And that she did everything she was told to do." Doctor Midland let out a long, exhausted sigh. "Okay. You did everything right. Her pregnancy and the growing baby just overwhelmed the ability of her body to use the insulin she's been taking. I'm going to give mom medications that will strengthen her baby's lungs. He has to come out. And soon."

"Should we call her husband and family?"

"Yes. I take it you didn't have much time before you came here, right?"

"Nee, we didn't. Kate, go call her family, please."

After placing the calls, Kate came back. "Can we go and see how she's doing?"

"In a few minutes, then we'll wait for her family to get here. I hope we'll get home soon enough to make supper." As it turned out, they did get home. Doctor Midland made the decision to admit Faith and observe her for forty-eight hours.

"We'll be giving her steroids to make the baby's lungs stronger. In about forty-eight hours, we'll take her in for that C-section. I'm the most worried about her blood sugar. Our endocrinologist will be working with her numbers to get them into a more acceptable range. Kate? Is that your name?"

Kate nodded. "Ya."

"You made an excellent catch. If you hadn't recognized her symptoms, she would have gone into a coma. And this would have put the baby's life at serious risk. Just keep studying, because I think you'll make an excellent doctor."

Kate floated on a wave of happiness all the way home.

"You should call Mister James to let him know we gave you permission to celebrate tomorrow. And you're wearing a Plain dress."

"Ya, I know. When he mentioned wanting to celebrate, I told him that I couldn't wear anything else."

"Gut. Do you like him?"

"Like him? In which way?" Kate felt tense.

"Like a man. Like someone you could date."

"Mamm, that's too soon! He's my tutor."

"Ya, he is. But it's my role to look out for your safety."

"He has *never* tried to do anything to me. *At all.* He's always respected that boundary."

"But, have you talked about the two of you as man and woman, not tutor and student?"

Kate exhaled, trying to think. "He's a nice man. But I've been too busy with studying and working on getting into school to think about whether I like him or not."

"Your Daed and I talked about it. Last night, after you went to bed. There are ways that, if the two of you decide to begin a relationship—"

CHAPTER 22

"Mamm!" Kate blushed.

Becky was implacable and would not let it go. "If he's a Christian, he can be baptized Amish."

Kate opened her mouth, about to speak. Her retort blew away, like so much smoke in a breeze. "If it comes up, we'll talk." She closed her eyes, stunned. *I'm so glad I didn't say anything else!* Going upstairs, she focused on her work, refusing to think of Casey in terms other than as her tutor.

Downstairs, Becky mused about what she had just learned. *So, she likes him. This will be much harder for her daed to swallow, let alone the elders. Is he Christian, and will he be willing to think about being baptized as an Amishman?*

Later that day, Becky and Kate completed each prenatal visit they had scheduled. On their way home from the final appointment, they decided to stop at the store to get items they needed at home. It wasn't until they had started to go home that Becky finally voiced her thoughts. "You know, daughter, we don't often welcome someone new into our community. Do you like Mister Casey?"

Kate sighed. There was no way out of it. Her response was slow and hesitant. "I… well, maybe… a little."

"I thought as much. Do you know if he's Christian?"

"Ya, he said he is. And he certainly speaks of Gott in a very loving, reverent way."

"Well, gut." Becky smiled. "Do you think he'd be willing to consider baptism in our community?"

Kate laughed. "Mamm, that's a long time away. If it ever happens. I don't really want to be juggling school, all that involves and a new relationship. I'll only have time and energy for one thing at a time."

"Well, I'm glad to hear you thinking like that. So, you want to focus on classes, then?"

"Ya, exactly. Mamm, I see it this way. I have a goal I want to reach. I have to devote everything I have to that, not counting what I give to Gott, you and Daed. If he…if Gott wills a relationship between me and Mister James, it will happen when it's supposed to happen."

"I hope he knows that. Mister James, I mean. I see him looking at you like he's just completely besotted."

Kate blushed. "Ya, well, we have spent a lot of time— Uh, there's Ursula over there."

Becky quickly brought up another subject, one that she and Kate were discussing as they pulled abreast of Ursula. "So, now that you have your GED, what are you doing about getting into that university?"

Kate was stunned. She sent a look of confusion to her mamm. "Ya, I have until the last day of May to submit my admission paperwork. Speaking of which…I'll discuss the essay with you at home. Hi, Ursula."

Ursula refused to answer. She had heard what Kate and Becky were discussing and she thought it was totally scandalous.

"Ursula? What's wrong?"

Now, she spoke. Hot, angry words spilled out. "What do you mean, putting yourself above everyone else here? GED? Admission to that college? What college?"

Kate, freed of all fear now that she had permission from the elders, spoke. "Eastern Mennonite University at Lancaster. They have a pre-med program."

Ursula opened and closed her mouth, unsure of what to say. Then, "I'm telling the elders."

Becky intervened. "There's no need, Ursula. First, they gave their permission to Kate. She's done everything correctly. Second, do you want to follow your parents in the ban?"

Unable to say anything, Ursula showed her reaction with a dark, blotchy flushing on her face and neck. Growling, she stalked off.

Kate waited a few seconds. "Mamm! It's a gut thing I asked the elders!"

"Ya. It is. And just make very certain that you do so for everything you do. Especially if you and Mister James decide to begin courting."

Kate nodded silently in agreement.

KATE STAYED STEADILY BUSY HELPING BECKY AND completing her admissions paperwork. On the day she had agreed to meet with Casey, she read through every document and tossed her handwritten essay on top of the pile. "I hope that's it." She hurried to the barn, where she hitched two of their horses to the buggy and left.

Becky, seeing Kate driving off, waved her arm in the air. "Kate!"

Kate stopped the buggy. "Ya?"

"I'm praying for you. Try not to say anything to Mister James about your feelings."

"Thank you. If he brings them up, then I'll discuss them. If not, then I won't."

"Gut. Be careful and try to be home by the time we start supper. We shouldn't have any deliveries today."

"Denki. I'll be home when it's time to make supper. Don't worry!" Kate smiled at her mamm.

IN THE LIBRARY, KATE AND CASEY WENT OVER her paperwork.

"I'm so grateful you have good penmanship. Have you ever typed?"

"What, me? Nee!"

"Okay, then, I'll type out your essay and print it. Then, we'll go in my car to the university and submit everything. Do you have the admission fee?"

"Is it still twenty-five dollars?"

"Yup. Let's go to the library and get this baby written out."

"Why don't they accept handwritten essays?"

"Not everyone has nice handwriting like yours. Try figuring out whether someone is saying 'cut' or 'out' when you still have two or three hundred other essays to score."

Kate's eyes widened. "That makes sense." She sat next to Casey as he rapidly typed her eight-page essay.

"Okay. Unedited, it comes out to five pages typed. Is there anything you think you can cut?"

Kate groaned. "Cut anything? But everything came from my heart!"

"I know. Everyone feels that. But, again, it's the time factor for the admissions staff. Let's see here…" Casey slowly read Kate's essay and pointed out a few areas he thought were unnecessary.

Kate approved cutting one section. "Those two, I think they should stay in. Let's see here." She read the typed words. "Okay. If we need to cut anymore, then, why not cut this section here?"

Casey removed the area Kate had pointed to. "Okay, much better. It's just under four pages." He looked through the forms once again. "Okay. It looks like you have everything. I'll print your essay out—no, don't worry. I have the money here." He indicated a small, plastic card which he inserted into a small device next to the printer. Soon, four pages spat out of the printer. Casey tapped them all into place, stapled them and slid everything into a manila file folder. "Let's go!"

AT THE UNIVERSITY, KATE LOOKED AROUND, wide-eyed. She saw Mennonite students in a variety of Plain and Englisch dress scurrying about. Some of the women wore prayer caps, some didn't. The male students looked like any college students at any university in the country—their dress wasn't Plain. Following Casey, she went into the Admissions Office, ready to start the process of becoming a student. After thirty minutes of waiting as the admissions clerk went over her paperwork and processed her payment, Kate was able to grin and hold the small receipt in her hand. "And I'll get paperwork in the mail about my acceptance?"

"Yes, you should be able to expect it to come within the next two to four weeks."

Kate's smile faded slightly. "That long?"

"Yes, I'm sorry. Right now, students have about two weeks before the final deadline, so it's getting pretty rushed. We'll get our decision to you soon."

Kate nodded. "Denki." She began to wait the next day, forcing herself not to rush to the mailbox at the end of the day. Instead, she tried to keep herself occupied with housework, cooking, studying and midwifery. The highlight of that month was going out with Casey to celebrate her achievements. As promised, she wore her Plain dress with an apron and prayer cap. By contrast, Casey chose to wear dress pants, a light gray dress shirt and a dark-silver tie. He took her to an Olive Garden restaurant in the heart of Lancaster. Out of respect for her community's beliefs about alcohol, he chose to drink iced tea instead of wine. "Kate, you have accomplished so much! And you did it by yourself."

Kate blushed. "No, I had your help, Casey." She smiled, sipping her tea.

"Well, true. But, if you hadn't had that drive, would anyone have noticed and reached out to help?"

Kate paused, thinking. "You know, you're right. But the Amish—we—don't like to take the credit that belongs to Gott."

"That's true. So, how does this work?" Casey

snagged an olive from the salad bowl and ate it. "You put a lot of work into a goal you have and God saw your struggle. He put people into your path to guide you."

Kate thought. As she did, she took a bite of the tasty bread stick. "Ya. I can accept that."

A few tables away, a family was staring at Kate, their eyes opened wide. The husband and wife were whispering, creating a sibilant flow of sound. "What's she doing here? And why is she dressed that way?"

Kate and Casey heard the whispering and Casey frowned. Raising a finger, he signaled to Kate that he wanted to listen. What he heard caused his eyebrows to lower until he was glowering. "Wait here." He strode to the other family's table, dodging tables along the way. "Excuse me. I just overheard what you're saying about my friend over there. And—"

"Who is she? Why is she dressed like that?"

"She's Amish and they dress plainly so they don't draw attention to themselves."

"Well, she sure drew attention to herself, coming in here."

"Are you from here?" As the husband shook his head, Casey closed his eyes, trying hard not to judge. "Okay. It's pretty common for the non-Amish to see the Amish in this area. They leave their community to take care of business. But they try not to mix too much with people not from their community."

"Well, if she don't want to dress reg'lar and 'mix' with us, why is she here? She's inviting our comments!"

'"No. She's celebrating a huge achievement. With me."

"Why can't she celebrate among her own?" The wife spoke up.

Casey's breath left his lungs in shock. "Do you know that, if you go into the Amish communities, you would be welcomed? They will answer any honest questions that are asked respectfully. And they will do everything they can to help out the 'English' visitors to their community. Just as Christ welcomed strangers." Raising a finger, Casey lifted one eyebrow. "Now, please stop whispering and revealing your ignorance." He wheeled around and returned to his and Kate's table.

"What happened?"

"N-nothing."

Casey, your expression doesn't look like 'nothing' happened. You're angry. I can tell." Kate waggled her fingers, as though asking for something. "Talk."

Casey sighed, not wanting to ruin the evening. "Kate, it's not pretty. What about later?"

Kate paused. "No, not later. If it's because they wonder what someone like me is doing here, I get it all the time."

Hearing this, Casey felt even more protective. He sensed someone coming up behind them. Quickly, he blurted out, "They wonder what an Amish girl is doing here."

"Ach. I see." Kate looked up into the angry eyes of the wife. "Ya?" Her slight German accent seemed to be more pronounced.

"Why can't you go eat at someone's house? Why are you in here, in a place that has to be...*foreign* for you?"

"Do you know that we welcome the Englisch to our community? They come in as tourists. Some of them are really respectful. They ask why we have certain rules they have to follow. Others are, well, more like you. They do things they aren't allowed to do."

"And? So?"

"As long as they respect our values, the Englisch are welcome in our community. If, like you, they don't, they aren't welcome." Kate put everything on the table. Having done so, she turned her chair so she wouldn't have to view the woman's husband.

Casey beckoned to their server, who came over. Looking at his nametag, he addressed him. "Travis, it turns out that this woman here was discussing my companion in negative terms. She then came over and began to harass her. Will you please…?" Casey pointed toward the area where the entrance was located.

Travis quickly figured out what was happening. "Ma'am, the Amish are polite and respectful diners, they are always welcome here. You and your party need to leave."

The woman's gaze swept to her family and friends. "But, we're celebrating his birthday!"

"I'm sorry. When you chose to go after her, you lost your chance to stay here. You'll need to cele-brate elsewhere. We'll be happy to bag your order."

"No! Forget it!" The woman, her husband and her friends grabbed their jackets and purses, walking out in a huff.

Casey leaned back, smiling at the server. "Thank you, Travis." *He'll get an extra tip tonight.*

Kate looked at Casey, shock in her eyes. "Mei

Gott! I have never experienced that kind of hate before!"

"That was eye-opening for me. You handled it very well."

Kate dipped her head in thanks. "You did as well. We know that prejudice is out there, but that's the first time I felt it like that."

After the couple finished talking about what had happened, they returned to their celebration. As they munched their salad and pasta entrees, they laughed and talked about what Kate would face as a first-time college student.

"Deadlines. Lots of deadlines. As soon as you finish one assignment, another one is rushing right at you."

"So, how…?"

"Stay organized. Write everything down in a planner. Because you can't use the internet at home, buy a planner at the store, one that has several spaces after the date. Then, you can write down assignments, their due dates, test dates and when papers are due."

Kate cradled her head in one hand. "Am I going to be able to help my mother?"

"Occasionally. When you're on winter and summer break. Don't count on having much time during spring break. Also, try not to get too tired during the semester. Rest. At home, when you have a few minutes, try to relax. Your family's land is beautiful. Take advantage of that and just fit in a few mini-breaks."

Kate let out a long sigh. "What have I gotten myself into?"

"For pre-med, a hectic life. By the time you get to med school, you'll be used to the routine."

The next few weeks passed quickly. Kate and Becky attended several deliveries, all of which were routine. Kate had thought that the time between applying for college and getting the answer back would drag. Coming in from helping to weed the vegetable garden, she saw a thick envelope from the college. Gasping, she dropped her gardening gloves, grabbed the envelope and tore it open.

CHAPTER 23

Opening the letter, she scanned the first few lines, and then let out an almighty shriek. "Mamm! I got in!"

Becky, who was upstairs, finishing some cleaning, heard the scream and jumped. Scooping up the dust cloth and furniture polish, she hurried downstairs. "What are you screaming about?"

Kate waved the packet and letter in the air. "I got into the Mennonite college!"

The cloth and can fell to the floor. Then, Becky uncharacteristically began to hop and scream, right along with Kate. "You're one step closer!" Then, stopping her frenetic jumping, Becky approached Kate, putting her hands on Kate's arms. "Girl, you had better do well. We have a gut plan, one that can benefit all the women here."

Kate felt the solemnity of the moment. Looking at Becky, she nodded. "Ya. I know. I will do a gut job in school. Mister James—that is, Casey—said that he would tutor me throughout the summer. Then, if I need, I can find a tutor at the university."

"That's a gut idea, but I don't think you'll need one."

"I pray that you're right, Mamm."

THE REST OF THAT SPRING WARMED UP. IT seemed to happen in the snap of fingers. One day, the mornings were still frosty, and the next, the Amish found that their homes were soon too hot for comfort, unless they opened every window, both upstairs and downstairs.

Kate came into the house one early summer morning. Lugging a loaded laundry basket full of dry laundry, she heaved out a loud sigh and blotted perspiration from her forehead. "Whew! It is hot out there!"

"Water. Drink cold water. Because I get the

feeling that, sometime today, we're going to have to go and visit Missus Schmidt. Her time is nearing and she looked so big the last time we visited."

"Are you sure she's not having twins?"

"Ya, I'm sure. I haven't heard more than one heartbeat in any of her visits. I think she's just big."

Kate considered. "Well, it's a gut thing she's big herself."

"Ya. Or…"

Kate winced, knowing what it would mean if Mrs. Schmidt was a tiny woman. For the rest of that day, she and Becky hurried, cooking both dinner and supper before it got too hot in the kitchen. Looking outside around mid-afternoon, Kate gasped. "Mamm! Look outside!"

"Oh, no! Those clouds aren't gut. And I don't like the looks of that wind, either." It had just begun to rain when Kate pulled dessert out of the oven. Hearing her cellphone ringing, she answered. "Hullo? Ya, Mister Schmidt…it is? How far apart? Five minutes. Denki. We're on our way, as long as the weather doesn't stop us."

"She's in labor. Hurry. I pray we can make it before the storm hits. We'll need to leave a message for your daed." Becky swung her heavy medical bag over one shoulder and locked the door as Kate stepped outside. Holding their breath and dresses, both women ran for the barn. Kate grabbed one horse and Becky grabbed the other. These horses were calm, stolid and not easily upset. As they stood in front of the buggy, Kate and Becky buckled them into their harnesses.

On the road, Becky held the horses straight and urged them to hurry. "Go! There will be hay for you in the Schmidt's barn. Go!"

The horses responded to the word "hay." Stepping up their pace, they covered the mile to the Schmidt's farm in record time. Danny Schmidt, the oldest son, ran to the barn and let them in. "Go ahead and I'll feed your horses."

"Denki." Kate and Becky ran into the house and upstairs. There, they found Angela Schmidt sitting on the side of her bed, breathing and focusing on getting through her contractions. She and Daniel were already the parents of six kinder, so she knew exactly what to do.

"How far apart are they?"

About two-and-a-half minutes, maybe three. Strong and steady."

"Gut." Becky and Kate helped Angela get into

bed, once they had spread out several waterproof hospital pads under her.

Daniel came into the room with supplies the two midwives needed. Because of the storm, he had been forced to close the window. Now, it was raining, a hard, driving storm that spit raindrops sideways against the windows. Two hours later, Kate took a call from Steve. "Daed, ya? We're at the Schmidt's. Angela is in serious labor. I don't know how long we'll be."

"Well, if it's still raining as hard as it is right now, stay there until it's safe to come home."

"Ya, we will. I'll tell Mamm what you said."

"You be careful, you and your mamm. I pray the new baby will be strong and healthy."

"I'll let Angela and Daniel know." The call ended and Kate slipped her phone into her pocket.

Angela, between contractions, had watched the exchange Kate had with her daed. "How does that phone work?"

"I don't know the technology. It doesn't require electricity, except for charging. We charge them on the generator."

"And you use them only for patients?"

"Ya. No social calls, no internet, no texting. Although they do allow people to text."

"Gut! I'm glad you have them. If this storm had been any worse, then there's no way you would have heard that we needed you."

"True." At a grimace from Angela, Kate went next to her. "Is this one a bad one?"

"Ya. I think I'm going into that transition phase." Two minutes later, Angela proved her words right. She threw up, as was normal for her, when entering transition. Now, she sat up and dangled her legs over the side of the bed. "Walk. I need to walk."

Kate and Becky supported Angela, one on each side. They slowly walked back and forth. Becky detected the subtle tensing of Angela's body that told her she was about to deliver. She looked at Kate, giving her one slight nod.

"It's time to sit down. Do you want to push lying on your back, or leaning over something?"

"Leaning. The gravity will help me." Angela gasped, breathed and moaned slightly.

Daniel, hearing her preference, pulled the high-backed chair closer to the bed. As he did so, Becky spread several fresh pads where Angela would be standing. Then, she and Kate helped Angela stand and walk over to the chair.

Angela gripped the back of the chair, holding on tightly. Bending slightly, she let the contractions and pushing take their way with her.

Daniel stood behind and slightly to one side of Angela, helping to support her as she labored.

Thirty, then forty minutes passed. Kate, kneeling in back of Angela, saw the baby's head show. Next, she waited as Angela let out a big push and groan. She caught the baby's shoulders. "You're doing well! Shoulders are out! Keep pushing!" Guiding the baby's tiny, slippery body, Kate supported it as Angela continued to push. The next few minutes passed quickly—then a tiny, squalling baby girl was born. "It's a girl! Your fourth!"

Now, Angela's legs buckled under her as she felt the expenditure of all of her energy. "Oh! So tired!"

Daniel, anticipating the loss of energy, scooped his wife up and gently deposited her on their bed.

Kate went to the small tray that held apple juice, crackers and cheese. "Here you go. Eat slowly, as you know."

Angela scooped up some crackers and cheese. As Becky was cleaning and weighing the baby girl, Angela ate delicately and sipped some juice. "Oh, so much better. Thank you." When the baby was ready, she eagerly accepted her, offering her the breast. The baby latched on quickly and began suckling.

After cleaning Angela and the room, Becky filled out the notification of live birth application that she would take to town the next day.

Kate looked out and was relieved to see that the heavy rain of several hours earlier was now just a steady rain. "Mamm, the rain isn't as bad."

"Gut. I brought the umbrellas. At least now, we won't destroy them. "Angela, we'll see you in two or three days. If anything seems to be happening, call one of us."

"Ya. I will, denki." Angela turned to her newest baby, enjoying the look of her tiny face.

The ride home was cool, humid and still rainy. Kate saw a few flickers of lightning in the distance, followed by low rumbles of thunder. She yawned. Then laughed as her stomach grumbled.

Becky noticed. "You're hungry, too? We'll eat a meatloaf sandwich, and then get to bed. Do you have plans for tomorrow?"

"Ya. I'm meeting with Casey to go over my lists of books. So I can budget money for them. Then, he's going to tutor me in algebra and biology. I want to be at least equal to the other students in my classes. So I won't fall behind."

"I have no worries you'll be able to stay current."

At home, Kate and Becky wolfed down the promised meatloaf sandwiches and drank glasses of milk.

ARRIVING AT THE LIBRARY THE NEXT MORNING, Kate and Casey found out about the outage affecting the library.

"This outage affected the power going to the library." Casey was watching the crowds of people wanting to go inside.

"Wow. So they can't open the blinds and let us in?"

"No, apparently not. I think it's a safety issue. We can go somewhere else. There's a Starbucks, a coffee shop, on the other side of Lancaster."

"Isn't this electricity outage—doesn't it affect everyone?"

"Not necessarily. Depending on where the lightning hit the electrical transformers, it will take power out in one area of town while another one isn't affected."

"Hmmm. Then, ya. Let's go somewhere else. I'd like to figure things out as far as my books and what I need to learn in math and science. I don't want to fall behind in my classes."

"There's little risk of that. As motivated and intelligent as you are, you'll be able to understand what your instructor is teaching you. I'll show you. Hop in, and we'll go to a coffee shop."

Fifteen minutes later, they arrived at a shop that had power. Sitting inside, Kate fanned herself—the humidity was back up—and waited for Casey. She smiled as she saw him walking back and balancing a tray with their drinks and snacks. "Mmm, iced tea. This is the first time I've ever had a scone." She took a bite, closed her eyes and sighed in bliss. "So, this is a scone."

"Yup. It's light, which is great for these hot days. Okay, here's a list of the books you need." He spread a folded list out in front of Kate. "Some of these books will cost you serious money. The science and math ones, specifically. I'll show you how to find and buy less expensive books. If you don't mind, we can find them online. I'll order them, then you pay me what they cost."

Kate thought this through. "Okay. Will you be able to find good deals?"

"Definitely. I've been buying my books this way for the past eight years. I'll tell you a secret. You don't have to pay full price for your college textbooks. Save that money for fees and tuition, and your lunches when you have to be there through lunchtime. Also, have you thought about applying for grants and scholarships?"

"Nee. I don't want to owe money."

"No, these aren't loans. You don't pay back a penny, unless you don't fulfill any of their requirements. Which are fairly easy to carry out."

Kate bit at her lower lip, thinking. "Okay, explain, please."

Casey explained how grants and scholarships worked. "When you find any that apply to your situation and your goals, apply. Your application, along with anyone else's, will be considered and the winner will be notified. Use the money for school expenses. If you'd like, I can bring my laptop and show you how we can find them and apply. The thing is, deadlines are approaching, which means you need to fill out the financial aid form. And I can help with that. It'll take about two hours, if we do it online."

Kate responded by looking at her planner. "Well, if you have time, I can meet with you later this week."

"Let me check. I don't think I have anything. "Tomorrow? Wednesday?"

"We don't have any deliveries, but we know what can happen when a mother goes into labor. It happens when it happens."

"Okay. Use that little phone and call me at this number. Let me know and we can change plans if need be."

All of these housekeeping details were settled, allowing Kate and Casey to begin working on the tutoring part of their meeting. By the time they finished, her brain felt stuffed with numbers and science facts. "I'd better get home. I promised Mamm I would be home to help with supper."

"Okay, let me take you home." On the way, Casey and Kate discussed having him pick her up for study sessions. "It's only going to get hotter and more humid. You don't want your horses to get overheated on the street."

Kate gasped. "Nee! Daed wouldn't be happy at all. Okay, ya. Pick me up for our meetings."

"That sounds good. So, if you're able to meet

tomorrow, why don't we meet at nine in the morning?"

"That works well. Then, I can help mamm and any women who go into labor."

THE NEXT DAY, SITTING IN THE LIBRARY, WHICH now had power, Kate and Casey went through the list of books Kate would need in the fall. Because they had reserved a small room, they didn't have to worry about whispering. "Okay, this will be your final cost. For all six books, three hundred dollars."

Kate gasped. "That much. I'll have to get money from the bank. I—"

"Don't worry. I know you'll pay me back. Should I order?" He paused, fingers above the keyboard.

Kate nibbled on her lower lip. "How much would I pay in the bookstore?"

"Let's check." Casey pulled up the Eastern Mennonite University's website and navigated to the bookstore page. Searching for the books Kate would need, he scribbled down prices and added them up. "Okay, you would have to pay just over one thousand dollars to the bookstore."

Kate gasped and slapped both hands to her cheeks. "Mei Gott! Insanity! How do students afford them?"

"Those who can buy at the bookstore. Others order online like you and I are. And honestly? I have to say that those of us who are looking for ways to pay less, are the smarter ones."

"Well, ya! Frugality has something to say for it."

CHAPTER 24

"Yes. Now, let's order your books and then start working on your financial aid application. It's late, but they'll still accept it." Two hours later, they were finished. "Whew. Now, with this PIN, we'll be able to log back in and check the progress of your application. We'll also have to use that to apply online for scholarships and grants, and then accept any awards you might get. I'll be checking online to find grants and scholarships that fit your situation. We'll apply for them, say in two days?"

Again, Kate checked her calendar. "Two days works out for me." She agreed on a time, penciling it in.

Two days later, Kate and Casey met several hours later than they had originally planned. Kate and Becky had attended the tragic miscarriage of a young, Amish woman who badly wanted to become a mother.

"You seem kind of down. Bad day?"

Kate sighed, hoping she could hold tears back. "Y-ya. One of our pregnant women is no longer pregnant. She and her husband have been trying for years. She can get pregnant, but she can never *stay* pregnant. This is her fourth miscarriage."

"Ouch. You know, I'm not totally up on causes of repeated miscarriage in a woman. But it sounds like something's wrong with her reproductive organs. She really should go see a doctor. Once she and her husband know what's happening, they can make adjustments ."

"You mean, like adoption?"

"Exactly. Are either one of them open to that option?"

"Ya, I think she is. But I'm not sure about her husband. His family is, well, fixated on having biological nieces, nephews and grandchildren. Not adopted. I think that might affect the husband's outlook on this."

Casey thought quickly. "Kate, I never told you this. But I'm adopted. My mother suffered from permanent infertility issues. And yes, it did take my father some time to adjust to the idea. But eventually, he did warm to the thought of being a father to a child who's not his flesh and blood. We have a close and very loving relationship."

"How did you find out that he was resistant?"

"Well, actually, that came out in a fight we had. I was a rebellious teenager and he had grounded me for something stupid I did. I was yelling at him. I hollered, 'You don't love me!' You know what he told me?"

Kate shook her head, wanting to find out right away.

"'I loved you the minute I saw you. You were about nine months old, a little scrap of a boy, with the deepest brown eyes I'd ever seen in a baby. You just looked at me. You didn't cry. Then, you reached up and grabbed my eyeglasses. You just waved them around in the air and it was a task to get them back. Then, when your mom and I separated, I requested custody from the family court. Your mom needed to take care of some things. She eventually came back and our relationship got strong again. But I was prepared for it to end.' I asked him how and why I'd ended up in foster care. He told me that my birth mom died after she'd been in a gang fight. 'Nobody in her family was fit to take care of a cockroach, let alone a little boy. I would give my life for you.' After that, I never accused him of not loving me again. Ever."

"But, how was he resistant?"

"It took time for mom to be able to convince him that adoption was the only way they'd become parents. They had tried using other methods to get mom pregnant. But, along with the infertility, she couldn't hold onto a pregnancy. It was from that day on that I became interested in medicine."

"Wow." Kate couldn't think of anything else to say. She simply shook her head and looked at her friend. "So, you do understand."

"Thanks. We lived it. Are you going to suggest to this couple that they think about adoption?"

"Ya. I think we can do that. Before I say anything, I'm going to ask Mamm and Daed."

"Good. Because there is hope. Even if they don't become parents in one way, they can in another way."

After hearing Casey's story, Kate felt immeasurably better. She was better able to focus on the search for grants and scholarships. "So, you're sure I won't have to repay these."

"Yeah. Positive. Except…read this one. This section right here." Casey waved the end of his pen at one particular section he'd pulled up on his computer.

Kate focused on it. "How do I get to read more?"

Casey showed her how to scroll up and down.

"Ya, I see what you mean. I would have to work in an underserved area. I wonder if Amish communities are underserved."

"The only way to find out is for you to visit the university's financial aid office and find out. I'll call them right now." After placing the call, Casey verified that, if she chose, Kate could work in an Amish community to fulfill the terms of any scholarships with that requirement. Hanging up, he smiled at Kate. "Well, good news. Just like a rural area in the Southwestern United States or a Native American reservation, an Amish community is considered to be underserved. I think Eastern Mennonite University got that wording for the scholarships it serves, because of its student population. I may be able to guarantee you that several of your future classmates might have some of the same plans. No matter what their majors are."

Kate leaned back, nodding and smiling. "That is such gut news! Thank you! Mamm will be very happy to hear this. And Daed, too. He's been kind of doubtful, even though he hasn't said anything."

"Kate...does this mean... Well, does it mean that he won't allow you to date me?"

Kate took a minute to organize her thoughts. "Casey, like my patients who can't have a baby the usual way, our situation requires a little imagination. Mamm and I were talking about this. She suspects that we like each other and she told me: she said that, even though you're a Christian, you would... well..."

"Have to be baptized into the Amish faith?"

"Ya...yes."

"I'd have no problem with that."

Kate temporarily lost the ability to speak. Her eyes widened as she gazed at Casey. "You..." She shook her head.

"Let's open up our options a little here. So, since I'm willing to become Amish, what would your folks say if we both converted...and became Mennonite?"

Now, Kate was completely confused. "Ah, uh."

She squeezed her eyes shut, trying to get control of her racing thoughts.

"Would they disapprove? Because I know that more conservative Amish communities do frown, even on the Mennonites."

"We think that kind of disapproval is mupsich... stupid. Our community is a little more progressive. And I'm glad. Because, there's enough division in our world that we just don't need anymore. So what if different communities have different beliefs? But..." Kate floundered again.

"But what?" Casey felt a little better, but was worried again.

"Daed has always dreamed of all his daughters marrying Amishmen. And it'll be hard for him to let go of that."

"So, we should be gentle when we break the news? That we want to date?"

"Well, I think it's a wunderbaar idea to let him know ahead of time. And I don't want to sneak around."

"No, I wouldn't ask you to do that. We just need to let him know that I'm a good man who loves God. Should I go to a few services with you?"

"That would actually be a gut idea. Talk to the elders, too. This way, they can give you some ideas about what you should consider before you make a final decision."

Casey covered Kate's hand with one of his own. "Girl, I've already made up my mind. Spending time with you over the past several months has already told me that your heart is in the right place. You love God. You're devout. And you're honest."

"There's one more thing." Kate shifted, feeling uncomfortable. "When I was dating Mike, he, well, he expected me to neglect my job, and he got angry when I refused. We got into several arguments."

"Kate, did he ever hit or abuse you?"

"What? Oh, no! Although I did fear him at first. A little before we started our tutoring arrangement."

Casey opened his mouth, ready to speak when Kate's phone chimed.

Kate, raising a finger toward Casey, opened the flip phone and answered. "Mamm?"

"Ya, you need to get home. We have a premature delivery. How long will it take you?"

Kate's eyes widened.

"Is that your mother? Delivery?" Casey was already standing and shoving his computer into its case.

Kate jumped up. "Ya. Premature delivery. How long will it take you to get me home?"

"Less than fifteen minutes."

Kate relayed this information. "Okay, ya, if you would get me home just as fast as possible."

The ride back to Kate's was quiet as Kate tried to remember everything she could.

"If the mom is anything more than a month away from full term, take her to the hospital. In fact, would you like me to stick around? Follow you to their house? That way, I can take you to the hospital. It'll be a lot quicker."

"Ah, maybe. I'll ask Mamm." Arriving home, Kate and Casey ran from the car and into the house. "Mamm, Casey offered us a ride. Just in case Missus Holder needs a ride to the hospital."

"Ya, she will. She's just past seven months. Denki, Mister James." She hurried to the car. She sat in the back, rustling through her medical bag.

"Mamm, did she wait for too long?"

"Ya, of course. She was trying to deny they were contractions. And now that they are three minutes apart..." Becky huffed impatiently, her lips thinned.

"Missus Lapp, is this her first child?"

"Nee, it isn't. She's had five other kinder. And two of them were premature. So she knows!"

Kate groaned.

At the house, they were pulled into the house by a frantic husband, who hurried them upstairs. "I told her she was in premature labor!"

"Denki. We're probably going to have to take her to the hospital. We don't have the medications necessary to stop her labor."

Mr. Holder's face paled. Turning, he asked his parents to stay with the kinder. After they said they would, he went to hitch his horses to the buggy.

"No, Mister Holder. I am Kate's tutor. I have my car and we'll go in that. She doesn't have time for the buggy."

Now, the frantic father's eyes widened.

After a quick, five-minute exam, Kate and Becky confirmed that Mrs. Holder was definitely in early labor. "Let's go." Becky's voice was quiet, but there was a slight, detectable thread of steel running through it. "You really should have called hours ago."

The ride to the hospital was frantic, punctuated with Mrs. Holder's cries of pain. Just as they pulled into the emergency bay, she shrieked. "It's coming! Neeeeee!"

Casey ran into the emergency room and came right back out, accompanied by several nurses and a gurney. He and Mr. Holder got Mrs. Holder out of the back seat and onto the gurney. Because she was already beginning to give birth, there was no time to get to the fourth floor. Becky, Kate and Mr. Holder were in the small cubicle, and Kate and Becky tried to comfort Mrs. Holder. Casey waited at the end of the small area, ready to go into action; he had told the ER doctor that he was an intern in pediatrics. Too soon, the tiny, wizened body of a baby girl slipped out of Mrs. Holder's body. The nurses grabbed her and, setting her on the Isolette mattress, began to stimulate her any way they could. Finally, the baby jerked her tiny arms into the air and took a tiny gasp. Casey sighed in relief. He stuck a tiny oxygen mask over the baby's face, praying she would make it. "Kate, we're going to NICU!" They left, bearing the tiny, too-early baby.

Mr. Holder held one of his wife's hands as Becky and Kate tried to comfort Mrs. Holder. A few minutes later, she was on her way to the L&D ward, with her husband, Becky and Kate right behind.

After thirty minutes, the NICU nurse came out with Casey next to her. Casey spoke. "Missus

Holder, your little girl is alive, but she's going to need a lot of medical intervention and prayers. She's on oxygen. She's a little fighter." He stopped speaking before his voice broke.

The nurse took over. "Missus Holder, we're going to do our best to make sure your little girl thrives."

Kate, her mother, Casey and Mr. Holder stayed for as long as they were allowed. Mr. Holder called a driver after telling Becky that he was going to stay at the hospital. "They both need me. Will you go tell my family that we have a tiny little girl?"

Becky smiled. "I would be happy to do so."

Casey took Kate and Becky home.

Becky was livid. She sat strapped into a seatbelt in the back seat, trying hard not to blow up. "We told her, Kate. Two years ago, after her little boy was born early!"

Kate was about to respond when Casey asked a question.

"Missus Lapp, how many more of her children were born too early?"

"This is her sixth baby. Three of them—three now, were born early! The prior two children have physical and mental issues stemming from the early deliveries."

"Why does she wait that long?"

"Honestly? Because she's denying to herself that she has something happening inside her body that makes it difficult for her to stay pregnant after about the seventh month. Now, they have three children with special needs."

"And they won't do anything to stop her from getting pregnant, will they?"

"Nee! There's no way! It's Gott's will."

"I have a thought. If you wouldn't mind, would you allow me to talk to her about the consequences of early delivery?"

Becky looked at Kate, who nodded.

"I trust him, Mamm."

Becky sighed. "Ya, if it will help."

"What kinds of issues do the older children face?"

"Developmental delays. One has a seizure disorder. And one is legally blind."

Casey blew out a long breath. "And what makes her deny that she's in early labor?"

"Fear. All of her sisters have been able to get to forty weeks of pregnancy and she feels like she's inadequate because she can't. So, when she goes into early labor, she tries to deny it to herself."

"Do you think Mister Holder would allow me to be real frank with her?"

"He may. You would have to ask him."

"Okay. If you don't have a labor and delivery tomorrow, why don't we all go down to the hospital? I'll check with the labor ward and see if they'll allow me to do so. I'm going to see if I can do my residency at this hospital."

Kate closed her eyes and sighed. "Thank Gott."

Becky, now used to the presence of Casey in Kate's life, sighed in relief as well. "If you would speak to her and just explain what she's doing to her children, I would be so grateful."

Casey sighed. "One thought occurred to me last night. Does the hospital know she delays getting your help if she goes into labor early?"

"Ya. They do."

Casey was stunned. "Wow. Because, if they were to put two and two together, they would realize there's multiple Holder children who are suffering from all these problems. And they would act."

"In what way?"

"Missus Lapp, what she is doing is harmful to her children. I realize she loves them. But, if NICU would put all of the pieces together, they would have a case."

Becky didn't know if she liked the direction in which Casey's thoughts were going. "What kind of case?" She was apprehensive.

Again, Casey sighed. "Even though it's not intentional, Missus Holder is, at the least, neglecting her children before they're even born. Child Protective Services can step in and take custody of the children who were born so prematurely. I don't want to see that happen. Instead, I would like to talk to her and let her know that there's a reason she goes into premature labor so often."

Becky nodded. Her thoughts had been going the same way, but with her ingrained fear of state organizations, she also didn't want to see an Englisch agency get involved with the family of one of her patients. "How do you suggest approaching her? Because, believe it or not, I do agree with you."

Kate did as well. She closed her eyes in relief.

"First, we offer her the diagnostic services she needs to find out what's causing all these premature labors. Once we get her connected with the right specialist, then I think either you or Kate should explain just why delaying getting your help until it's literally too late constitutes neglect. And how CPS *could* take action."

Kate's blood chilled at this last sentence.

Becky was quiet for a long time. "Ya. I'll do it."

AT THE HOSPITAL THE NEXT MORNING, THEY checked on the tiny baby, who had been named Ruth. Seeing that she was fighting and holding her own, they got the nurses' agreement to call them right away if anything happened. In Mrs. Holder's room, Becky sat on Mrs. Holder's bed. Casey and Kate were also in the room, but sitting at a distance from Becky.

"Missus Holder—Sarah—we were talking yesterday." Becky didn't identify the "we." "There's a reason why this keeps happening. We need to find out what it is so that, if you get pregnant again, we can stop it from happening ever again."

"What do you think it is?" Sarah cuddled the tiny baby closer to her.

"It could be anything. Your cervix may be too weak to hold your babies inside you. Your uterus may be tipped in such a way that your body can't help but go into labor. You and your husband have struggled with this for so many years and waiting for so long to call us when you do go into labor has put three of your kinder in danger. And they suffer the effects today. We need to make sure that stops, if you're able to have any more children."

"Any…" Sarah coughed, choking on her shock. "But we want to have more!"

"If it's Gott's will, you shall. But——" Becky's words were cut off by the entrance of a young woman in a lightweight pantsuit.

"Missus Holder? And Mister Holder? My name is Kat Lovett. I'm a social worker with the state of Pennsylvania." Kat extended her hand, which held two business cards.

"Social worker? Who called you?" Sarah drew her knees up, protecting herself and Ruth.

Mr. Holder stood up. "Now, wait a minute! We don't abuse our kinder."

"Paul, help me!"

Kat approached Becky and Kate. "I believe you're the midwives mentioned in our report, right?"

Becky responded. Licking dry lips, she nodded. "Ya, we are. Who called?"

"I'm sorry. We're not allowed to reveal that information. I need to speak to the baby's parents, and then I'd like to speak with you. Please don't leave yet." Seeing Casey, Kat's eyes widened. "And you are…?"

"Casey James, med student. I helped get the family here yesterday, since I have a car."

"Thank you. I'll also need to speak with you, since you saw everything that happened."

Becky motioned to Kate and Casey. They found a soft bench a little way down the hallway and just waited.

"I wonder who called." Kate's voice was low and shaky.

"At a guess, one of the nurses or the baby's doctor. I know you don't like having this kind of intervention."

"Nee, we don't. But, we have—" Becky stopped as the sound of a high, keening wail came from Sarah's room. "What is going on in there?" She stood up, as if to run in.

Casey grabbed her arm. "Missus Lapp, please wait. It's possible that Miss Lovett has just given her some shocking news."

Inside the room, Kat had just told Sarah and Paul that their children were at risk of being placed into foster care. "By waiting so long to get medical care when you've gone into labor early, you haven't given your midwives or doctors the opportunity to stop your labor when it's still possible to do so. This has placed your babies at physical risk and now, from what the doctors say, at least two of them are suffering from traumatic injuries related to premature birth."

A nurse bustled into the room. Seeing that the parents were having trouble absorbing what Kat was telling them, he explained it to them. "If you had only come to your midwives earlier in your labors, they could have gotten you here sooner. And we could have stopped each labor with medications. Or we could have given you medications that would have strengthened their lungs."

"Oh. I was only just praying when I went into labor—we prefer to rely on Gott. Did Becky or her daughter call?" Sarah's eyes, wet with tears, narrowed in anger.

The young nurse shrugged. "I have no idea who called. That's above my pay grade."

"I will ask them."

Kat intervened before the conversation was totally derailed. "That's your right. But we have to talk now. Mister Holder, we need to see your children and make sure they are being properly cared for. Will you be here all day long?"

Paul didn't know how to answer. He felt torn, not wanting to leave Sarah or the new baby. Yet, he also felt he should be at home, watching over the older kinder.

Kat, who was highly compassionate, saw his quandary. "Mister Holder, we only want to see them. We won't be taking them. At this point, your sixth child has been born and it's going to be some time before her doctors know if she's suffered any ill effects from her premature birth. We need to get child education professionals in to meet your children and assess just what kind of health issues they suffer from. Then, we can work *together* to help them so they can make progress that will help them live more normal lives. They aren't going into foster care."

Paul visibly relaxed. Putting a hand on Sarah's shoulder, he told her quietly that they had nothing to fear. "I think they want to help us and the kinder."

Sarah's tear-filled eyes switched back and forth from Paul to Kat and back again. "Oh. Well…in that case. . ."

"Miss Lovett?"

"Missus Lovett, actually."

"Oh, sorry. Missus Lovett, we live on Cardinal

Lane. Number 17. It's the fourth house on the left. White with dark-green window shutters."

Kat quickly scribbled the information down. "Thank you. Can I please see your baby? I promise I won't do anything."

Reluctantly, Paul placed the newest Holder baby into the social worker's arms.

Kat cooed at the baby. "Well, hello, little one. I'm going to be working to make sure you and your older brother and sisters won't be too affected by being born too early. Is that okay?" She chuckled softly as the baby rooted at her chest. "I think she's looking for something that only mom can provide." Tenderly, she handed the small, squirming bundle back to Paul, who gave her to Sarah.

"Do you need me there?"

"No, not at all. I'm going to speak to the midwives and the medical student first. Can you call your house and let them know I'm going to be heading there, probably in the next thirty minutes?"

"Ya. I will. And...on those services—are they definitely going to happen? Because two of the kinder, they do need help."

"Yes, they will be happening. We'll be placing your family into a category that means we supervise you while everyone stays at home. Even your kids."

Sarah nearly started crying again at this news. Instead, she nodded and held her baby a little more securely as she nursed her.

Outside, Kat directed Casey, Becky and Kate into a small room at the end of the hall. There, she started asking questions. "Why does Missus Holder wait until it's pretty much too late to stop her labor?"

"She's afraid. She knows something is wrong with her body. But, every time she goes into premature labor, she denies that she's in labor. She's probably trying to convince herself that it's gas or illness or something."

"Very natural."

"Ya. But I have told her many times not to wait. Now, I don't know who called you, but I hope that my daughter and I—or her friend, Mister James— won't be blamed. We have to work with her, if she's able to get pregnant again. And we live in the same community."

"I can't reveal who called. What we want to do is work with the family for a short period of time. Refer the children to services to assess what's wrong, to what degree, and set up a treatment plan so they can, hopefully, catch up. So that, by the time they start school, they'll be functioning at or near a normal level for their ages."

Kate closed her eyes in relief. "Thank you. Mister and Missus Holder don't mean to hurt their kinder. But they just don't realize the consequences. Mamm, are you going to talk to her doctor?"

"Ya, I think so. Because something in her body is not allowing her to reach full term."

Kat left, telling Becky that she would be contacting her later on.

Becky gave Kat their address, and then they went into the Holder's hospital room. "Sarah? We heard the gut news. They're going to try and help the kinder."

"Ya, what does that involve?" Sarah wasn't the brightest woman in the community.

Casey spoke up. "Missus Holder, we have intervention programs for small kids like yours. If the kids have some kind of delay, whether it's in their mind or body, specialists can find it, figure out what it is and set up a treatment plan that helps the child or children to catch up, to use that term."

"And the kinder? Will they be at home the whole time?"

"You mean, living with you? Oh, yeah. They will.

Now, some appointments may take place away from home. But you'll just have to go to the agency's office to meet with the educational specialists or pediatric therapists so they can work with your children and give them exercises to do. You'll have to do those exercises several times a week at home so the children will get used to working on the problems they have."

"What kinds of problems?"

Casey realized that Sarah, herself, was also slow. He brought his explanation down a few levels of simplicity.

"Well, for instance, one child might have a hard time understanding spoken words. They may not be able to speak right. They'd get speech therapy. Or they may have problems in moving their legs, arms, mouth, or tongue. They would get physical therapy."

"Oh... So they want to help us? Not take the kinder away?"

"Right. Now, I get the feeling that the doctors are going to want to talk to you about all the premature labors and births you've had. There could be something wrong with your body. And you and your husband are going to have to make some decisions."

"Like what?" Paul knew Sarah had some challenges, but he loved her. He tried to protect her as much as he could.

Becky, silent, looked at Paul. "Something is wrong inside your wife's body. We don't know what it is. Her doctor asked me about her history of pregnancies and labors. He told me that, with three premature births, they need to run tests on her. And, it may be possible that they'll tell her not to have any more children."

"What? But, if Gott wills it…"

"Paul, this may be Gott's way of saying He doesn't want her having any more children. Be honest with yourselves. Do you want any more of your kinder having problems with their health?"

Sarah was about to answer Becky's question when the baby in her arms began seizing unexpectedly. "What? Baby, what's wrong?"

Paul ran out and hollered for a nurse to help. Within a few seconds, two had run into the room and grabbed the still-seizing baby from Sarah's arms.

"We're taking her to the NICU to stop her seizure. We'll let you know as soon as we can." The nurses began injecting a solution into the baby. Getting the seizure stopped, they ran at full speed for the baby nursery.

Twenty minutes later, the pediatrician came back into the hospital room. "Okay, Mister and Missus Holder. Here's what we have for you. Your daughter was born so early that she's having trouble processing the nutrients you're giving her in your breast milk. So, we're feeding her through a tube. Small amounts that she can tolerate, but still enough that she gets the nutrition she needs. Long story short, she may need to stay here in the hospital for a few weeks, just until she reaches a good weight, something that tells us her body is taking in and using nutrients."

Paul choked back a deep sob. "Will she…will she have some of the same problems that our older kinder have?"

"You mean movement problems and problems learning?" Here, the doctor paused, thinking. He didn't want to frighten the parents. "We don't know yet. We're going to be watching what she does over the next few weeks."

CHAPTER 25

As it would turn out, this baby's problems would be the most severe, as she had been born the earliest. Testing showed she suffered from cerebral palsy.

On the same day, Sarah's obstetrician came to see her and Paul. His suggestions didn't make the couple happy. "Mister and Missus Holder, your history of premature labor and births tell us that there's a problem inside your organs—those that make and nourish a baby. And we need to deal with that. We're going to run some tests to find out just what's wrong. That way, we can offer suggestions for your future."

For the next two days, Sarah underwent several diagnostic tests. By the time these were done, the doctor came back with a diagnosis. "Missus Holder, your uterus is abnormally shaped. Normally, it looks like a pear. This makes it much more likely that you're going to go into labor early." He held up a picture of a woman's uterus that looked like it was bending over in a strong wind. "This is what your uterus looks like. It's actually a miracle that you've been able to stay pregnant to full term with three of your pregnancies. Your waters broke early, which led to early labor. And we cannot, in good conscience, suggest that you continue trying to have more babies. Since you're Amish, you and your husband should talk with your elders about what precautions you can take. Given that this baby has had seizures and seems to be having problems with normal movement, she's going to need a lot of services."

A psychologist entered the room. Seeing Sarah sitting in the bed, her eyes puffy with tears, the psychologist sighed. "Missus Holder? Mister Holder? You've been taking a lot of bad news over the past few days. I'd like to speak with you and see if we can get you to a point where you can deal with everything that's happening."

"Our elders…" Paul wasn't sure they would be allowed to talk to the lady doctor.

The psychologist smiled. "Mister Holder, I am a Mennonite. I earned my undergraduate degree at Eastern Mennonite University at Lancaster. While I don't wear Plain clothing, I still practice my faith, every day. I won't tell you to do anything that goes against your Ordnung."

Now, Sarah could hear the soft, subtle accent in the doctor's voice. "What's...what's your name?"

"Millie Chadwick. Dr. Millie, if you want to call me that."

Oddly, Sarah felt more at ease. She smiled slightly through her tears. "I'm glad you're Plain. Well, sort of Plain."

Doctor Millie was wearing a long, light-green dress with tiny, blue and yellow flowers. Over that, she wore a long, white, crocheted sweater with a nametag on the front. On her feet, she had black, low-heeled shoes. Her hair fell down to her shoulder blades and she had it caught up in a loose ponytail. "Now, let's figure things out. Your doctor and your baby's doctor talked to me. There's a lot going on with your family right now. If you're feeling confused and as if God has abandoned you, that's normal. And I'm here, specially chosen, to help you get through this time. Let's start like this. You ask me the questions you have, and I'll answer those that I can. I'll try to help you feel just a little better, so that, as things calm down, you'll feel like, with God's help, you can deal with everything. Okay?"

Paul looked at Sarah and she looked back at him. Then, Paul looked at Doctor Millie. "Okay. First, are we at any risk of having our kinder taken away from us?"

"From what I understand, no. That's not being considered. The social workers and doctors made the decision that you didn't understand the risks to your kinder. And you're willing to work with the social worker and the child development agency that's going to work with your kinder. Both of these are in your favor. If you had refused to work with them, then yes, your kinder would be more likely to be placed in a foster home."

Paul sighed, feeling marginally better. "We trust Becky and Kate. Will the doctors—including you—include them in your work with us?"

"Your midwives have been a highly valuable source of information regarding your wife's reproductive issues. About what they tried to get you to do when it came to premature labor and early births. So, we need them on your team. And, Mister Holder, that's what we all are. A team. We're all going to work together to help you and your kinder."

Sarah and Paul both exhaled in relief. "Gut. Because they have only tried to help us. But, out of fear, we didn't listen. We thought we could make her body stop going into labor too early."

"And now that I know I have a body part that's shaped wrong, I have a better idea of why my pregnancies ended the way they did."

"You have three kinder who were born at full-term, right?"

"Ya."

"You are blessed. You are truly blessed that you had that happen. Has your obstetrician told you about the forms of birth control that you might find acceptable?"

Paul flushed and looked at Sarah.

Sarah also had a slight flush on her cheeks. "Uh, ya. Something called the rhythm method? What is that?"

"Quite simply, it literally relies on your body's monthly rhythms. You'll learn about what physical signs to look for. These signs tell you when your body is most fertile—when you should avoid being intimate. You'll also learn when your body is least fertile. And, of course, we Anabaptists view physical intimacy as a means toward procreation. Gott also intended us to use this intimacy as a way of showing affection and love to one another. You don't have to partake only as a means of becoming pregnant. And, Sarah, Paul, in your case, you shouldn't try to become pregnant. Even though it's the Amish practice to have large families, right now, you have six children. Three of them were born too early and suffer from physical and mental or what we call intelligence issues. What kind of work do you do at home, Sarah?"

"I bake."

"Okay. Your midwives…" Millie checked Sarah's file. "…Kate and Becky are going to be involved in everything we do. Therefore, you should expect to see them in team meetings when it comes to the care of your disabled kinder. Whenever we have meetings, we're going to invite them. If they aren't attending births, they'll be there. Once the childhood intervention teams begin to work with your kinder, you're going to be learning so many things that will make you feel overwhelmed. That's where I come in. I'll help you to talk about what you're feeling. I'll also supervise the team that's helping you. If you have questions or concerns, I want you to bring them up to us. These are your kinder, so you should let us know what *you* want to see happening. Because you're their parents, you'll lead the team in what you want done. Understand?"

"Ya. Where will we meet?"

"Your house. It's so much easier for us to bring the interventions to your house than it is to have you load two or three disabled kinder into your buggy. Paul, what kind of work do you do?"

"Carpentry. In a shop right in between my father's house and ours."

"Good. That's actually perfect. Sarah, you're going home tomorrow. The baby has to stay here. She needs to have her diagnosis firmed up. We need to determine which treatments will best meet her needs. Now, do you have a generator that powers most electrical items in your house?"

"Ya, but not the upper floor."

"Can you get long power cords that go from the first floor to the second?"

"Ya, I'm sure I can. Why?"

"The baby will have equipment that runs on power. Since you don't have electricity, it'll all have to run from the generator."

"Ach, I see."

"Doctor, how long will our baby be here?"

"That depends on how well she gains weight. How quickly the doctors find medications that slow or stop her seizures. Because, she's had a few in the nursery. Were you wanting to breast feed her?"

"We did, but she didn't do very well."

"She's too small. Instead, you're going to pump your milk and freeze it for her. She'll have to drink your milk from a bottle. A lactation specialist will be coming in to show you how to use a pump so you can express as much milk as possible. You can freeze your milk—what kind of freezer do you have? Does it share a door with your refrigerator?"

"Nee. We had to buy a new one a couple years ago. Each has a separate door and ours is on the bottom, with the refrigerator on top." Paul was beginning to feel overwhelmed.

"Good. Sarah, your milk will last from three to six months if you freeze it there." Doctor Millie paused. "You're feeling overwhelmed. Why don't we start again after lunch?"

Both parents nodded with relief. When the lactation specialist returned, they were ready to ask their questions and attempt to absorb the information she had for them. "So, we're going you have to bring milk here for her. After you pump it into the little bags we're going to give you, freeze them right away. Don't take them out until you come here to see your baby. Bring them here in a small ice chest with ice in it. We'll thaw them out and feed them to her. Once she's ready to suckle from a bottle, we'll help her to make that change. Are you with me so far?"

Paul nodded, but Sarah seemed more hesitant. Raising one hand, she asked, "How will you feed her since she couldn't feed from me?"

Here, the lactation specialist paused. "We're going to have to insert a thin tube into one nostril and into her stomach. It doesn't hurt. That tube will stay there night and day, so we can just feed her when it's time—or when she tells us she's hungry."

Sarah's guilt returned tenfold. She started to cry. "Why didn't I call them earlier?"

"Missus Holder, what's done is done. All you can do now is look forward and do what you can to help her. She is getting a little stronger. She isn't so premature that she won't make fast progress. But, she does have a fight ahead of her. And it's up to all of us to work together, as a team, to help bring her to a point where she can start feeding independently and go home. At this point, having her feed from your breast or a bottle doesn't matter as much as just getting her to that point."

Sarah heard the message and understood. Wiping the tears from her face, she sniffled and nodded. "Okay. Ya, I understand. Do you know how long she'll be here? Her brothers and sisters will want to know."

"That's up to the nurses taking care of her. We'll keep her in the nursery to make sure she stays stable. Once we know she will, we'll bring her here to room in with you."

Finally, the long session with the lactation specialist and nurses was over. Sarah leaned back on her pillow, more than ready for a nap. Her eyes drooped.

Paul noticed. "I'll go check in on the baby and let you know how she looks. Then I'll go home to take care of the farm. Do you want me to come tonight?"

"Ya, please."

Paul paused. "Would you like to go see her?"

Sarah got to the nursery in a wheelchair. Seeing her tiny daughter in the nurse's arms, she smiled. The smile wavered slightly. "She looks like her oldest sister."

"Ya, she does. And she does have a temper."

Sarah giggled. "Ya, she does."

Back in her room, Sarah was finally able to relax and nap after Paul had left.

AT THEIR NEXT MEETING, AT A STARBUCKS, KATE and Casey discussed the premature birth of the Holder baby. "So, what do you think will happen?"

"CPS will oversee the family and help to coordinate services for the three who are disabled. They and her doctors will make sure she is using procedures that ensure she's much less likely to become pregnant. And the parents are going to work as hard as they can to make sure this newest baby begins to gain ground. She needs to gain weight and start drinking independently so she's not on tube feeding for too long."

Kate sighed. "I feel horrible for them. At the same time, Mamm and I told both of them, many times, that they had to call us much earlier, when they even just suspected she was in labor. They didn't. A small part of me is just looking at them, saying, 'We told you. Now, you have a third child suffering.'"

"Yeah. I know just what you mean. On one hand, they really made some big mistakes—three times. On the other hand, they clearly love each other and their kids. Are you and your mom going to be keeping up with them?"

"We talked about it. We're so busy already, but we feel like we have to, just to make sure they don't allow her to get pregnant a seventh time."

Casey grimaced. "Short of spending time in their bedroom at night…"

Kate shuddered. "Please, no."

"Yeah, that's a 'gimme the eye bleach now!' moment." Casey grimaced.

"Eye bleach?"

"Just an expression that's popular on Facebook, which is a social media site. It just means, 'I don't want to see that in my mind.'"

Kate nodded. "There is so much I don't know about the Englisch world."

"You have time. Just learn one thing at a time. I have a question. I know the Amish don't believe in using computers or electronic technology, including social media. What about the Mennonites? Do you know?"

Kate considered for a minute. "I think they are allowed to. We heard through the grapevine that a leader in the Mennonite community was accused of abusing young Mennonite women. He was also accused of sol…soliciting prostitution." Kate looked down, ashamed of saying the last two words. The sister of one of his victims wrote on this Facebook about what happened, and it was read by so many people. Will I have to use social media?"

"No. Not if you don't want to or can't. Eastern Mennonite University doesn't require students to use it. Although…"

"What?" Kate was apprehensive.

"Nothing bad. You might have to create an email account so you can communicate with your professors and fellow students. That's one of the most preferred methods, short of visiting professors in their offices."

Kate groaned. "What am I getting myself into?"

Casey wrapped his hand around Kate's wrist. "Learning. I'll be there any time you need my help. Just breathe in. It's a lot to consider, but you'll catch on. Besides, your fellow students are already used to the internet, email and social media. As you make friends, they'll be happy to help when I can't be there."

CHAPTER 26

K ate felt sadness pulling her down.

"What's wrong?"

"I'm going to miss being able to ask you questions or have tutoring sessions."

"I will, too. But we're both going to be busy with classes. I'll have my intern hours and you'll have lab sessions. Don't be afraid to make new friends. Just... I don't know if I should say this yet." Casey looked uncharacteristically shy.

"What? Tell me, please." Kate's voice was gentle.

Casey sighed. "I'd love to consider us a couple. But, if it's too soon, I understand. Can I ask a huge favor?"

"Sure, go ahead." Kate's face betrayed her excitement with a slight blush on her cheeks.

"Okay, here goes. As you make friends at the university, would you please look at the guys as just friends?"

Kate lost her breath. Inhaling slightly, she blushed again. "Ya. I can't see myself dating more than one man at a time, so that will be easy. You really…?" She motioned between the two of them, not able to find the words she wanted.

"Yeah, I do. I would love to date you. And consider you as my girlfriend." Now, Casey blushed. "Ah, let me get some more coffee before I make a total fool of myself."

Kate busied herself by rearranging her notebooks and pen. As she did, she had a slight smile on her face.

"Here we go. So, what do you think?"

"Casey, do you know about one of our traditions in the Amish community?"

"N-n-no, what are you talking about?"

Kate grinned. "It's nothing big. Or too hard to accomplish. The Amish don't really talk about their romantic relationships. While it's not a huge secret, people still do have to guess whether a couple is truly a couple or not. It's not until they get engaged that things become truly clear. Although…"

"Although, what?"

"Mamm and Daed already know that we like each other. But we still have to be discreet. Especially…"

"Since I'm an Englisher, right?"

"Exactly."

"What will people in your community say when they suspect that we're seeing each other? Will they be real hard on you?"

"Some will try. Others won't particularly care. Those that don't care are more likely to be younger or a little more enlightened."

"And what about your ex-boyfriend?"

"I would hope he'll say nothing, because he's dating someone new."

"Good. I just hope he's a lot more understanding of the work she does."

Kate giggled. "Ya, she's definitely not a midwife."

"Kate, would you like to go have something to eat this weekend? Say, on Friday or Saturday evening?"

"I would love it"

"Also, I have some great news for you.

Remember those local scholarships and grants we applied for? You got them!"

Kate's mouth dropped open and her eyes widened. Closing her mouth, she shook her head. "But, that's so fast."

"We got them in just in the nick of time. They were about to start going over each application and you did a wonderful job on yours. Read these." Casey opened his laptop and clicked on the first of three emails. "Here." He turned it toward Kate.

Kate began reading.

"In reading your essay, we were most impressed by your stated work ethic. It's clear that you have chosen to learn independent of the Amish community so you can help the pregnant mothers in Lancaster. It's not very easy learning about pregnancy-related topics—reading that you had to tackle advanced chemistry and math equations impressed our committee. We are confident that, as you start your classes at Eastern Mennonite University, you're going to have a successful academic career. Therefore, we would like to offer a scholarship in the amount of $1,000."

Kate gasped. Then, learning from Casey, she figured out what she needed to click on. The remaining emails were each in the same vein. By the time she finished reading the last congratulatory email, Kate realized that she had a little more than sixteen thousand dollars to use for tuition, books and fees. Fighting tears of joy, she pressed her hands to her cheeks. "Oh, my! So much money!"

"Hold on. That's not all." Casey clicked on an email that Kate hadn't seen.

"Dear Miss Lapp, We are pleased to offer $10,000 per calendar year in scholarship funding. Please note the terms of this funding require you to commit to serving in an under-served community for five years once you have graduated. Failure to fulfill this commitment means that the scholarship will have to be paid back to our committee. In reading your application, you indicated that you plan to serve within the Amish community of Lancaster, forming a clinic with your mother. This satisfies the "underserved community" require-ment of your scholarship.

"Also, this scholarship automatically renews for three subsequent years, meaning that, if you complete your under-graduate education in four consecutive calendar years, you will be able to use this scholarship in full. Sincerely, EMU Schol-arship Committee."

"Mei Gott! That's twenty-six thousand just for the first year!"

"Even better, you don't have to use every penny in the year for which you apply. You can hold onto some of the funding in one year and use it the next."

"Wow. Oh, my." Kate fanned herself, trying not to cry. "Do students normally get this much money for school?"

"Oh, no. Every scholarship committee you sent applications to were just impressed with what you said, with your plans. I didn't open them before I showed them to you. But looking at the subject headers, I could see that every one of them gave you money."

"I won't be able to use it all on school-related stuff."

"No. You won't. At least, not this year. So, buy food in the student union. Buy gas for your drivers. Buy new dresses."

"Or, buy the fabric. We make most of our clothing."

"Caps included?"

"Ya. And aprons. We do buy the men's pants and shirts. Some of our craftier women make socks, scarves and capes for their families."

"What would your family say about wearing non-Plain clothing?"

"Oh, no! I'm being *allowed* to advance in my education because it aids the community. But beyond that, I can't."

"Hmmm. They wouldn't allow you to use a laptop at home."

"No. No electricity and whatever it is that allows me to get on the internet. I could probably buy a computer like what you have. I wouldn't be able or allowed to use it within the community. As long as I'm quiet about it, I may be able to use it at the library."

"Yes, they have free Wi-Fi. That's the signal that allows you to connect to the internet. And I'm glad to see you're thinking of buying one—many libraries across the country only allow their patrons to use the library-provided computers for one hour a day. That's not much when you have notes to read, lab reports and papers to write."

Kate's eyes widened. "That's all?"

"Yeah. I'm guessing that libraries have so many patrons visiting a day who need their computers that they have to limit how much time each patron can be on a computer."

"Wow. Then, along with books and fees, I'd better look for a laptop. Are they expensive?"

"The least expensive are about three hundred and you can pick one up at Walmart. The most expensive are produced by Apple. And they cost anywhere between one thousand and thirteen hundred dollars."

Kate's mouth dropped open and she gasped.

"I'm thinking that, because you're getting so much money this semester, you should go all out. Buy an Apple laptop—they're nicknamed 'Mac' computers. As long as you keep software updates current, it'll last you for years."

"Casey, what's a software update?"

"Sorry. Those are the programs that are pre-loaded on each computer in the factory. Like the word processing program. And, even though Mac computers are less likely to be invaded by viruses, you should find a good antivirus program, too. I can help. A virus is a bad program that does bad things to computers and other electronics. Antivirus programs help to find those viruses. They isolate them and remove them from computers."

"Whoo. So much to learn." Kate bracketed her face with her hands.

Casey took one of her hands. "Relax. I'll help you with all of this. I'll find someone at the university who can help you if you have problems with your computer."

Kate gazed at Casey with fear in her eyes.

"Casey, please tell me that I haven't taken on too much."

"Honestly, you have taken on a lot. But, looking at the woman who attended three births, one right after the other, I think you can handle it."

Kate snorted. "You would bring that up."

At the end of the day, Casey drove Kate back home. Before they turned into the Amish community, he stopped the car. Putting it into gear, he set the brake and looked at Kate. "You're so brave." Pulling Kate into his arms, he kissed her.

Feeling Casey's lips on hers for the first time, Kate's heart rate sped up. Too soon, she felt the kiss being broken. "Where did that come from?"

"I really care for you, Kate. I didn't want to kiss you in front of your family's home and get you in trouble. We're really going to have to be careful."

Kate nodded, pulling herself out of Casey's arms. "I'd better start behaving now." She indicated a buggy coming their way.

"Whoa, thanks." Casey started the car and began driving down the road to Kate's home. As he drove, Kate waved in the direction of the buggy-driver; it was one of the community's ministers.

"Who was that?"

"One of the ministers." Kate's voice was shaky.

OVER THE NEXT FEW WEEKS, AS KATE SIGNED paperwork for her grants and scholarships, she began to get used to the idea that she would soon be a full-fledged college student. As the first day of classes came closer and closer, she became more and more nervous. Her emotions weren't helped when Ursula Mast tried once again to force her to abandon her plans.

The two were at the Amish market, with Kate buying groceries and baking goods for Becky. Ursula was there for the same purpose.

"Kate, can we talk?" Ursula was trying to dial back her normal aggressiveness.

Kate looked at her with puzzlement. "Ya? What is it?"

"Do you have a few moments?"

"Ya. What is it?"

Ursula looked around, wanting privacy. "Let's go outside and talk there." She led Kate to the side of the building. "Okay, I have to say this. I've been praying about it. I know what the elders said, but… I don't know. You're still breaking the Ordnung, permission or not. And this is going to put you in a bad—"

"Wait! Ursula. Wait. I already have the permission. I've been accepted to the Mennonite University. I have my scholarships, and I know what books I have to buy. I'm getting a little more tutoring just to make sure that I'll be able to keep up with the other students. What's more, I'm wearing Plain dress, every day that I'm in classes. I'm taking my buggy to school. I'm coming home every day so I can be with Mamm and Daed. I'm not living in the dorms."

"So…but…" Ursula couldn't continue because Kate had explained just what she was going to do to stay within the Ordnung. Finally, "Well, why do you feel the need to set yourself apart?"

"I'm not setting myself apart. Mamm and I are going to start a clinic. She'll continue working as a midwife. I'll be the doctor she refers her patients to, so they don't have to travel that far, especially if the weather is real bad. We're going to work together, so how is that so bad?"

Several silent seconds slipped by. Then, Ursula began to huff as she tried to look for a valid rebuttal. She couldn't find any. "Fine. Whatever. Destroy your soul. See what I care." Whirling around, she stomped off and clambered into her buggy.

Kate stood, fists on her hips and just stared after Ursula. "When will she stop?"

"Who?"

Kate turned and saw Deacon Kopp. "Oh, Ursula Mast. She was saying that I'm endangering my soul by going to the Eastern Mennonite University. It's ten, eleven miles away."

"I'll talk to her before she gets home. You just don't worry about her. She's only doing what her mamm and daed have been doing. And, if she continues past her baptism…"

Kate nodded. She knew exactly what the deacon meant. "Denki."

"When do you start school?"

Kate's stomach clenched with nerves. "About six weeks. I've been working on signing my scholarship paperwork. After my tuition and fees are paid, I should be getting whatever is left over from the financial aid office. I'll be putting that into the bank. Deacon? When I was talking with Mister James, he told me that I should get a computer. Because I'll need it for assignments."

"I know. Have you decided what to buy?"

Kate was stunned. "You know?"

"Oh, ya. Mister James came to us and told us

what you needed to do and that included buying a top-lap."

"Laptop. Do you know I have to learn to use the internet?"

"Ya. I can tell you that it was a hard decision for us to make. But he reassured us that you wouldn't violate any rules we'd give you. Do you have a few minutes?"

"Just a few." Kate sat on a nearby bench.

"First, don't abuse your privilege. Don't waste your precious time on that Face-something site. It could only get you in trouble."

"I think you mean Facebook. Mister James explained it to me and I agree. I might open an account on Twitter, so I can communicate with fellow students. I know I have to sign up for an email address. And he's going to help me."

"What is Twitter?"

"From what I remember seeing, it's a site where people can talk with each other in very short bursts."

"I hope you can't get into trouble on this Twitter. Hold off, please, until I talk to Mister James."

"Okay, I will. I'd better go. I have perishables for Mamm." Kate jumped up.

"Okay. We'll be visiting you before long, about

this Twitter." As it happened, the elders had an opportunity to speak with Casey. He was leaving Lancaster after dropping Kate off a few days later.

"Sure, I have a few minutes."

The deacon started. "We spoke with Kate a few days ago. She told us about Twitter? How does that work? Can she get herself in trouble there?"

Casey paused, knowing he had to say things just right. "No. Not as long as she knows how to conduct herself on a platform that renders her effectively faceless."

CHAPTER 27

"'Faceless?' What do you mean?" The bishop was concerned by this.

"When people communicate on the internet, they can't be seen by others. They're anonymous—faceless. Knowing Kate, she won't abuse that. However, others do abuse it. And I do plan to talk to her about that and show her how she can protect herself if it happens. But as courteous as she is—as is her habit—I can't see her making anyone else so upset that they'd say anything bad to her. But just in case, I do plan to explain the etiquette of the internet."

"Is this necessary for her schooling?" The bishop was worried.

"The internet and email, yes. Twitter, because

some of her fellow students might have an account there, yes. If she is going to connect with fellow students so they can talk about their classes, assignments and exams, it is necessary."

The elders looked at each other, all of their glances seeming to say one thing.

Casey, seeing this, rushed to explain. "I have a computer. I'll spend some of my free time with her this weekend. I'll show her my own account and how people talk."

"How will this equip her to be on this place?"

"Once she sees how people interact, she'll be more careful about how she says things. I've been spending a lot of time, tutoring her and helping her to get scholarships. I'm confident she's going to do well. She'll also adapt to the internet, as long as she uses it only for class-related conversations."

"Can you show us such a conversation?"

Casey scrolled down through his list of connections and clicked on one. As it opened, he scrolled more slowly, allowing the elders to read what people said to one another.

"So, you and your fellow students talk about classes and exams. Your internships and where you hope to be residents, ya?"

"Yes. And we have what we call a 'code of

conduct.' If anyone violates that code, they are made to leave the group. If they continue, well, they develop a bad reputation."

"That won't do them very well when they go on to become doctors."

"Oh, definitely not! Their reputations become well known and not only do fellow students avoid them, attending physicians do as well. It makes it harder for them to make connections at hospitals, and they find themselves isolated."

"Hmmm. Banned, in a way."

Casey nodded. "Yes. It's not formal, but that's the same effect."

The deacon relaxed. "Kate certainly knows all about that, having seen at least one person being given the ban. Okay. I'm glad you explained it this way. Will you wait here while we talk?" After getting Casey's agreement, the four men went to an area away from him, where they had a low-voiced conversation. After a few minutes, the men returned.

The bishop started talking. "We give permission for Kate to sign up for this Twitter place. We'll tell her our expectations and we do expect you to give her a good education in how it operates."

"Thank you. I will."

At the Lapp house, the elders explained the limitations under which Kate could be on Twitter. "If there are other programs like this one, you would have to find a valid reason related to your classes to join them. Talk to us and we will talk to your tutor. He is going to show you how people behave on this place. And, Kate…"

"Ya?"

"If anything…*untoward* happens, I expect you to tell your parents and us. Also, Mister James."

"I will. I promise." That night, before falling asleep, Kate reflected on all the new privileges she had been granted. *Gott, I know we restrict ourselves from Englisch inventions for gut reasons. Denki for making it easier for me to get through school. I will treat these privileges with responsibility.*

Over the next week, Kate was busy, going from one task to the next, as she completed her preparations for her first semester of college. Casey picked her up early on Wednesday, so she could report to the financial aid office and sign for her financial awards. This included the check which represented the funds remaining after all tuition and fees had been paid for the fall semester. Tearing the sealed envelope open in Casey's car, Kate gasped at the amount shown on the check. "Oh, my! So much money!"

"Do you have a bank account? I can take you to deposit that."

"Ya, please. I should hold on to it for as long as I can."

Casey peeked at the amount on the check and whistled. "Yeah, I'd say so. Although, at a guess, you're still going to have some of this left next semester, if you're careful. It's a good thing you don't drive. No expenses for gas, vehicle maintenance or insurance."

"But, when the weather gets bad, I will be paying a driver."

"You know, once you get used to the routine at school, you might ask your parents and the elders about staying in the dorms. You'd be living with other Anabaptists, so little to no temptation for anyone to worry about."

"I don't know. Are the dormitories divided by gender?"

"Strictly, I believe. Whereas, at Penn State, where I go? There are coed dorms mixed in with the male-only and female-only dorms."

"Everyone would disapprove of that at home."

"Seriously, Kate. If you live in the dorm, the time you'll spend going back and forth will be better spent in class preparation."

"Good point. I'll think about it. How much would it cost?"

"The housing office can tell you. Do you have that paper map with you?"

"Ya, because I want to practice the walking routes between classes so I won't get lost."

"Good point. We'll deposit that check and go back."

Kate winced. "I'm sorry. I'm making you use gas you need for your own errands. Here, let me…" She pulled a twenty from her wallet and stuck it in his hand.

"Kate, I don't—"

"Casey, please. I would feel better."

"I….okay." Casey stuffed the bill into his front jeans pocket. After arriving back at the EMU campus, he showed Kate some of the best ways for her to get from class to class. "Find shortcuts. That way, a fifteen-minute walk takes about half that time. That's critical when you have classes ten or fifteen minutes apart." Kate practiced the routes a few times, until she had figured out landmarks she could use to keep her on the right paths. "That coffee shop. The math building. Student union. Science build— why do they have all the different subjects in different buildings? Isn't it a waste?"

"Not when you look through the course catalog and see that the university offers multiple classes in science, math, history or English. And that, in each subject, there are several different classes for, say, English 101 or Math 111. They need every class-room they have."

"Wow. That makes me feel like..."

"Like you're one of many students all striving toward your goals."

"That's true. We're all like a *club*, right?"

"There you go."

"When do classes start for you?"

"At the same time. Pennsylvania's higher educa-tion system has to operate on a schedule. So, most colleges, vocational schools and universities will start within a few days of each other. I'm going to stay in touch with you, via phone calls and emails. Have you learned how to text yet?"

"No, should I?"

"It may come in handy if you're making plans to study with other students in your classes. I'll show you how. Let me see your phone." Casey tried a few things with the texting function. "Okay, here you go. Look. Each number button has two or three letters printed on that. You need to press the number key associated with the letter or letters you need. For instance, look at the two. If you need to text something with 'a, b or c,' press that button once for a, twice for b and three times for c."

"Let me try." Thinking of a word with two of the letters mentioned, Kate tried to write "candy." It took a few tries for her to write it correctly. "I get it. So, now, I can send texts to my classmates."

"And, to me. If, for instance, I text you and you're at the library, where it's supposed to be quiet, we could have a whole conversation. Just set your phone to 'mute' when you're there."

"Okay, if you can have patience. I'm sure to be slow until I know what I'm doing."

"That's fine. I understand. If you're by yourself at the library and you're stuck on something, text me. In fact, I have an extra copy of my class schedule for this fall. It's in my car. I'm giving you a copy. Familiarize yourself with it so, if you need, we can chat, no matter where we are."

"Even at a distance?"

"Oh, yeah. Because our phones connect or ping with close-by cellphone towers. That's how the messages and phone calls get sent back and forth."

"Oh. I think I get it. And I'll text if something is confusing me."

"Good. That way, I can still be your tutor, at a distance."

"I did see something here about free tutoring."

"Yeah, every school provides them. If you need to, sign up for it."

"I will."

IN THE TWO WEEKS REMAINING BEFORE SCHOOL started, Kate and Becky interviewed their choices for the midwife apprentice who would take Kate's position. After talking to the three young women, Kate sat with Becky in their kitchen, going through their notes. "It's a shame Katherine Ernst was unavailable, she would have been perfect. But I liked Emma the most of these applicants. She is smart and compassionate."

"Ya, but I liked Daisy even better. She's not afraid to consider doing something new. Like birthing in a tub. Or on a birthing ball."

"Kate, I don't think our mothers are quite there yet."

"Nee, they aren't. But we already know that

lying flat on our backs in bed is the least effective laboring position, right? So, once our mothers know this, they may be more open to trying something else."

"I don't know; I need a little time to think about that."

So, it's between Emma and Daisy?"

"Ya. Pretty much. Isabel didn't impress me very much. She was tentative in her answers to our questions, even though we told all three of them to be ready and sure of their answers."

"She's always been shy and not very sure of herself. I agree. If she's not sure of herself in a difficult delivery, it could be bad for the mother."

"As well as for the baby." Becky leaned back. She pushed the pages full of Isabel's responses to the side and looked back and forth between Daisy's pages and Emma's. "You know, I think you're right. While it could take some time, we could get our mothers used to other birthing positions. This way, when you graduate and come back with your medical license, we'll have even more services we can offer."

"I agree. Kate checked the time. "If we leave now, we can go visit all three applicants and let Daisy know she'll be my replacement. We don't have much time. A week and a half. I want to get her in with us right away so she knows how we work."

Becky rose. "Let's go. When we get home, we'll have to start supper."

At Daisy's family's house, Becky and Kate gave her the good news. "Because of your willingness to look at new delivery modalities, you're our choice. You know that, when Kate comes back, she'll have her doctor's license. This way, you, Kate and I can become a full team, offering a full list of services."

Daisy's pretty face was wreathed in a large grin. "Ya! I love the idea! Will you be available during our patients' pregnancies, too?"

"Oh, ya. If problems develop, I'll be there, helping them right alongside you. That way, maybe we can avoid hospitalization. Or, if we know we'll have to take the mamm to the hospital, it won't be such an unpleasant surprise to her."

"So, can you start tomorrow?"

"Thursday, right?" Looking at the wall calendar, Daisy nodded. "Ya, I can. I'll tell Mamm."

The next two stops were fairly quick as Becky and Kate simply offered the news that they had chosen another candidate for the now-open position. They told Emma that, if she was available, she would be chosen at any time they decided to add more midwives to the group.

"Okay. Although I do have an interview in the next community."

"That's three miles away. Will you be able to make it at short notice?"

"Ya. Between the three of us, I am engaged to a young man over there. We're getting married during the Wedding Season and I'm going to live there. So that distance won't be a problem."

Kate grimaced. "Well, that puts paid to our thoughts of expansion."

"Maybe not. You still have several years of schooling. I'm sure candidates will be available at that time. Besides, we aren't quite there for expanding."

THE DAY FINALLY DAWNED. KATE WOKE, FEELING eels squirming in her stomach. Getting dressed with shaky hands, she had to re-do her braid twice before she was satisfied. Downstairs, she eyed breakfast with doubt in her face.

"I know you're nervous. But you need to eat. What will you do for lunch?"

"I have extra money. I'll eat at the student union."

"Do you have your books ready?" Steve eyed Kate's backpack.

"Ya. I know what classes I have today, so I'm taking everything I need. It's already in my backpack. I also know where I can leave the buggy and the team as well."

"And you'll hire a driver for bad-weather days?"

"Ya, that's something Mister James and I already discussed."

"Gut. Just use drivers we've already hired in the past. A woman alone—"

"Ya, Daed. I know." Slowly, Kate ate her breakfast, willing it to stay in her stomach. After several minutes, she was sure she wouldn't be sick from nerves. Before leaving, she helped Becky with dishes. "I'd better go. I practiced the walking routes. But I don't want to forget where I'm supposed to go. So I'd better leave early for the next few days."

"Gut idea. Gott be with you and be careful. Will Mister James be tutoring you during the semester?"

CHAPTER 28

"We don't know yet. Our classes will be keeping both of us busy. He did tell me that I could call, if I had any difficulties."

"Gut. For classes only!"

"Ya, Daed. Classes only." Kate left, not wanting to get lost on-campus. Arriving, she parked the buggy and paid the attendant for water and grain for the horses. "I'll be back at three or thereabouts when I leave today."

"Okay, we'll see you then."

Kate sped off on foot, worried that she was about to get hopelessly lost. Gripping her map in one sweaty hand. Under her breath, she muttered to herself. "From the barn to the math building.

The first landmark is the, uh, the student union. Ya, there it is."

"Your first day, huh?" A young, Mennonite girl was walking next to Kate.

"Ya, it is. I'm so scared!"

"You'll be okay. Just keep that map, and also, write down what landmarks you need so you remember more easily."

"Gut idea!" Kate whipped a pen out of her handbag and scribbled the student union down next to the math building. She walked into the building with the girl, who was named Penny.

"What are you majoring in?"

"Pre-med."

"But… You're Amish."

"Ya. I got special permission from my elders and parents to do so. I'm—or, I was—a midwife. I can offer better service to our patients by—"

"Becoming a doctor. That's wunderbaar! Will you do midwifery on school breaks?"

"Possibly. That depends on my mother. She and I just hired my replacement a week ago."

In that meeting was born a friendship that would last years as Kate accustomed herself with the Mennonite lifestyle.

During the rest of her day, Kate hurried from

math to history, then lunch in the student union. After lunch, she took her biology class. Leaving, she was muttering to herself.

"What are you saying?"

Kate turned. A young Mennonite man was grinning at her.

"I-I think I made a mistake, thinking I could get through college-level science."

"It's difficult, for sure. If you'd like, I can help you."

"Well, my tutor told me I could just text him."

"He's not here?"

"Nee. He goes to Penn State. He's in medical school."

"Wow. Okay, so, help me out here. If you're Amish, how can you text someone?"

Kate smiled. "I got permission; actually, Mamm and I got permission to carry small flip phones. I just learned how to text. My tutor told me to let him know if I needed help. And I just may be doing that, once I get home."

"Is this your last class?"

"Ya, it is. I need to get home so I can help Mamm. Unless she has a delivery right now."

"A delivery?"

"She's a midwife. She told me that, if she and Daisy needed help, they would let me know."

"That's good news. I'm glad to see your community allowing you to do this. I left my community when I wasn't allowed to go to school to become a teacher."

"You're Amish?"

"Was. I'm Mennonite now. I met my fiancée here. She didn't have classes today. She'll be here tomorrow."

"Ya, my one day away from school will be Fridays. That way, I can study and help Mamm. Were you banned?"

"No. I hadn't been baptized yet. By the way, I'm Sam."

"Kate Lapp." She shook Sam's hand. "I'll be seeing you in class."

"You brought your buggy. What are you going to do when it's snowy and Icy?"

"Hire a driver."

"When you hire a driver and we've had an ice storm, it's just as bad for them as well. You'd do better in reserving a room in the guesthouse."

"I'll tell my parents."

"Good. The rooms aren't expensive. Twenty dollars a night."

Kate swallowed. "Okay. Ya, I have funds, but I just want to make sure they last."

"Gotcha on that. Be safe on the way home."

"I will." Kate smiled. For her first day, she'd already made a couple friends. "I hope I get to meet your fiancée soon."

"I'm sure you will. Just let me know if you need help studying."

"I will." Kate waved as she jumped into her buggy and started home.

That night, she did the homework she'd been assigned. She was worried that she wouldn't be able to keep up at first, and then she realized Casey had told her the truth. *Well, that's for my English class. Wait until I get into the assignments for math. Science is going to break my brain.* Looking at the time, she realized she could still call Casey. Shoving her books and notebook back, she placed the call.

"Hello? Kate?"

Kate giggled. "I still can't get used to how you know it's me before I speak."

"You'll get there. How was your first day?"

"Not bad, actually. I met some fellow students and it looks like I'll have, um, *study buddies?* Is that the term?"

"That's exactly it. What are you going to do if study meetings are set up for evenings?"

"I'll just request that they be set up for afternoons or even Saturdays. I have a question."

"What is it?"

"My biology class is going to break my brain. Can we get together for tutoring this Saturday? Please?"

"Sure, if the morning is okay with you. I have hospital hours from three in the afternoon until close to midnight."

Kate sighed in relief. "That works for me. What time and I'll put it in my calendar?"

"How about nine-thirty? I can buy brunch or lunch for you."

"Ya, okay. That works. Thank you." Kate was conscious that her parents were in the next room.

"So, how were your classes for your first day?"

"Not bad. But the biology was the only hard one. English and even math were easy."

"Okay, good. Just let me know as you go to each class which you'll need help with. We'll focus on them."

"Thank you. I'd better go. I have homework to finish."

"Okay, see you Saturday."

Slipping the phone back into her apron pocket, Kate resumed her studying. She quickly finished her English assignment, realizing she would have to work in the library on the days she got the assignments. Her professor had stressed that he wanted all assignments typed, not hand-written.

"How is it going?" Becky came into the kitchen.

"Gut! I'm going to have to find a fellow biology student who understands our assignment better than I do. I'll also have to write out my English assignments—rather, type them out—in the library on the day they're assigned. My professor won't accept handwritten ones."

"Oh, my! I hope that will work for short ones. For longer ones, you'll have to spend several days in the library."

"Ya, I will. But as long as I can get all my research and notes, that shouldn't be too hard. I remember Mister Beiler giving us long English assignments. Even though I had to handwrite them, I could finish my research and do the writing in about a week."

Becky sat down across from Kate. "So, do you have a list of topics to choose from?"

Kate opened her notebook to the syllabus,

which she had slipped into the front pocket. "It's on the fourth page, I think. Here you go."

Becky quietly read what Kate would be required to do. "Do you know which topic you want?"

"It's between the one on learning, or the one on the use of technology. I'm leaning toward the technology one."

I imagine you could give quite an individual perspective on that one."

"Ya, that's why. I might be the only Amish student there, given how we're expected to leave school at fourteen. I'm so new to using a cellphone and computer that I might write about how we're forbidden from using them—but for me to complete my medical degree, I have to do so."

"Do you think the bishop should read it?"

Kate thought. "I don't think so. What do you think?"

"I think it'll be an eye-opening experience for him. Think about it. Showing your classwork to the elders may make your new path easier for them, as well as you."

Kate nodded slightly, thinking. "I can do that."

~

THE FOLLOWING SATURDAY, CASEY PICKED KATE up and they went to a Starbucks close by the community. "Okay, let's see the biology." Opening to the page Kate indicated, he quickly read through. "Do you have the homework handy?"

"Ya, right here. It's due Monday morning."

"Let me show you something. I want you to think independently and learn, but until you get a better understanding of biology, you're going to have to read the assignment questions first. See these numbers? They're the page numbers where you'll find the answers."

"Ya, but, that's too easy."

"Not really. You have to read—*really* digest the pages indicated in your assignments. Once you do that, you'll be able to find the answers to the question your professor asks in these handouts."

"Let me see that, please." Reading the question, Kate leafed to the page indicated on the handout. She read slowly, digesting each word. "Oh. I see. So the answer to that question is right here."

Casey retrieved the book and checked where Kate was pointing. "Exactly. But you may get some trick questions, where the answer could be this, or it could be that."

Kate groaned. "Why do they do that?"

"To make you slow down and think about what you're reading. That way, it sticks in your mind longer."

Kate quickly wrote the answer down. "So, I should be able to remember these answers on Monday morning?" She was clearly skeptical.

"Most of them, yes."

In this vein, their study session went productively, until a young Englisch man approached their table. "Hey, I thought the Amish dropped out of school. What are you doing in college?"

Kate indicated she would answer. "I see how I can help the women in my community by requesting and receiving permission to go to school. I'm a midwife, but we don't have the education to handle some situations. I don't know if you're married or not, but would you want your wife to have to travel from an Amish community at midnight, in the middle of a blizzard or rainstorm? Especially if something has gone wrong?"

The young man paused. "Ah, well, no. I wouldn't. So, what? Are you in medical school?"

"Pre-med. And, if you don't mind too much, I still have some studying to do." Kate turned away.

"But—"

"Excuse me. My student told you she needs to study. Please respect that." Casey's voice was firm.

"Sir, is there a problem?" A Starbucks manager was standing next to their table.

"Yes, Tammy. My student and I are going over one of her assignments. And this young man won't leave her alone."

"But, I just wondered why…"

"Tony, we warned you last month. We accepted you back in here on the condition that you wouldn't harass other customers. You're banned permanently. Effective immediately." Tammy pointed toward the door.

Tony, defeated, left. "I'm going to find out more about you, Amish girl."

Kate's eyes widened as she looked at Casey.

"Miss, whenever you need to leave, let me know. I'll send two of my male baristas out to make sure he won't bug you."

"Denki." Kate's voice was small. She felt fearful of the questions the now-banned man wanted to ask her.

"Kate, don't worry. I'm taking you home, remember?"

"Ya, but what if he follows us?"

"Then, we deal with it at that point."

When Kate and Casey left Starbucks, Tony had long since left. Still, Kate hurried to get into Casey's car, not wanting to see the strange, young man. When she got home, she found a note on the kitchen table.

"Daisy and I are assisting at a birth. We left at ten this morning, and since it's a first child, it could take a while. Please make dinner and supper for you and your daed. Use the recipes I put on the counter."

Kate sighed.

Steve came into the kitchen. "Your mother's gone and won't be back for a while."

"Ya, I saw her note. She and Daisy are helping with a first birth. I'll be making dinner and supper. I hope…"

"You'll do well. You just need to be confident. Just as confident as you are when you're helping a mamm have a baby."

Kate groaned. "Biology was easier." Pulling the first recipe toward her, Kate began making dinner for herself and her daed.

"This isn't bad. See, what did I tell you?"

Kate tasted the savory meatloaf. "So, if I don't try to add this or that to it, then it tastes like it should. We'll have leftovers so Mamm and Daisy can eat."

After answering a few of the biology questions for her class, Kate looked at the time. Putting her studies away, she started working on supper. Quietly, she thought to herself that it would be nice if her mamm would come home. Using the second recipe card, she made spaghetti sauce. Tasting it, she turned the burner down and tossed spaghetti into the boiling water so she could boil it.

"See what I told you? This is wunderbaar!"

"Denki." Kate smiled, feeling more confident.

Becky came in as Kate was washing dishes and cleaning the kitchen. "It smells gut. And I am starving." She put her bag in the pantry, against the far wall. "I'll dish my supper up. How did it turn out?"

"Daed and I loved it. I followed your recipes to the letter."

As she ate hungrily, Becky was happy. "You did a wunderbaar job. I always knew you could. And the baby was finally born. A little boy. They named him Jonah."

"That's gut. Are we making anything for tomorrow's lunch?"

"Ya. A cold fruit salad. We'll mix the whipped topping in when it's time to serve. But for tonight, we'll just chop the fruits and mix them all into a large bowl."

Kate helped with chopping fruits as Becky had planned. By the time they finished, it was after seven. "I'd better finish these questions. They're due Monday." By the time she finished her biology homework, Kate was heavy-eyed.

"How much did you get done?" Steve lowered his mystery book.

"Biology. I'll work on the American history tomorrow, after lunch. That's only reading. I also have to scan through topics to decide what topic my semester paper will be on." A yawn caught Kate by surprise. "Oh! I'd better get to bed. It's been a long day. Mamm? You'd better get to bed, too."

The entire family went to bed early, as they were all tired.

AT THE NEXT DAY'S MEETING, KATE WAS uncomfortably aware that she was being stared at. Without being obvious, she figured who was doing the staring—Ursula Mast and some of her friends. Sighing, Kate leaned over to her mamm. "Mamm, do you see them staring at me?"

CHAPTER 29

"Ya. I'll be right back. Stay here."

Becky, highly upset, went to the deacon. "Deacon, Ursula and her friends are staring at Kate. Should she say anything?"

"I saw them. Nee, she shouldn't. Leave them to me." The deacon went to where Ursula and her friends sat. "Miss Mast, come with me. Your friends, too." Asking the host of the meeting if they could talk quietly, the deacon got permission to use a first floor bedroom. His wife joined them, as a chaperone. "Ladies, why were you staring so much at Kate Lapp? What has—?"

"She's breaking the Ordnung!" wailed Ursula.

Deacon Kopp closed his eyes and sighed. "No,

she is not. As we have told you, she came to us long before she returned to school. She is doing so in order that she and her mamm can work together as partners, helping mothers to have their babies."

"Midwives are gut enough."

"Until a mamm has a problem. Are you going to stop bothering her?"

"Nee. She's breaking Gott's rules."

"Well, I just hope that, when you are expecting a baby, you won't have any problems. Any of you." The deacon, feeling so much better, stalked off. He told the bishop what had happened, including his own outburst.

"You are human. We'll go talk to her and her friends tomorrow morning. Unless you have anything you need to do?"

"Nee, nothing that can't wait."

THE NEXT MORNING, AS KATE WAS GETTING ready for her Monday classes, the elders all stopped at Ursula's uncle's house, where she was now living.

"Ya? Is something wrong?"

"We need to speak with Ursula. Privately."

Ursula's aunt let the elders into the house

without saying anything. She had always thought her brother and sister-in-law were wrong to hold such a conservative point of view. "Ursula! Before you go to work, the elders need to speak with you! She'll be in the kitchen."

"Denki." In the kitchen, the four elders sat on one side of the table as Ursula sat by herself on the other side.

"Ya, what is it? Are you going to finally discipline Kate Lapp for what she's doing? Oh, what a relief!"

"Nee, we aren't. She did everything exactly as she was supposed to do it. She discerned a need. Prayed about it. When she still felt that she was supposed to be doing this, she didn't just go ahead and get enrolled in her classes. She came to us. And she met every single one of our requirements. . ."

"Is it true she uses a computer?"

"Ya, it is. None of her teachers will allow her to hand in assignments written out in longhand. So, she bought a computer and she brought it to us. She showed us that she has no accounts with any of the media-social groups." The bishop mixed up the wording for "social media." Not aware of what he had done, he continued. "She applied to the Mennonite University in Lancaster and was accepted. She'll be coming home at the end of every school day, rather than living in the dormitories. She does her homework, helps her mamm and, before her school started, she helped to select the new midwife and trained her. So, she has been very busy."

"Miss Mast, I have a question for you. Do you want to see the obstetric services improved for the mothers here? Or do you want to see mothers and babies dying needlessly?"

Ursula couldn't answer. "I...nee, I don't."

"You don't what?"

"I-I don't want mothers or babies to suffer." Ursula was almost totally breathless now.

"Well, that's funny. You could have fooled me." The bishop was heavily sarcastic. "Miss Mast, we realize you haven't been baptized yet, but you are approaching that time. You saw what happened to your mamm, then your daed. They were banned for harassing Kate and her mamm."

Ursula couldn't say anything. With huge eyes, she just stared at the elders.

"Now, do you want to be baptized into our community, only to come before the community some years hence? *Do you want to run the risk of being banned, like your parents?*"

"Uh, nee, I don't." Ursula's heart was pounding.

"Then you had better stop hassling Kate Lapp. Do you understand?"

Tears began to flow down Ursula's cheeks. "But…"

"What?"

"I'm just used to living more conservatively."

"Ya, and that's fine. You live *your* life as conservatively as you please. Just do not try to impose your preferences or beliefs on others around here, do you understand?" Bishop Troyer's voice was a low roar by now.

Ursula leaned back into her chair, pressing her back hard against the back of the chair. "Y-ya, I un-understand."

"Missus Trobel, will you please come in here?"

Deborah Trobel came into the living room. "Ya?"

"I'm sure you heard just a little of our conversation."

"Ya. I couldn't help but."

"We're sorry for that. Ursula has been harassing Kate Lapp."

"The one in school, right?"

"Ya. She's in the pre-medical program at Eastern Mennonite University at Lancaster."

"I'm glad. We need more people like her. My brother, sister-in-law and now, Ursula, are refusing to accept that we can petition you to get exceptions to our Ordnung. As long as we have gut reasons for doing so. Ursula, Kate isn't leaving here every day just so she can go out, party, get drunk, then come home at the end of every day. She's working hard! Taking classes that go beyond what our eighth graders learn. And this will help the women and families here by and by."

"I agree. Ursula, if you don't change your practices, you're going to be sent to go live with a family member who is even more serious about being conservative than you, your daed or your mamm are. Do you want that?"

"Will I be banned?"

"You haven't been baptized yet. Therefore, we can't ban you. But we could require that you move elsewhere, if you refuse to stop this disruptive behavior. You were glaring at Kate before our Sunday service even started! You weren't focusing on Gott and preparing your heart for the day's lesson."

Ursula had begun to cry. "Nooo, please don't make me leave! I promise you, I'll stop!"

"Are you being honest about this? We've told you to stop in the past. You promised to do so, only to continue with your actions."

"Nee, I do promise. I don't want to leave here. It's home. Even though I can't communicate with Mamm and Daed, I can see them, at least."

The deacon began to speak. "Ursula, continue holding your conservative beliefs, if that's what you're most comfortable with. But, be warned: If you continue, you will be gone from here!"

Ursula nodded, completely frightened.

"Now, who are the friends who have been supporting you in your actions?"

Ursula looked at the bishop, a question in her eyes,

"Ya, you do need to tell us."

She sighed. "Okay, Mary Best, Otto Hoffstetter —my beau—and Rachel King."

"Denki. I urge you to pray sincerely about your wrongdoing. Pray for forgiveness and promise Gott that you'll never act in that way again."

Ursula's eyes began to leak tears again. "Ya, I will." She knew just how close she had come to being made to leave the community.

"You are forgiven. We forgive you." The elders made quick trips to each of the young people Ursula had named. Their message to each of them was identical to what they had told Ursula. "You have two choices: Quit what you're doing. Or go live elsewhere, with other family members." In the end, only Rachel King decided to leave. She left the next morning for her sister's house, located in Ohio.

"So, what did the elders tell you?" Otto was in his buggy, Ursula next to him.

"That, if I didn't stop hassling Kate, they would force me to live elsewhere. And I can't. I'd lose you."

"Ya, that's why I decided to stop as well. She's going to do what she's going to do. It's her soul and her business, I guess."

"So, what do we do?"

"Ignore her. Since we can't get the elders to bring her before the community, all we can do is to ban her in our minds."

Ursula thought about it. "It'll work. They can't control who we talk to or not."

"Ya, my thoughts, too. Do you want to

tell Mary?"

"Ya. I'll be going to the market to sell my quilts tomorrow. I pass by her family's house, so I can stop on the way."

"Gut."

The next day, Mary was upset as she talked to Ursula. "Why did they do that? It *does* violate the Ordnung to go on further with our educations!"

"Ya, Mary. But Otto put it well. He said we should just ignore her and, in our minds, ban her."

Mary had been about to say something. She closed her mouth, thinking about Ursula's words. "Well, ya, that will work. I never liked her, anyway. She's too liberal for my tastes."

Thus the "ignore Kate" plan went into operation. When Kate realized what was happening, she just shrugged. *The less hassle I get from them, the better.* As she went about her classes and life at home, she felt lighter, as though she had one less thing to worry about.

BECKY AND KATE WERE AT THE STORE ON A DAY when Kate's first class wasn't until ten a.m. As they put their selections into their cart, Becky spoke. "I just saw Ursula, Mary and Otto. They clearly saw you, but said nothing. In fact, it was as if they were looking through you, rather than ignoring you. Do you know what's going on?"

Kate nodded. "Ya, I think I do. When they couldn't get me in trouble with the elders, they decided the best way to deal with me is to 'ban' me in their minds. By ignoring me, they're sending a clear message to me. But I don't really care. It's one less worry for me. Now, I can focus on school and helping you."

Becky closed her eyes and shook her head. "I only have one thing to say. When it comes time for any of them to have a baby, even Otto, they will need to hire another midwife. And, if they have medical issues with the pregnancy, they'll have to travel to the hospital in Lancaster. We are not going to be serving them. Now or in the future."

Kate nodded. "I agree with you."

Mary and Ursula overheard Becky and Kate discussing their 'ban' of Kate. Looking at each other, their mouths fell open. Becky was known as the most skilled, compassionate midwife in their Lancaster community. Ursula grabbed Mary's arm and pulled her to a different area of the store. "We can't have that. I had hoped that, when I do get pregnant, Becky would be my midwife. She's the best."

"Ya, but what can we do now?"

"Nothing." Becky stood behind Ursula. Her blue eyes, usually so friendly and warm, glittered like icicles today. "Kate has figured the two of you out. And I do have the right to decide who will be my patient—and who won't. You have been giving Kate trouble for so long that we are just done with it. And you. After you get married and start having babies, you'll have to rely on another midwife—and another doctor, if something goes wrong." Turning, Becky walked away fast, before she said something she knew she would regret.

THE FOLLOWING SATURDAY, KATE AND CASEY SAT at their usual table at Starbucks. Kate listened carefully and took notes as Casey explained her algebra equations. After trying a few of them, she felt more comfortable. Once they finished that and her biology, Kate set her pencil down. "Do you know what happened earlier this week?"

"No. I hope it was good."

"Mm. Gut in a way. The elders found out that

Ursula and her friends were still bothering me. They were all just staring at me before church, glaring at me. We told the elders and they went to talk to them. Well, as it turns out, they were told to stop or face consequences."

"But they can't be banned, can they?"

"No. They haven't been baptized yet. But the elders told them that, if they didn't stop, they would still be made to leave the community. For good."

"Wow! And what did they say?"

"Ursula, her boyfriend, Otto, and their friend, Mary, decided they would cooperate with the elders. They would leave me alone. But their friend Rachel decided that she couldn't ignore my 'violation' of the Ordnung. So, she was made to leave. She's in Ohio now, living with her sister."

"Well, good!"

"You know what's even better? Mamm and I saw them at the store this week. Mary and Ursula were ignoring me. That's their solution: in their minds, by ignoring me, they are banning me. That is absolutely fine by me! But…"

"What? This is good."

Kate snickered. "We midwives are able to decide if we're going to work with a particular mother or not. And, because of what the three of them, including Otto, are doing, we aren't going to give them prenatal services or help at their childbirths. They need to hire another midwife. And, if something goes wrong with any of their pregnancies, I won't be the doctor to serve them. I hope."

"Yeah, if you're the O.B. on call at the hospital, that could be a problem."

"No!"

"Unless…"

"What? Please! Is there a remedy?"

"There may be. I'd need to check. If a doctor has been bothered in the past, they can tell the hospital administration that they won't serve the harasser. This is important, because, if something goes wrong…"

"Oh, my. Ya, I see where you're going with that. So, there might be a way that I could do that?"

"Yeah, but let me find out for sure. If so, you can tell the head of the Labor and Delivery floor about your history with these three. And, because they tried to get you banned, that may be enough to get the administration to ban them from Lancaster General. They'd have to go to another hospital in Lancaster or even in another township. Like East Petersburg, Leola, Bird-in-Hand, or Paradise."

Kate was stunned. "Wow! They're at a distance,

though. Their midwife would have to figure out fast if there's something wrong."

"Exactly. But, given how they've treated you, there's no guarantee that they'd be any nicer during labor and delivery."

Kate grimaced. "Nee! They would definitely be worse. I'll keep it in mind and tell Mamm."

As the remainder of Kate's first semester in college went on, Kate grew more accustomed to her new routine. She began to feel more comfortable with her classes and studies, even biology and chemistry. Slowly, her dream of becoming an obstetrician became ever clearer.

Gott had put her exactly where she needed to be, and with work, she would achieve her dream.

The End.

You can **learn more about my other books here**. There is also a sample of the first chapter of another of my books in the next chapter so you can get a further taste of my work.

And if you are interested in getting email updates from me, **click here**.

Lastly, if you'd liked this book and have 2-3 minutes to leave a review, I would be incredibly grateful. Reviews are life and death for indie authors like me because they let potential readers know what folks like them think of the book.

And if you find something in the book *yikes* that makes you think this book deserves less than 5-stars, drop me a line at rachelstoltzfus@globalgrafx-press.com and I'll fix the problem if I can.

All the best,

Rachel

A sudden illness. A shocking diagnosis. Can she be healed?

When fourteen-year-old Margarete King begins to suffer from weakness, nosebleeds, and a strange rash, it soon becomes clear that her life hangs in the balance of a tragic illness and the whims of a callous hospital administration. Will this family be strong enough to save Margarete? Will Margarete's grandmother seize a surprise second chance at romance?

Find out in this uplifting 3 novella series collection of strength, faith, and hope.

Chapter 1

Margarete, hurry, please! Those cookies aren't going to bake themselves, and we still have so much work to do!" Leora King was exasperated at the unusual slowness of her daughter, who had just recently become an apprentice in her baking company. She looked over at Margarete's progress, alarmed to see that she had just barely begun to mix the shortening, sugar and eggs together for the snickerdoodles.

"Ya, Mamm, I'm hurrying. I'm sorry." Margarete swiped her three-quarter length dress sleeve against her sweaty forehead. *That's funny. It's bone-chilling cold out and raining. I shouldn't be hot! I'm not even close to the ovens.* Shaking her head, Margarete tried to clear the odd tiredness from her mind and body.

"Daughter, are you okay? You look flushed." Leora hurried to Margarete's side and, with one hand, tested her temperature. "You are burning up. Go. Take some acetaminophen and drink some cool water."

Margarete nodded thankfully. After taking the pills, she sank into a kitchen chair, feeling more and more exhausted by the minute. Not wanting to think about why she was so tired, she sighed and looked outside. Today at her mother's bakery, she had been grateful to be inside. Now, she would give everything she owned to be outside cooling off, if only for a few moments. But she couldn't gather the energy to do so. Feeling the waistband of her dress slipping down her hip, she pulled it up and pinned it more closely to her waist. She looked at her mamm, not wanting her to know she had lost weight. Then, she looked back outside, watching large fluffy flakes of snow falling. After thirty minutes of resting, she felt a little better. "Mamm, I feel better. What do you need to have done?"

"Mix the snickerdoodles, please. I still haven't been able to get to them. Denki!"

Getting busy, Margarete made good progress on the cookies and started to scoop the dough out onto several cookie sheets. As she did so, she felt her nose beginning to run. Sniffling a few times, she finally left the dough scooping and went to the sink, where she yanked off a square of paper towel. Rubbing it against her nose, she was alarmed to see that her nose had begun to bleed. "Mamm! My nose! It's bleeding!"

"Tip your head back! Pinch the middle of your nose between your thumb and two fingers. I'll be there in a second." Leora looked around. When she saw the amount of blood on the paper towel, she gasped. "Margarete! Are you okay?"

Margarete couldn't speak without choking. She shrugged, doing as her mamm had told her. After a few minutes, the bleeding slowed and finally stopped.

Leora, seeing the crisis appeared to be over, sighed. "You must be coming down with something. How do you feel?"

"Just…tired. Weak. And I felt fine yesterday. Do you think it's a cold? Flu?"

Leora tested Margarete's forehead again. "Well, you're not hot anymore, just clammy. Drink some more water. At home, I want you to take more medication and rest. Supper will be easy. I am making spaghetti."

Margarete tried to be enthusiastic, but even knowing her favorite food would be served did little for her appetite. "Gut!"

At home that night, Margarete did as her mother said. She went upstairs and rested, trying to regain her usual energy. As she changed position, she winced—her bones hurt!

A week later, Margarete felt gut again. Her strength was back and her bone pain was gone. She wasn't feverish and hadn't had another nosebleed. On Saturday, her cousins came over and Margarete split her time between helping her mamm and sisters and watching over her younger cousins. Just after supper, the strange feeling of tiredness hit again. She collapsed into a chair after helping to put dishes away.

"Daughter, you okay?" Leora had continued to keep a close eye on her daughter.

"Ya. Just tired all of a sudden." Feeling a bone-deep chill, Margarete shivered and wrapped her arms around her. As she rubbed her upper arms, the bone pain came back. After everyone left, she went to bed with another fever. She fell asleep quickly, but her sleep was broken by fever dreams. She tossed restlessly. By the time morning came, she was almost unable to get out of bed. She sneezed and coughed. "Mamm! I think I have the flu!"

Leora came running into Margarete's room, followed closely by Samuel "Sammy" King, her daed. "What? We have church services this morning!" She felt Margarete's forehead and shook her head. "Husband, she's feverish. I think she's right. You go to service and I'll stay home with her."

Sammy sighed. He'd always had a special spot in his heart for his daughter. Caressing her hot cheek, he tried to smile. "You do everything she tells you so you can get better. I hate to think of you being sick. Wife, I wonder if one of the kinder made her sick."

Leora thought for a few minutes. "Nee, I doubt it. She was only with them yesterday, and it takes days for a cold or even the flu to make its presence known. If she's not better by the time you come home, we'll take her to urgent care in town. I'm sure they'll diagnose flu."

Living in Somerset County, Pennsylvania, the King family wasn't very close to medical care—they had doctor's offices, an urgent care center and a small community hospital.

"Ya. That sounds gut. I'll take the muffins and bread and bring your containers back."

"Breakfast first. Daughter, do you feel like you can eat?"

Margarete sighed. "Nee. No appetite. I'm sorry."

"Nee, don't worry. Just rest and I'll bring some tea up to you."

"Samuel! You'd better be dressed! It's going to be just you and me. Your sister is sick."

Little Sammy popped his head out of his bedroom. His shirt was partially buttoned and he had only one suspender pulled over his shoulder. "Aw! That's not fair!"

Sammy glared at his son. "Son, shush! She has a fever and she's sneezing and coughing. Something tells me you wouldn't want to have that."

"Sorry, Daed. Nee, I wouldn't." Now subdued, Little Sammy hurried downstairs. "Does she have a cold?"

"Mamm thinks it's flu. We're going to take her to urgent care this afternoon if she's not better."

By the time her daed and brother came home, Margarete was feeling much better. Her strength was back and she wasn't feverish. However, she was still coughing.

"What do you think?" Leora's glance was full of worry.

"I'd rather take her and feel like a fool when we're told it's just a bad cold rather than not take her and have it be something really serious." Sammy's words were a foreshadowing of more problems with Margarete's health. Bundling her up, they took her and little Sammy to urgent care.

After an examination, the doctor spoke to the family. "It looks like a bad cold to me. Her fever is gone and she says she feels better. That nosebleed last week may have just been irritation from working with flour and other baking ingredients. Margarete, I want you to drink lots of fluids and try not to overdo it. Get lots of rest and try to eat as many healthy foods as you can. You're just a little underweight for your height."

Margarete was stunned. She had never been described as "underweight" in her life. Closing her mouth, she coughed slightly and nodded. "Ya, I will."

For the next few weeks, she recovered from her cold and went to the bakery with Leora, helping her to bake the goods her mamm sold. Her good health and appetite soon returned. Only occasionally did she feel that odd tiredness, mainly when she'd been extra-busy in the bakery, helping her mamm with the baking and customers. She was puzzled, finding it necessary to go to bed earlier so she could regain her normal energy and strength. One day, when she had been really tired, she sat on her bed, feeling frustrated and helpless. *Gott, I don't want this horrible feeling! Please take it away from me!* Resting her forehead on her knees, she sighed, willing the tiredness to leave her body. Slowly, she dozed off, sliding down so her head rested at the side of her pillow.

"Margarete! Supper's ready! Come on!"

Margarete roused, feeling better than she had all afternoon long. Standing and stretching, she finger-combed her bun back into order and straightened her head covering. "Denki, Sammy. I'm on my way." As she woke up, Margarete was relieved to realize that she felt normal once again. Hurrying downstairs, she was happy to find that she was, once again, ravenous. She loaded her plate with meatloaf, vegetables and mashed potatoes. By the time supper was finished, she was pleasantly full and ready to help Leora with dishes and cleaning up the kitchen.

"Well, daughter, let's get the redding up done. I'm tired and I want to sit down."

That night and for several days, Margarete was happy to see that her health had apparently returned to normal. At the bakery, she was back to her normal activity level, baking cookies and cakes. She helped at the front counter, selling items customers wanted. One day, close to the end of the day, several Englischers came in. They seemed to all be in the same family. Margarete patiently helped them out, explaining what each item was. "This is snitz pie, and it is delicious! Ahh!" Margarete pointed at one of the youngest kinder, who was trying to reach into the side of the case. He had his eyes on a large chocolate chip cookie.

"Travis, get over here! If you don't behave, you won't get anything."

That seemed to be the signal for all bedlam to erupt. Travis, on hearing his mother's warning, dropped to the ground and began kicking the base of the display cases and wailing loudly. "I want that cookie! I'm not going to stop until I get that cookie!"

Margarete, unaccustomed to such behavior, just stood and watched. Soon, the caterwauling gave her a headache. She looked around, hands over her ears as her mamm came hurrying to the front.

"What is going on here? It sounds like someone is being killed!"

Margarete shrugged. "She told him that if he didn't behave, he wouldn't get anything! That's when he started this!"

Leora, accustomed to strict but loving parenting, shook her head. Putting her fists onto her slender hips, she moved over to Travis. "Young man, if you don't stop this nonsense, your mamm is right not to give you anything. And ma'am, do not give into his screaming. That's what he's trying to do."

The other mother nodded. "Okay. Then, we'll take the other cookies and that pie your daughter was telling us about. No cookie for Travis."

Travis, who had stopped wailing, began to rev up for another round.

"Stand up, young man. Now." Leora waited, kneeling, until Travis slowly obeyed. "Do you know what we do in our family? If any of our kinder do what you just pulled, we give them a good pop on their behinds. Margarete can tell you. They get sent to their room to think about their wrong. And they do not get what they were screaming about. And that's what's going to happen to you today. I don't allow kinder to misbehave in my bakery."

Margarete, working with the mother and giving her change, smiled slightly. She nodded. "Ya, that's *just* what happens."

Travis, looking back and forth from Margarete to Leora, sniffled. His eyes welled with huge tears again and his lower lip stuck out. Crossing his arms, he looked down and moved next to his mother.

"Thank you. I'm going to remind him of this scene the next time he thinks of throwing a tantrum." The mother was red-faced, from both anger and embarrassment.

"You're welcome. Ma'am, don't allow him to try

and…what's that word? Manipulate you, ya, that's it. Just tell him what you expect and, if you can get him a treat, do so."

The rest of that week, Margarete continued to feel good. It was the next week when she noticed tiny red spots dotting her body. They were everywhere. She thought that maybe she'd been bitten by insects. Later in the week, she was body-slammed by fatigue—she wasn't able to shake it off. Finally, two days later, her parents took her to the doctor. That morning, when she had gotten up, she felt bone-deep achiness. Wondering if she had come down with another case of flu, she was ready for the doctor to tell her parents she had to stay home until she was well.

"Margarete, tell me what your symptoms are." The family doctor, Emily Morgan, was busy looking into Margarete's throat for signs of infection.

Margarete hesitated for a few seconds, trying to think of every symptom she'd recently experienced. "Uh, fever, achy bones…at least I think it's my bones. I was feverish a few weeks ago, coughing and sneezing, so we thought I had flu. Earlier this week and when it started, I just felt worn out, draggy. I'm losing too much weight. I had a bad nosebleed… nee, two of them. I have all these red spots on my skin. I think they're bug bites. And lately, I've been sweating a lot."

"Do you flood the mattress when you sweat?"

"What do you mean?" Margarete was confused.

"Do you sweat so much that you have to change your nightgown or even your sheets? And the surface of your mattress is noticeably wet?"

Margarete thought. "Nee, not quite that bad. But my gown has been damp. And, even though it's cold, I get sweaty in the daytime."

Dr. Morgan was busily writing down everything Margarete told her. She sighed. "I want to admit her to Somerset Hospital for a few days. Something's going on." Reluctantly, she raised her gaze to Mr. and Mrs. King. "Missus King, the sooner we get a handle on what's causing her symptoms, the sooner we can start on making her better."

Leora was extremely unsettled. She'd gotten to know Dr. Morgan well and the look in the doctor's eyes was sad.

"Margarete, go ahead and get dressed again. I'll see all three of you in my office in just a few minutes." The doctor left the room with Leora hot on her heels.

"Doctor, may I talk to you for a minute, please? I've never seen that look on your face when

Margarete or Sammy have been sick before. Something serious is wrong, ain't?"

Emily sighed. "I won't lie, Leora. I think it's something that's potentially serious. We need to admit her to the hospital for all the tests, so we can get an accurate diagnosis."

THANK YOU FOR READING!

You can **grab this book and learn more about my other books here**. There is also a sample of the first chapter of another of my books in the next chapter so you can get a further taste of my work.

And if you are interested in getting email updates from me, **click here**.

All the best,

Rachel

ABOUT THE AUTHOR

Rachel was born and raised in Lancaster, Pennsylvania. Being a neighbor of the Mennonite community, she started writing Amish romance fiction as a way of looking at the Amish community. She wanted to present a fair and honest representation of a love that is both romantic and sweet. She hopes her readers enjoy her efforts.

You can keep up with her new releases, discounts and specials when you sign up for **Rachel's email updates list**.

www.ingramcontent.com/pod-product-compliance
Lightning Source LLC
Chambersburg PA
CBHW021213260626
47172CB00002B/409